FOLK SONGS FOR TRAUMA SURGEONS

STORIES

"There's a busted heart beauty to Rosson's dazzling collection full of misdirection and literary mutation. Like some kind of punk rock Kelly Link, he takes you on a singular voyage through world-weary resignation and enchanted love in a way that feels sincere and earned and more than a little magical."
—Jeremy Robert Johnson,
author of *The Loop* and *Skullcrack City*

"Deadpan tragedies, comic transcendence, elegant ambiguities: in *Folk Songs for Trauma Surgeons*, Keith Rosson knows everything's always about to go sideways, so strike up the band, let's dance."
—Kathe Koja, author of *The Cipher*

"Each story in *Folk Songs for Trauma Surgeons* is a bullet. Fast. Weird. Funny. Horrifying. This is a collection of unique grace and pleasure amongst all the oddities and twists. A major accomplishment."
—Tod Goldberg, author of *Gangsterland*

"There's a fierceness to Rosson's intellect, a wildness to his imagination, a crackling energy in his prose. The stories in *Folk Songs for Trauma Surgeons* are often strange and sometimes funny and always irresistible. Like a brakeless train tearing through the tunnel of my mind, the propulsion and potency of this collection woke me up in the way only the best literature can."
—Alan Heathcock, author of *Volt* and *40*

"Keith needs very few words to paint the sum of someone's character in vivid color. Each of these fifteen stories tells a tale of someone that feels familiar. I love how immersive his writing is, even in short stories, where you're only with the characters for a few thousand words. You can't help but understand their deepest emotions."
—Aconite Cafe (5 stars)

FOLK SONGS FOR TRAUMA SURGEONS

STORIES

KEITH ROSSON

Meerkat Press
Atlanta

"The Lesser Horsemen," originally published in *Redivider;*
"At This Table," originally published in *PANK;*
"Baby Jill," originally published in *Cream City Review;*
"Their Souls Climb the Room," originally published in *Ink Heist;*
"Hospitality," originally published in *Camera Obscura Journal;*
"This World Or the Next," originally published in *Aggregate*
"Gifts," originally published in *Rivet;*
"Coyote," originally published in *The Nervous Breakdown;*
"Yes, We Are Duly Concerned with Calamitous Events," originally published in *Phantom Drift;*
"Winter, Spring, Whatever Happens After That," originally published in *Gulf Stream;*
"Forgive Me This," originally published in *Noble/Gas Qtrly,* later reprinted in *Grasslimb Journal;*
"Dunsmuir," originally published in *December Magazine;*
"Homecoming," originally published in *Phantom Drift;*
"Brad Benske and the Hand of Light," originally published in *Outlook Springs*

ISBN-13 978-1-946154-52-1 (Paperback)
ISBN-13 978-1-946154-54-5 (eBook)

Library of Congress Control Number: 2020948773

Cover design by Keith Rosson
Book design by Tricia Reeks

Printed in the United States of America

Published in the United States of America by
Meerkat Press, LLC, Atlanta, Georgia
www.meerkatpress.com

For Robin
a continuous light in the dark
and
Evelynn and Rosie
minute and beloved whirlwinds

CONTENTS

THE LESSER HORSEMEN...1

AT THIS TABLE.. 17

BABY JILL..25

THEIR SOULS CLIMB THE ROOM 32

HOSPITALITY.. 44

THIS WORLD OR THE NEXT..58

GIFTS..70

COYOTE 84

YES, WE ARE DULY CONCERNED WITH CALAMITOUS EVENTS 94

WINTER, SPRING, WHATEVER HAPPENS AFTER THAT 110

FORGIVE ME THIS 125

DUNSMUIR.. 131

HOMECOMING 148

THE MELODY OF THE THING 159

BRAD BENSKE AND THE HAND OF LIGHT.......................176

ACKNOWLEDGMENTS.. 191

ABOUT THE AUTHOR...193

THE LESSER HORSEMEN

Call Him whatever you want: The Good Lord, Jehovah, Yahweh, The Beginning and The End, *God;* we loved Him and we feared Him, and perhaps it was intentional but when He was in human form, we were also a bit disgusted by Him. Disgusted because He seemed, in all honesty, like a cad. A scumbag. Seemed, in fact, to revel in it. To become so abjectly the type of man who sucked his teeth and followed with his small and shiny doll eyes as young girls passed by on the street, his hand in his pocket; the type who relieved himself at bus stops and shouldered old ladies aside for a better seat somewhere; a man who when in restaurants left very small tips, in coins, as some kind of statement. A man who stank of cheap cologne and had hair, probably, riding up his back in the shape of a Spanish moss.

Our palaver had long become toxic.

The handouts He gave us featured a smiling cruise ship amid a cobalt sea, a smiling sun perched above, and smiling clouds scattered around. There was even, I saw, a smiling seagull perched on the deck's railing. He sold it to us as part vacation, part team-building exercise. He used those exact words. His office sat across the street from the methadone program they ran out of St. Joe's, and you could see the clusters of addicts hanging out, bullshitting out front after they'd gotten their dose, people loose-limbed in the sun and happy now to be alive again.

It was a five-night, six-day cruise from Portland to Glacier Bay, Alaska, He said. "Real nice. All the amenities. Shuffleboard, Wi-Fi, breakfast buffet. They even got a little paintballing gallery below deck. You guys can get some of your aggressions out, shoot each other in the beanbags and whatnot."

"This an optional trip?" I asked, and the Good Lord laughed.

Famine said, "Death isn't coming, I take it."

"Don't worry about Death," He said.

There were four of us, of course, but you'd never know it—Death for millennia now on his own trip, the three of us continually left in his wake.

War said, "Don't worry about him? And that means what, exactly?" and the Good Lord fixed him with a warning look. Quick enough, but filled with that terrible distance that none of us, not even Death on his best day, could come close to matching.

He pointed a finger at the three of us. "Listen. Death isn't the problem here, okay? You dicks got me?"

Was I pissed, hearing this? I mean, do I even have to say it? When had Death *ever* been a problem, right? No, the impetus was always on us, the fractured thirds. This trio of recalcitrance.

War couldn't help himself; he snorted contemptuously, exhaled a cloud of anthrax that settled on his shoulders like dandruff.

The Good Lord popped a butterscotch candy into his mouth, cracked it like a femur between his teeth. He shook His head. "Nah, it's you three I have issues with. The sniping, okay? The constant infighting. It showcases a serious lack of cohesion as a department, is what I'm saying. Even now? Handing Me this attitude? It's bullcrap, is what. So here's the deal: you go on the cruise, you eat some tacos, play some bocce ball, whatever. And do these team-building exercises. Learn to trust each other again. Talk it out. Because as it stands now, you're just straight up screwing the brand, okay? You've become ineffective."

"Except for Death," Famine muttered, toeing the carpet with a duct-taped high top.

"You're *goddamn right* except for Death!" the Good Lord roared, and slapped his desk hard enough to make his coffee cup jump. The addicts across the street, without knowing why, suddenly remembered pressing engagements and drifted away. All of them unanimously stricken with unease. This one little outburst and I could imagine all too well a mine collapse in some crumbling shithole town in Kentucky somewhere, a tsunami or mudslide enveloping some poor third-world enclave, thousands of bodies snuffed to lifelessness within moments. It wasn't a heartlessness—you could say a lot of things about Him, but the guy *felt* everything very strongly, was *seized* at times with feelings—but there was, what seemed to me at least, an unawareness of environment or consequence that could sometimes be construed as cruel or uncaring.

Then again, he was the Divine Creator and I was but one quarter of the Great Cessation—and a low-ranking one at that—so what the hell did I know?

He said, "Enough about Death already," glaring at us again while he sopped up his coffee spill with napkins. He ran a pudgy hand over the errant hairs on his dome and smoothed down his wrinkled tie. "Now I want you to get on that boat, and I want you to relax. Look at how pretty the water is and shit like that.

But above all: Drop the attitude and learn to work together. Because if you don't, what's the saying? How's the saying go?"

"We perish alone?" Famine offered weakly.

The Good Lord leveled a stubby finger at him. He smiled at us for the first time that day, showing rows of butter-colored teeth. "That's it. Exactly. You work together or you perish the hell alone."

• • •

We stepped outside as knives of sunlight winked off every glassed thing on the street. The stink of exhaust enveloped us. Sewage warming in the gutters brought out the scents of the human soufflé: piss, heated blacktop, burnt plastic.

Famine hiked his jeans up—we had our trappings, each of us, our strange cosmic shortcomings that kept us tethered here, not nearly human but certainly more than *ideas*, and Famine's was, obviously, his constant hunger. Not so obvious was that he could never find a fucking belt that fit him. He took off down the avenue muttering something about an all-you-can-eat bouillabaisse shop on Mississippi, the cuffs of his pants scraping the ground, arms wrinkled and red at the elbows, striding along with one hand bunching the acid-washed fabric at his waist.

War folded his cruise handout and sighed, squinting at the empty street. "We leave in three hours? Man, He's not dicking around."

"He's not known for that, is He?"

"True. Guess I better go grab my gear," he said, and then paused. He seemed poised for some comradely dig, but we were long past it. Centuries, at least. "See you on the boat," he managed.

The Good Lord certainly had a point. I could admit that. We'd long since become fractious, four different arrows arcing toward four different targets at four different times. No harmony, no shared intention. There had been a time when that was not the case, but now? Only Death was constant.

The Good Lord was staring at me through the window, his hands cinched over his little stovepot of a belly. He raised a hand and shooed me along, the look in his eyes absolutely flat, dead as deep space.

I went home to pack.

• • •

"I'm pleased, more than pleased, *ecstatic*, truthfully, to welcome you aboard the *Stately Queen*." We'd dropped off our luggage in our rooms and the ship's captain now stood quaking before us, a small man with a trimmed and quivering thumb of white mustache. His crew peppered the wheelhouse, mortified and silent, busying themselves with their gauges and instruments. "I'm sure you'll find our accommodations to your liking, *more* than to your liking, but if there's *anything* you need, please don't hesitate to ask."

Famine: "Where's the buffet, hoss?"

War, had he eyes, would have rolled them. "Jesus Christ," he said.

I laughed. "Don't bring him into this."

The captain's eyes pinballed between us, sweat already dampening the collar of his uniform. It felt strange being there—I wasn't used to hanging around people unless I was, you know, working the crowd. Maybe I was alone in that regard, that restlessness of mine, but I kept wanting to just lay into the captain and his guys—maybe bubonic-plague him so bad and so fast his shirtsleeves would rip at the seams, his armpits and throat swelling up black, but that was probably just habit. When you have a fast car, you want to drive it.

"The buffet, like all of our ship activities," said the captain, "is available for you twenty-four hours a day. You'll find itineraries in your rooms, which will give you an outline of planned activities, as well as scheduled free time throughout the week. Being who you are," and here he gave a stiff little laugh, "you have free rein of the ship, of course. We live, as they say, to serve."

"*If you live,*" I moaned like a low-budget horror movie ghoul, flexing my sore-spotted hands toward him. The captain quailed, lurching back into another sailor. War laughed, readjusting his grenades.

• • •

We had long been a motley band. Death was the only one among us with any style, haunting in his wending cloak, his scythe, his ghastly pale skull. He was *cool*. Then the three of us, trailing behind: Famine with his acid-washed jeans and faded Joe Camel tank top, bleach-spotted pink at the hem, a thing skinny as a nightmare, a thing ceaselessly, painfully starved. And then War with his shit-smeared cammies, his jutting AK-47 clip and pineapple grenades where a living man's reproductive materials would lay, those steel barbs that ran along his scorched flesh like veins. And me? A theme park for maggots. A grunting amalgam of wens and boils and pustules. My body crafted from red and green mountain ranges of ruined skin, a body volcanic with expectorate. I shuffled and left a trail like a slug.

We were made expressly to bring about the end of the earth. We were, I knew, *of* the Apocalypse. Built for it. Intellectually, I understood that.

So why, in those quiet moments that were becoming commonplace as we grew more and more ensconced in our four-part discord, why was I just not fucking *feeling* it anymore? Which had come first? Our group's lack of cohesion, or my lack of interest in my work? Because let's face it—my work was my identity. I took that shit home with me. As a group we were falling apart, it was true, but it had been such a long time coming, a slow boil over millennia, that I was finding it hard to care. We could no longer stand being around each other, us Horsemen, and perhaps even more strange: I had reached a point where, in lieu of my colleagues, I had found myself drawn to the living in odd and incalculable ways. I still loathed their physicality, their fragility, their penchant for weakness and disease. I still desired to bathe in their gore, their viscera, their inviolable *liquidity*. But it was for this same reason that I almost admired them. Their tenacity, their resolution. Their grim insistence in culling from this world the majestic, the meaningful.

I had started writing *sijos,* a Korean style of poetry birthed around the time Taejo of Goryeo was kicking ass and taking names in 10th century Korea and Manchuria. Entrenched within metaphors, puns, allusions, there's a grace to these poems, this style, a deceptively simple playfulness that encapsulates everything about the living's fierceness toward life. Oh, how they want to live, people do, how fiercely they cling to it all. I'd written over the years my own loose gathering of *sijos,* and had been for a number of months now submitting my collection of poems to various publishing houses under a moniker. I'd told no one, though I'm sure the Good Lord knew. I called the collection *You Bags of Liquid, You Sacks of Air,* and had so far received dozens of rejections. I couldn't figure out if it was due to the outmoded nature of the form itself or the possibility that my work was simply not very good.

But I kept at it, each email a fervent missive sent out into the void, hoping against hope. Like people themselves.

• • •

I woke in the middle of the night to see Lucius perched on the edge of my bed. My quarters were dark, the single oval window showing a night full of star-dotted ink. Writhing like a wisp of smoke before the wind takes it, Luce was a mess of images that coalesced, momentarily, before vanishing again into shapelessness: I saw a tangle of wetted veins, and small pale crabs burrowing in blued flesh. Coals banked in pools of gore. This was Luce: a joined-man of fire and a dark joyousness. He was the devil, he was in my room, and he smelled like dogshit on fire.

I coughed. "Open a window."

Luce laughed and took solid form. He wrapped his arms around his knees and pointed a cracked black fingernail at me. "You know He's gonna cut you out, right?" His voice: like a dozen howling children shoved into a rock tumbler.

I sighed and laid my pillow over my head. "Beat it, Tempter."

He unhinged his jaw and a cloud of smoke spiraled forth. As it dissipated, a hundred tiny screams batted against the corners of the room before fading away.

"Don't do that in here, dude. That's nasty."

"Sorry," Luce croaked. "I ate some bad Thai," and then bugged his eyes at me and screamed laughter at his own joke. He hopped to the floor and it was both sinuous and physiologically wrong. "But I'm serious. I've read the memos—'Everybody stays, except for Pestilence.' Plagues are old school, You-Know-Who says. Tacky. He'll be letting you go soon, hoss."

"Look," I said, "I know it's your job to sow discord and all that, but I've got a big, sucky day tomorrow. So beat it."

"Okay," Luce said. "But ask yourself, why would I lie?"

"Because you're the Prince of Lies."

Luce nodded. "Okay, that's fair."

"Because that's, like, your whole shtick, lying."

"Point taken. But I'm being square with you on this one. He's sick of all the dick-swinging power plays between you three. And you just happen to be the little fish."

"Us four, you mean."

He grinned and shook his shaggy head, and I saw one set of jaws housed inside another. "Come on. Don't be an idiot."

"Because Death's perfect," I said.

He ticked it off his fingers: "Death's perfect, War is inevitable, and with blooming ecological devastation being what it is, Famine's gonna be a busy little beaver within the next half century or so. But you? Honestly, when's the last time you were great?"

I thought about it and lifted the pillow from my face. "Spanish influenza," I said, quietly.

"What's that?" Luce hooked a hand over his misshapen ear.

"The Spanish influenza," I said, louder.

"Right. Which was what? A century ago? Look, I'll admit, it *behooves* me to see you guys in disarray like this, but I also, as you can imagine, like to root for the underdog. And you, my boil-laden friend, you are the underdog here."

"Whatever."

"Okay," Luce said, clucking his tongue. "If you say so. It's no skin off these balls either way."

He disappeared in a cloud of that terrible dogshit-and-brimstone stench, and I was alone again. It took a long time to get back to sleep.

• • •

"Guys," Linda said, "I want you to close your eyes and picture yourselves floating."

Famine said, "Like floating on our horses?"

"Floating," said Linda, "on a pod of air. Floating peacefully in the sky."

"But on our horses or not?"

Linda smiled. "Not on your horses."

"Are we, like, *on* the pod, or *in* the pod? Because—just being honest—I'd be worried about falling off if I was on top of it."

"For fuck's sake," War said.

"Whichever works best for you, dear," Linda said. She was unmoved and not remotely frightened by us. I wondered what kind of training was provided to a "Licensed Trust Therapist" that allowed her to work so fearlessly with even three of the Horsemen of the Apocalypse. Linda didn't look like much—who among them did?—as she wore a frizzed bowl of red hair and had cinched herself into an emerald pantsuit, with big gaudy rings laddering each hand. She looked like a tranquil leprechaun, I thought. But as far as a cathedral of microbes went, I liked her well enough. Pizzazz and chutzpah galore, and unafraid. Each of those were rare among the living, but all combined together?

It was our first day of training. We sat in a circle in one of the ship's conference rooms. I couldn't even tell we were moving, really. A blue wedge of sea and a paler sky hung outside our window. There was a glossy black table where we could have sat, but Linda instead had us take our chairs and circle up at the end of the room, so close our knees practically touching.

So we pictured ourselves floating. My pod, I decided, was milky white, like a caul, and airless. The inside of a marble, or the bowl of a skull, maybe. I wondered what that meant, or if it meant anything.

Finally, Linda said, "Now that you've floated in your pods, I want you to picture it dissolving. You're falling," she cooed. "Falling and falling to the earth. You're rocketing and plunging," she said, and opened her eyes, smiling as she looked at each of us. "And who catches you?" I saw how green her eyes were, flecked with gold, a singing green that matched that terrible outfit. "Who saves you?" she whispered to us.

The moment stretched out, and I surprised myself by breaking the silence.

"Nobody," I said. "Nobody saves me. I fall."

Famine nodded. "That's what I was going to say."

War shrugged and finally nodded agreement, his arms crossed.

Linda beamed at us all. "Good! Excellent work, friends. *Nobody saved you.* What do you think this means?"

"That these guys are dicks?" War said.

"That we shouldn't float around in a bubble of air?" Famine offered.

Linda smiled. "It means," she said, "that nobody saved you because *there was nobody that you trust.*"

We looked among each other for a moment.

"Well, yeah," I said. "That's kind of a given, Linda."

Linda patted my knee, and did so without flinching, even though I was wearing shorts and a boil burst, spraying yellow pus on the back of her hand, something that must have burned terribly. She only smiled and looked at each of us in turn. That gaze so fully moored in kindness.

"You're here to learn to work together. To rely on each other." She wiped her hand with a handkerchief. "So!" And she stood up in a zip of polyester and bouncing red hair. "Let's get started. I need a volunteer for this next exercise. Who wants to go first?"

The day stretched out before us. Lunch, and freedom, and more rejections for my terrible poems, was at least three hours away.

Surprising myself yet again, I raised my hand.

• • •

We were anchored outside of Seattle. The city's lights lay before us like a blanket of jewels, the stalk of the Space Needle limned in moonlight. It was *pretty*, is what I mean, and as I stood on the deck I toyed around with the notion of another manuscript, another series of poems. But was that really sustainable, an entire section of poems about *lights?* Who would read that?

More importantly, what was *happening* to me?

A magician's burst of shit-smoke and there was Luce drumming his nails on the railing and squinting out at the skyline. When he looked at me—even through the turned-out skin, the purple ovals of leeches covering his face—I could see the disappointment, the mockery.

"What was *that* bullshit today?"

I looked back out at the city. "Shut up, Luce. Why are you even here?"

"I'm trying to help you out, bro."

"You don't 'help anybody out,' Luce."

He pulled out a yellowed tibia from a pocket of his overcoat and packed the bored-out socket full of leaves. He offered it to me, but I held up a hand. "Look. I hear you," he said, lighting up. "I'm untrustworthy. But it's systematically and categorically true, isn't it: the Four Horsemen of the Apocalypse will cause more destruction, heartache and sorrow than the Three. And I'm into *that*. That, as they say, is my jam."

I didn't know what to say to that.

"Can I be straight with you?" he said, his voice pinched. Smoke leaked from the corners of his mouth and his eyes burrowed into slits as he held in his hit. Whatever he was smoking smelled like piss, the deep fug of wood rot. "You guys looked like idiots today. When you and Famine did that *trust fall?* I almost died."

"Beat it," I said. "That bird don't fly."

"What?"

"There's trees to bark up, but this isn't the right one."

"Wait," Luce said. "Are *you* high? I can't understand what you're saying."

"What I'm saying is, I'm doing exactly what I'm supposed to be doing and you're the Lord of Chaos. Confusion runs through your blood, okay? I get that. I know what you're trying to do. So *beat it.*"

"If Death was here—"

"Well, he's not. It's just the three of us, and this is what we're doing. So just give it a rest."

Luce thocked the bone against the railing and ashes tumbled to the dark water below. "Okay," he sighed. "Guess I'll catch you on the flipside."

"No, you won't," I said.

He shrugged and vanished again, and I looked down at the water, where hundreds of dead fish bobbed at the surface, their bodies riding the small swells that butted against the ship's hull, their silvery corpses reflecting the city lights.

• • •

"I don't know *when* the resentment started," War said. We were back in the conference room. Our fourth day. "I don't know when we started hating each other. When things went to shit."

"I do," Famine said. "The Crusades."

"No way," I said. "Things were tense way before that. Egypt? I'd even gamble on the Lelantine War. Remember? We weren't even talking to each other by then."

"That's right," War said, nodding. "Me and you took Chalkis, and Famine and Death took Eretria, and we totally played against each other."

"And we kicked your *asses,*" Famine said.

"Oh, spare me," War said.

I turned to Linda, who sat and watched us with polite interest, the gentle stoicism of a woman following a tennis match.

"The Lelantine War took place in Greece," I told her, "between these two city states, okay? Sixth century. *Everybody* got into it, pretty much all of Greece, since these two cities carried a lot of weight as far as politics and resources went, right? It was miserable. I remember at one point, War—"

Linda held up a hand. "Let me stop you right there, dear. *Why* was it miserable?"

That stunned us. You could see the gears turning. Why had it been such a miserable time? An event like that? We should have flourished. We should have loved it.

"I remember being really pissed at you guys," Famine said. "You were such dicks."

"It was just a little good-natured competition," War said. "What's the big deal?"

"No," he's right," I said. I doubted we were capable of epiphanies, but this felt like something close to it. "We were supposed to work together, and we blew it."

"Good," Linda said softly, clasping her ringed hands together, looking pleased. "Good."

· · ·

We had the night off, and I was considering tracking down one of the guys, maybe playing some air hockey or barking out some terrible karaoke in the cavernous banquet hall. I was feeling expansive, it was true. Between the trust falls, the counseling, the role-playing, I was feeling closer to War and Famine than I had in millennia. I marveled at the centuries wasted, and how large-hearted I felt toward them now, after just a few days of Linda's mediation. Who'd have thought that such a human thing—oh how they babbled these days about the necessities of *communication*—could have turned out to be true?

We had entered Canadian waters by now and the air had a slight chill to it. I rarely got a sense of just how big the ship was, how massive, but there were times like now, as we cleaved our way through rougher water, when it felt as if I was just some tiny thing on the deck, inconsequential and meaningless.

A damn strange thing for a Horseman to feel.

Which was precisely when a waiter came by, one I'd never seen before. He lifted the silver dome from a serving tray to show me a glistening cross-section of sliced human organs.

"*Hors d' oeuvre,* sir?"

"Luce, for the last time. Leave me alone."

Luce sighed and hurled the plate like a frisbee out into the glossy, moon-rippled sea. His uniform disappeared in that rot-whiff of smoke and he was back in his usual: overcoat and turned-out veins. A human thumbnail jutted between two incisors.

"We've simply *got* to stop *meeting* like this."

"You've got something in your teeth."

"It looks like you made some real *progress* today. I hope that feels good." He leaned in close, and that bouquet particular to the Prince of Darkness washed over me: mustard gas, gunpowder, small woodland animals dunked in a deep fryer. "But have you considered"—and here his voice purred like a zipper coming undone—"just what it is that Death and The-Putz-I-Cannot-Name are *up to* in your absence?"

He was so good at this. Tilling these crops of fear and mistrust, tending these poisonous weeds.

"I haven't thought about it, no."

"So you're being *willfully* blind, then."

"I'm trusting in the process," I said.

Luce laughed. "Have you considered that this may be a situation in which I have as much to gain by telling the truth as I do by lying?"

"I haven't, no."

Luce finally grunted a frustrated little cough and rose a foot from the deck. For the first time, he unfurled his wings and flapped them; a fine filigree of blood spattered the walls behind him, delicate as lace.

"You're an idiot, Pestilence, and I'm done with you."

"Fine," I said.

"Fine."

"Goodbye."

"Yeah," he said. "Oh, and by the way, I read your manuscript. *You Bags of Liquid, You Sacks of Air?* Are you kidding me? It was the most hackneyed, trite, and painful collection of writing I've read in probably five thousand years. Make no mistake: you are, at your core, a terrible writer."

A puff of smoke, and there was nothing left. Just me. Me and Luce's blood stippling the wall, almost pretty in its delicacy.

• • •

The four of us sat in our usual circle, arms folded, looking down at the ground.

It was our last session, and Linda was fifteen minutes late. War sipped a latte, and Famine was eating Funyuns from a bag as large as his torso.

"If it was anybody else," I said, "I'd say we just leave."

"But it's Linda," Famine said, his mouth full.

"And Linda rules," War said.

"Listen," I said. "I'm really sorry, you guys." I meant it, too. "I wasted *centuries* being jealous of you guys. Talking shit. Me just looking out for me, you know? You guys were just doing your jobs, same as I was. I see that now."

"We all were," War said. "I'm to blame as much as anyone."

"We wasted a lot of time," Famine said.

"But we're a *team* now, right?"

"Damn straight," War said.

"Once we're done with this cruise," Famine said, "we are gonna kick some ass."

Which was when Linda walked in, followed by the Good Lord, and finally, ducking his cowled head in the doorway, Death.

• • •

"Hello, boys," the Good Lord said, as Death propped his scythe against the wall and leaned his bony ass on the table behind us.

Linda sheepishly took a seat and gave us a look, heavy with apology.

"I'm proud of you boys," the Good Lord said. "That was some gut-level honesty you walked through this past week. Moving as shit, to tell you the truth. I'm glad you patched things up." He nodded at Linda, who with a seeming reluctance reached into her bag and handed us each a folder. On the front of mine:

TRANSITIONS:
NAVIGATING THE EXCITING SHIFT FROM FULL-TIME
EMPLOYMENT TO ON-CALL FREELANCING!

"Papyrus font?" Famine said, his mouth puckered.

I said, "You're *firing* us?"

The Good Lord held His hands up. "I am *not* firing you, Pestilence. Absolutely not. You will *all* be highly valued contractors, hired on an as-needed basis."

War stood up. "As needed? We're *the Four Horsemen of the Apocalypse*. What is this 'as needed' shit?"

Behind us, Death rumbled, "Sit your ass down."

War turned to him and gestured at his grenades. "Pull the pin, dude. Do it. I *dare* you."

"Boys," the Good Lord said. "That's enough."

"So what do we do when we're not on call?" I asked.

"You stay here," He said.

"Here? On the boat?" Famine said. "You kidding me? And what about *him?*"

The Good Lord shrugged and then held out a hand toward Linda. "You worked terrifically with your Trust Therapist, and the three of you are a tight-knit unit now—you're not perfect, but you'll get better. I'm impressed. This world wouldn't be what it is without War, Famine and Pestilence. Okay? You are *not* redundant." He shrugged again. "But we're downsizing. I've hired a new guy who, apart from the specialty work I'll occasionally need you guys for, can handle things just fine with Death. It'll be just the two of them working the field most of the time."

"What?" I said.

"Unbelievable," War said.

"Who?" Famine said.

And in walked the new guy. Eight feet tall, matted fur, rattling like a diesel engine just standing there.

Linda, justifiably, shrank back in her seat.

"He looks like a big otter or something," War said.

Famine scowled and pointed a Funyun at him. "Dude looks like a blood-splattered chipmunk. The hell. This is your guy?"

"Ladies and gentlemen," the Good Lord said, bowing like a game show host. "I bring you . . . Terror."

"Hey," Terror said, lifted one sopping paw.

• • •

Glacier Bay, if you stare at it long enough, becomes pretty unspectacular. Clots of shimmering lights that glow twenty out of twenty-four hours now that winter was upon us. There is the occasional dark ink of a whale pod breaking the surface, and the cries of seals drift low across the bay. But as far as the world of men? It's just the three of us docked here. The ship is crewless. Linda teleconferences in every once in a while, but it's not the same. She's withdrawn; that fearlessness is gone. She's become afraid. She's ashamed of herself.

The three of us get along fine but we've grown sullen.

We have the internet. A small movie theater. There's a bowling alley below deck that War has spent weeks oiling and refurbishing; he speaks of eventual tournaments. We've become unhealthily obsessed with the board game Risk, if only to feel a little in control of our fates. Famine is a shrewd dictator, but it's War's diplomacy that surprises me.

It's worth noting, I suppose, a recent incident during a particularly frenzied game of foosball. A foosball rod hooked onto the pin of one of War's testicles, and before we could find it, the testicle exploded. No one, of course, was injured. A testament to our isolation: the Good Lord repaired the damage offsite, without even visiting, offering not a single word of consolation.

A boat comes twice a month to drop off whatever supplies and sundries we dream up, things we supposedly need. It's been seven months now, and War has been allowed a handful of day trips; he's come back from each one sulking and silent.

"I'm supposed to be showing Terror the ropes," he told me, shaking his head. "But he's fucking great at it. He's a natural."

"Yeah?"

"We're never getting off this boat, man."

Famine's gone out a few times as well, and is taking online courses on hydrology; you can hear him muttering about water scarcity and dispersion patterns as he walks sleepless up and down the stairwells of the ship at night. The Good Lord promises that the growing water crisis will get him some real movement soon, the thing that's going to get him off-ship a lot more frequently.

I haven't left yet.

The supplies come in a little cigarette boat piloted by a Frenchman named Bertrand. It takes less than two minutes for him to zip out from the docks and lash his little boat to the railings of our ship. We've got a little dumbwaiter that War's worked out, and we winch the supplies up because Bertrand's pants-shittingly terrified of us.

We've joked about it: Bertrand is so tempting, if only for his singularity. A collection of microbes, earwax, cilia, mushy genitals, a thrumming heart; the whole vibrant, messy human package. The only human we see these days. We want to rend, destroy, starve, cripple and dismember him. We want to see his belly swollen with hunger. We want to liquefy his internal organs. We want to see him perish.

We say that it's habit, just those old muscles wanting to flex again, but really, we are lonely.

We miss our old lives, the then-unknown abundance of them.

Famine has coined us the Lesser Horsemen. War has already ordered bowling shirts.

Bertrand sets boxes on the dumbwaiter and War and I take turns cinching them up, while Famine opens them and takes inventory. We love the days

Bertrand comes. Our copies of *Rolling Stone* and *The Economist*. Boxes of Ho Hos. Netted sacks of grapefruit. Bondage pornography from the 1970s. A trio of medieval swords. Twenty-yard rolls of bubble wrap, the popping of which brings some measure of solace to us somehow. We thirst for the tactile, the vibrant. We ache for it. We hoist and hoist and the sliver of moon hangs above us like a broken arrow, like our intentions, busted and forlorn. It is nine degrees and cold enough that I wished I could breathe, that fog would roil from my mouth as I worked.

"One for you," Famine says, handing me a box with my name on it.

I rip the tape with a nail and there they are, stacked and tiled cleanly in the box. How people seem to love that, to rail against disorder, to lean against it. They love their right angles, people do, their stacking and their straight lines.

Inside the box is my book.

One hundred copies of my chapbook—self-published, thank you very much. *You Bags of Liquid, You Sacks of Air*. Forty-eight pages of my *sijos;* vellum inner covers, saddle-stapled and trimmed, formatted by a professional graphic designer. It's beautiful.

"Is that it?" Famine asks.

I pause. I'm not sure why—maybe to extend the moment just a little? To keep it mine for just a second longer?

"Yep," I say. "This is it."

I give copies to each of them. They begin thumbing through it, even as Bertrand waits patiently below us in the dark, scared and alone. Fuck Bertrand, I think, who will leave here after he's done, to his family or his depression or his mother; fuck Bertrand and his luxury of movement. His *living*. And then I think, What the hell, and I lean over. Bertrand's face is a pale oval in the small dark boat.

"Hey, Bertrand," I say.

"Oui?" he says.

I put one of my books on the dumbwaiter and lower it down to him.

"That's my book," I say. "You can have it."

"Oui," Bertrand says, wiping hair from his eyes and looking up at me, terrified, like I'm going to ravage him with a super *e coli* any second now. Which a part of me still feels like doing, honestly. But instead I say, "That's my book of poems. Maybe you could read it and let me know what you think next time you come around. If you have time."

Bertrand lets out a pinched little laugh and says "Oui" again, and finally War says, "I don't think he speaks English, man."

When I push away from the railing, Famine is thumbing through his copy. "This is awesome," he says. "Congratulations."

"You're like a real author," War says.

"Well, self-published," I say.

"*Pssh*," Famine says. "Whatever. This thing looks great. I can't wait to read it."

I open a copy to the dedication page and something quickens in me. Not a quickening of the heart, of course, but maybe as close to a heart as I'll ever come. Just this brief little stutter of time—an *almost* wild, *almost* singing joy in getting something right, at least a little bit. It lasts for just a moment, there and gone, but it's a real thing, this feeling. Bertrand's speedboat zips off and I stand there in the cold and smile, looking at the dedication:

To War and Famine,
The other Lesser Horsemen,
who afforded me an unexpected grace.

Oh, and Death and Terror
can kiss my ass.

AT THIS TABLE

The table is in a restaurant in a building that was built in 1885. The building was remodeled in 1915 and again in 1952 after it was found that a broken sewage pipe had been weakening the foundation for decades. The building is located in a significantly gentrified area of a medium-sized city in a medium-sized state on the Pacific Coast of the United States of America. And also, your hands are damp. The restaurant is a restaurant that claims to cater to the health- and cruelty-conscious but really mostly caters to the cynical and ironic, things that you both claim to staunchly ridicule but secretly fear you are. There is one spear of watery sunlight that falls from the windows in the front of the restaurant onto the table you are sitting at. It bisects your menus and her hands as she moves them, as she arranges and rearranges her silverware that is no longer bound in a napkin; as she touches ragged cuticles with nicotine-colored fingertips; as she flattens tiny bits of detritus on the table.

You have hardly spoken. The sunlight halves the table as you try to speak.

And at this table, as the woman sits next to you and looks at your face or down into her lap or over your shoulder where outside everything is shot through with a cold winter sunlight, seventeen different individuals have left without paying their tabs over the past nearly-twenty years[1] and that number is about to increase in about five minutes. Approximately fourteen individuals with the name or a derivative of the name "Harold" ("Harold," "Harry," "Hank") have eaten breakfast, lunch or dinner at this restaurant within that span of time, which has only within the past eight or ten years made the jump from traditional diner fare to optional substitutions like Boca Burgers™ and free-range eggs or tofu, rather than bacon or sausage; "Harold" no longer appears to be a very common name. *It's not you it's me,* you say and she rolls her eyes and does not look at you. She fingers a crease in the menu in front of her. *Please,* you say, *I'm sorry please try to understand.*

---

1. Yes, you will be one of them.

(Except that what *has* been said so far is less even than a half-truth. They're hardly anything at all, these words you're saying. It's the same old shit, really: cowardice couched in a supposed truth.)

This table has been painted many colors, in bright and cheery designs, as have the other eight tables and the concentric half-circle of a bar that rings the waitressing station to your immediate right. The table at which the two of you sit has on it a smiling sun that is holding a coffee cup in one of its rays. It is painted in acrylic. The colors on the table are blue, green, yellow, black and white. Along with the sun, there are also many five-pointed stars painted on the table, and a Cerulean blue background that is obviously meant to denote the sky. The table, aside from being painted, has also been varnished. She says nothing, is now looking down into her lap again. You are worried that she will begin to cry soon. You do not want her to cry in a busy restaurant. There is a small, almost imperceptible blemish slightly to the right of the exact center of her chin; it is almost the exact same hue as her lips, which are beginning to tremble now. You have spent weeks steeling yourself for this exact moment. This one right here.[2] But in picturing it, you did not imagine her crying.

The varnish on the table is very thick—there are slight ridges that you can feel under your fingertips.[3] And while your fingers do that, your mouth—your lips and tongue and teeth—is about to form the words *I'm just not ready to commit to being with a woman* but then the waitress—thin, with bright and lovely tattoos arcing up and down her arms, a small metal spike through the middle of her bottom lip—arrives with your plates of food.[4] The woman next to you, the woman who has repeatedly told you she loved you over the past three months while you have done everything short of electrocuting yourself, throwing yourself out of the sole window in her chilled studio apartment in order to stop these words from tumbling gracelessly, hollowly from your own

---

2. If and when you ever become familiar with the act of self-reflection, you'll realize that you have always prepared yourself for these moments within the first minute of meeting someone—at the very least, long, long before your body ever collides with another, long before the thought of whatever new lover makes your heart flutter in your ribs like a trapped bird. It's all part of the process, isn't it? Always finding yourself here once the luster fades? Or once someone begins to expect something from you?

3. The varnish is made up of a synthetic resin called *polyurethane*, which is defined as polymer units that are linked by various urethane groups and used chiefly as constituents to paints, adhesives, foams and, yes, varnishes. You could not define *polyurethane* if your life depended on it, but this doesn't make you a bad person. What you are doing right now in this restaurant to this person doesn't even make you a bad person. It just makes you afraid.

4. For you: The *Ve-Gan-Do-It!*, consisting of spinach, tomato slices, artichoke hearts and cubed and marinated tofu and two slices of unbuttered, 16-grain bread. She is having the *Not Eggs-Actly Eggs*, which is pretty much just seasoned tempeh and a vegetable medley slathered with a pesto-cheese sauce. Still, a not insignificant part of your mind abstractly thinks that you should have ordered that instead.

mouth, bows her head like a supplicant, like someone about to be knighted or beheaded. And yes, her lips, her lips are definitely, one-hundred-percent beginning to tremble now.

You two need anything else, the waitress asks.

No thanks, you say, smiling up at the admittedly hot waitress to show that you are polite, but not too suggestively or brazenly, in order to subtly reinforce the notion to this woman sitting across from you that, despite the fact that she has brought you to orgasms strong enough to make your hands lock themselves into claw-like shapes while the veins in your neck leapt out in stark relief, despite the fact that the first time you kissed her, her tongue darting gently into your mouth, there was the familiar and lovely warmth that spread up into your belly, the same fluttering of that stupid, relentless muscle under your ribcage, the same sense of falling toward something *good* as you told and listened to each others' stories, no, you are most certainly not a lesbian at all. No. The time she cawed laughter when you fell on your ass on the ice and somehow it wasn't mockery at all and something inside you broke free at that, at the realization of that. It was like some dark, previously closed-off space inside you was flung open and her laughter was simple joy and not hurtful and how incredible that feeling was, do you remember that? And yet it is not *possible,* even as the idea flits and batters itself against the dim lamplight of your heart, that you are afraid of love itself. No? It is not *possible,* in spite of the fact that this is the fifth woman in your life that you have said those *exact words to?* It has no bearing on the situation now, at this moment. All of those women in your life you have left with bitter tears, the small ghosts of them murmuring inside you. All of them left stunned and surprised once some interior warning bell begins to clang inside you.

But what you do not know is that there are ghosts *everywhere* in the world, everywhere, even here in this room. *Especially* in this room. Because another thing you do not know is that there was once a man murdered in what is now the kitchen of this restaurant, though it was not the kitchen of a restaurant when the man was murdered.

The man's name was Aaron Shelby Dobbs and it happened in 1934 when the restaurant was not a restaurant but an upholstery shop. Dobbs was the proprietor of the shop and was feverishly pro-union, which was sometimes an incendiary thing to be in 1934, and also other times too. Worse still was to be a soapboxer, an outspoken, *loud* pro-union man in a time when citywide general strikes were going on in San Francisco, Minneapolis and elsewhere, and men were being killed by police and strikebreakers and there were many riots, sometimes even in this medium-sized city. Dobbs was a man like that. He had been trying to organize a union among other upholstery shops (those with employees *and* bosses: Dobbs's shop was small, his son being his only employee, both of them sharing equally in profit and responsibility) and the owners of these upholstery shops would get very upset when Dobbs soapboxed and sang songs on Saturday mornings on what was then and still is the city's major thoroughfare, Water Avenue[5], and would get very, *very* upset when Dobbs would sometimes pass out leaflets and/or handbills to the workers of various other businesses in the mornings as they went into work, forsaking his own business in favor of trying to Organize The People. This upset many wealthy men in the area, and after certain incendiary events elsewhere had come to pass[6], and after they had spoken about him for some time over beers and tumblers of whiskey and the fanned-out hands of playing cards and over the telephone sometimes too, certain actions were unilaterally agreed upon.

Admittedly, this would not interest you. But what *would* interest you is the fact that very near to this table you are sitting at, as you unwrap your fork from its little cocoon of napkin and wish briefly but ferociously that you could take it all back, everything, not just with this woman but with every woman in your whole life, that this is where Dobbs became a phantom. Right there, actually, right over there! And also, that he could simultaneously be construed as "near you" and "not near you" as the woman definitely sitting next to you allows one fattened tear to slide down the contours of her face.

As you look on helplessly. Locked in the arms of your own wordlessness. Your cowardice.

And what happened was that Dobbs was working late one night—he had spent much of the morning leafleting a cannery in the industrial section until various midlevel management types had shoved him away, one threatening to "kill his ass dead," though his demise had been in the works for some time and orchestrated by men other than this—and had a backlog of work to do. At that time of night, he was refurbishing a set of a dozen chairs for a billiards-and-whiskey club on, again, Water Avenue. It was past eight o'clock in the evening when there was a rap on the door. Dobbs pulled up the shade, saw a bearded man with one of his leaflets in his hand, with dark and shifting eyes like a rat. Dobbs had excitedly unlocked the door and the man had stepped inside and they began to speak. The man was very nervous, wiping the back of his hand across his forehead repeatedly, but this seemed reasonable to Dobbs—the machinery of capitalism

---

5. Named thusly because this medium-sized city in this medium-sized state on the Pacific Coast of the United States was then a port town and still is.

6. See the San Francisco Longshoremen's Strike, the Teamsters Strike in Minneapolis, the Auto-Lite Strike in Toledo, Ohio, etc.

did not *want* workers to be united, to form an entity larger than themselves, one crafted toward their own interests rather than that of their bosses. Of *course* the man was scared—he was risking so much by coming there, Dobbs believed. It was after Dobbs had invited the man in, after he had turned away from the man to retrieve additional literature he kept in his shop, literature that he had kept high on a shelf for just such an occasion as this—*first a trickle then a tide* he would tell his son daily—that the bearded man, who was from Spokane, Washington and was hired by men who knew that he did such things, that he was capable and willing to do such things for money, placed a small .22-caliber pistol against the back of Dobbs's head and pulled its trigger.

So I guess this is it, the woman says to you, peering down at her plate. It is nearly a whisper.

I just don't think I'm ready to be with a woman, you say, and this, yes, this could be a lie, you realize. It is not her womanhood that frightens you, is it?

It's simply her *thereness.* This other person.

The yawing, expansive trust that's complicit in love.

Dobbs had fallen without fanfare, without blood—the bullet entering and then ricocheting within the curved bowl of his skull—and the man stood over him and fired two more shots into the side of Dobbs's face (per instructions) and dropped a typewritten letter his employers had given him onto Dobbs's stilled chest (per instructions) and walked out the door and went without molestation or interference to his rooming house after first making a phone call from O'Malley's Tavern on, yet again, Water Avenue, that the job had been completed (per instructions). The way the world works is sometimes riddled with coincidence: the dozen chairs Dobbs had been reupholstering were from O'Malley's Tavern. The letter has since been lost, its contents unknown. The man spent a quarter on a pint of beer in O'Malley's after he made his phone call, drinking it wordlessly at the shining oaken bar. (This was decidedly *not* per instructions, but the man had an awful, raging case of piles at the time, and a pint helped him sleep.)

Do you want some of my food I'm not very hungry, the woman says, knuckling another tear away from her eye, her voice growing husky and thick. And it is a small knife in your heart, those words: that you have hurt someone like this, that those tears belong to you, they are your property, that you did not say *I love you* back to her when you could have any of those times, that three days ago you feigned other pressing, just-remembered obligations and left her bed immediately afterwards and ignored her plaintive messages on your cell phone and have not called her since, this well-known dread galloping up and down your spine. You, reaching your saturation point. You, leaving.

How tired you feel in your skin sometimes. All these trappings. The same maneuvers repeated endlessly.

What would truly interest you: Dobbs's ghost still haunts this restaurant. How Dobbs's ghost is actually standing and not standing right next to the two of you. Also how the cooks and waitresses will sometimes talk about it, him, the ghost in the restaurant, to their lovers and friends or their managers or each other (the owners are wealthy and are usually vacationing.) The employees will speak of vegetables suddenly mounded and prepped in perfect heaps when previously, only seconds before, they were lined haphazardly on the stainless-steel counters. They will speak of stacks of dishes moved from one shelf to another, all in a moment when their backs are turned away and they are alone in the kitchen. At this restaurant, you do not know it but there is a high turnover of staff. The ghost of Aaron Shelby Dobbs is not a physical entity per se but does physical things, and that is interesting because he is standing next to you and also not standing next to you right now when the physical thing *you* do right now is say *No thanks* to the other woman at this table.

This body of yours, lungs and voice box, corporeal and incredible, all of it a machine apparently designed to bruise the hearts of others.

You say *No* to this woman, that you do not want a bite of her food and then you say *Please understand* and she barks laughter and says *You keep fucking saying that.* You are afraid now of her face, those trembling lips and the one beautifully crooked tooth and the green-flecked brown eyes, one of them always looking slightly off-center no matter what.

You're just scared, she says flatly, still looking down at her plate, and the hand that holds her fork, all of those knuckles are white there, she's holding it so tightly.

No it's not that I swear.

You're just scared of being with anyone, she says. *Being a dyke has shit to do with it.*

No.

Bullshit Lara you're just fucking scared, she says. Her voice is rising and, even more than hurting her, what you are afraid of is making a scene in public.

I'm not a fucking dyke, you say (more vehemently than you meant to—people are definitely looking at you now) and now the woman stands from this table, her food untouched. She slams her thighs against the edge of this table as she rises and orange juice spills onto the face of the sun and she practically pushes you to the ground as she muscles her way past you into the aisle and people are watching still because your coffee cup falls from the table and shatters when it hits the painted concrete floor[7]. The woman storms down the aisle, past the

---

7. See footnote 3.

other customers, all of them twenty-something, all of them shot through with tattoos and ridiculous haircuts and clothes that are so unfashionable they are somehow fashionable—in short, people just like her and just like you—and, with one hand curled loosely around the door handle, she turns to you, her face a rictus tracked with mascara and hurt.

You are a selfish bitch, she says to you from across the room, enunciating each word but spaced with tremors, and what happens next is that all the silverware in the restaurant, all the knives, forks and spoons, all the metallic napkin dispensers and salt and pepper shakers and rounded placard-holders with the breakfast specials clipped inside, they all suddenly balance themselves on their points or begin to spin around rapidly in counterclockwise circles[8]. The exodus toward the door and the picturesque, sun-dappled sidewalk is immediate and frenzied. A punk, his hair quilled like a porcupine, his face peppered with piercings, is the first to reach the door. He pushes the woman to the side and makes his exit and soon there are others, a massed throng, everyone screaming—the cook comes galloping from the back shrieking *The fuck was that the fucking knives stood up and started spinning around* and someone else says *Earthquake it's an earthquake*—and she hits the floor and lays there dazed and something happens to you when you see her there like that.

And you rise from this table. You do. The silverware thrums and spins on the tabletops and along the arm of the counter as if they were dozens, hundreds of tuning forks or divining rods or dervishes, and the people are pushing each other through the doorway onto the sidewalk where there is sunlight and nothing strange, where inexplicable things do not happen. Some of them keep running once they get outside but some of them turn, their faces filled with wonder now that they are ostensibly safe; some of them begin taking videos with their phones or mill around and peer through the window, faces

---

8. Ghosts who have died without seeing their executioners—an incomplete list includes fleeing soldiers throughout history, the victims of suicide bombings, various politicians and one long-dead upholsterer who laments the fact he never got to share a pint with Joe Hill—are both gifted and cursed with the shifting and occasional knowledge of their own disembodiment. In short, Aaron Shelby Dobbs, even though he is both here and not here, sometimes *understands* that he is a spirit. Is sometimes aware that he can manipulate the physical, yet is himself without physicality. This awareness does account, of course, for the strange and unexplainable acts—which are, to his credit, nearly always to the benefit of the workers (chopping vegetables, cleaning up, etc.)—which take place around the restaurant. And the act of the shattering cup has served as a kind of electromagnetic claxon call to his wending spirit and, for the moment at least, more there than not there and feeling the emotional current between you and the woman much in the same way you would feel if you put a battery to the tip of your tongue, he has attempted to stem the tide, to give you both pause, to stop you in your tracks. In short, and despite the fact that the air is soon punctuated with screams and, in one unfortunate case, the loosening of bowels, the spirit of Aaron Shelby Dobbs is trying to help the two of you out. In the spirit—no pun intended—of pure kindness, something the living so rarely manage, he's trying to give you the opportunity for a different ending.

slack with awe, and also one woman continues to scream even though she is outside and you, you walk over to the woman on the ground, your lover, while the silverware thrums and jitters on its points, while there are small bits of spasmodic sunlight, thousands of them, dappling the wall. You walk over to the woman and crouch down, your hand on her shoulder—her skin is warm through her T-shirt with its ironic saying and you have no idea why you are not afraid right now, or if not fearless at least not stunned by this strange menagerie because mostly what frightens you is everything ending like this with this woman and you say, *Please talk to me I'm sorry I love you too I do it's just that I've never made it past this part before.*

You have no idea where this bravery comes from, how you can ask her forgiveness among the spinning blades and shivering forks wiggling upright on their tines and though you do not know it, this will serve as a catalyst for you throughout the rest of your life. This is a definable moment in time in which you were brave, in which you have thought of someone else. This is possibly the first time you have been brave for someone else but it will not be the last now because it gets easier with time. And what you do next is you say *Please wait for me Esther* and even though it is only a dozen feet, maybe twenty, you walk back to this table and grab your bag and Esther's bag among the calliope of light dancing on the walls and you come back to her and she is no longer crying but has the same look on her face as the people peering through the windows—that of awe and punch-drunk wonderment—and, laden with both your bags, you help her rise and hold her hand in yours as you both step out the door into sunlight. You are brave, you are brave, and when you step out the doorway there is a clatter and rattle like bright music as everything in the restaurant falls down, down, down.

BABY JILL

On Wednesdays, Gary comes to collect the teeth.

• • •

The things Gary has parked in the driveway on various Wednesdays: a pop-topped Vanagon with a constellation of faded stickers across the rear window. A pink Corvette. A Hummer the color of a traffic cone. A motorcycle and sidecar. A mail truck. Usually just regular cars, regular things, but sometimes ones like these.

I wonder sometimes about the neighbors.

Also on Wednesdays: how I jump when he rings the doorbell. Every time. You'd think I would grow used to it after all this time. I see his form through the dimpled, hazy glass of the front door, and I open it and there is Gary. He's a short man, handlebar mustache, the fabric unspooling in the bill of his baseball hat. I have never seen him smile. I've watched him grow old, seen the back of his hands grow their first few mottled spots, faint enough but there. Before Gary was Luis, and before him, Etienne. Before that, I don't even remember anymore, which bothers me when I let it.

Hi, Carol, he says.

Hi, Gary.

Got everything squared away?

Sure thing, I say. Come on in.

Always like this: Gary steps into the house and takes off his hat and stuffs it bill-first into the back pocket of his jeans. We walk into the spare bedroom, Gary taking the lead. I trace the hallway wall with one hand; it makes a noise as faint as a whisper. Gary stands in the doorway with his hands on his hips, assessing.

Every week we do this. Every Wednesday.

The room is empty save for the tens of thousands of teeth carpeting the floor. Mounds of them. Hills and valleys of little pale teeth. The room is not particularly big, but still. Sometimes Gary has to really force the door open, really work at it. Skeins of daylight sift themselves through the gauzy curtains.

Gary, not one to be impressed by the quality of light or much else, grunts and says, Looks like a twelve-binner.

Or a ten, or a fifteen. He's never wrong, either. He always calls it just right. He packs them snug—I'm not allowed to touch the teeth once they're home, but I can carry the bins—and he's always right. They're heavy, those packed bins, and it's a chore to carry them out to whatever car's in the driveway.

Speaking of which, it's a rust-shot Plymouth Newport this time, unwieldy as a battleship. Gary grabs the bins from the trunk, puts gloves on and begins shoveling the teeth in. Always by hand. I don't know. When he's filled one, he stacks it in the hallway, where I'm standing and smoking.

This is how it's always been. Before Gary was Luis.

Gary says, Shouldn't smoke, Carol.

I laugh, blow a jet of smoke at the ceiling.

At least not inside, he says. Brings down the property value. His voice echoes; besides the teeth, the room is empty.

It takes a while, but he fills the last bin and we do a sweep of the carpet, making sure we haven't missed any whole teeth. There are always fragments, every time, the common detritus of their living: crumbled teeth, flaked enamel, the tiny nubs fractured off from decay or simple fragility.

Gary starts taking the bins out to the car. Sometimes I'll help; usually I stay inside and vacuum the carpet. Recently—maybe before Baby Jill and maybe not—I have felt a curious halving at the sight of all that newly-returned blue, that sky-blue square of carpet where previously, just moments before, thousands of teeth lay mounded and still like little carapaces. Part of me is overjoyed, a sense of completion at what we have done, a sense of wholeness. But there is a part of me that feels a clanging hollowness, a kind of sad and empty thunder. Like I'm, I don't know? An automaton, maybe? A marionette. Just performing a function.

Before Luis there was Etienne.

Gary pokes his head in. His hat is still in his back pocket; he'll put it on somewhere between the front door and the car before he drives away. His hand is wrapped around the molding of the bedroom door and I see the crude green lightning bolts tattooed on each finger.

Gonna get going, Carol.

Okay, Gary.

See you next week.

I'll be here, I always say.

Gary drives away and I am in the house.

I've done this for so long it has become more than the simple cadence of ritual. By now it's become mythology.

• • •

After Gary leaves I get on the computer in the den, telling myself I will not look at anything about Baby Jill. I will not. This resolve lasts for exactly two cigarettes and then I am back to scouring the news sites and watching the videos of the fire on YouTube. The video of her rescue has been viewed over four million times. Maybe people are looking for other things than I am. But I think I am trying to find some sign of whether she will live or not live. As if we could divine any answer from the grainy, jittering footage of a house fire.

People have left terrible comments on many of the websites and I spend hours refuting them, challenging them, intimate with its futility, my stomach cinched in a tight knot, a mixture of fury and hopelessness—almost the same way I feel looking at the just-vacuumed carpet. The sun limns the houses across the street, paints the sky a searing pink fading to purple.

I stare at the photograph, the terrible and now-famous one where some photographer snuck into the hospital where Baby Jill lay in a bed. She has, we know, received third degree burns over ninety percent of her body. In the photo, she is swaddled in bandages that look so white and heavy around her tiny little frame. The only holes in the bandages are where her pink mouth shines, and around one glittering blue eye. There's an obscenity about it, mostly in the slowly unfolding horror: She looks like a snowman. A snowbaby. She does.

• • •

Enamel. Dentin. Cementum. Pulp.
Periodontium, alveolar bone, gingiva or gums.
Tiny teeth, baby teeth.
I was birthed and sustained in lore.
In tradition and belief and all the trappings of ritual that accompany them.

• • •

There are moments, okay, where I hardly seem to be here at all.

• • •

The child is sleeping, of course. The night is deep with shadows. I hear the dim murmur of traffic downstairs—this is an apartment building—and also the metronomic snore of a man in the room next to this one. The child's comforter is blue with little white dogs on it.

Simply being here is all that's necessary. The tooth is gone from beneath the pillow, cast to the floor of the house I live in, the money is there beneath the child's head. The family will remember everything differently—the mother tiptoeing in with a few dollars, taking the small tooth in trade. She will feel a bittersweet tug in her chest when she thinks of it tomorrow. This is the great and silent engine of myth at work, the locomotion of it that propels us all.

I don't know how long it is that I stand there, but the man in the other room coughs and it brings me back. This has been happening more and more, this curious drift within me. This distancing.

I should be gone—it should only take seconds, my presence is really all that's needed—but I do something I've never done before and tuck a curl of hair behind the little boy's ear. His eyelashes flutter and one hand flexes in sleep and then relaxes.

• • •

Harlan Fero pled guilty at his arraignment today. He cried. I saw it on the news. Baby Jill's father owed him money, he told the judge. A gambling debt. Baby Jill's father refused to pay and Fero set the house on fire in retaliation. I didn't think anyone was home, he said. No lights were on, no car in the driveway.

What we all want to say to him: They were sleeping. The car was in the shop, Harlan Fero.

You people, I think. All of you people.

I watch the video of the rescue again and again, the jumpy footage of the fireman in his mask and greatcoat pulling the little smoking thing from the house, the doorway itself bloomed with fire, his arms wrapped around the darkened little form cradled in his arms that we all know now is Baby Jill.

• • •

I am surprised when Gary is at my door and it is a Friday afternoon. The floor of the guest room is scattered with teeth. But not enough, of course.

You come on Wednesdays, I say stupidly, squinting against the sunlight out there.

I wonder what this feeling is that I'm having.

Gary looks bad. He's sallow and pale and even with his hat on I can see the flesh under his eyes is purple. He says, You're blowing it, Carol.

I look out at the driveway and there's nothing there.

How did you get here, Gary? Where's your car?

He shrugs and says, I walked.

It's not Wednesday, I say. Come back on Wednesday. I'm afraid. I start to shut the door but Gary puts his hand out.

You can't touch the kids, Carol. Rule number one. You've known that forever. What's going on?

Take your hat off, I want to say but don't. And also: Let me see your eyes.

Instead I say, I'll see you Wednesday, Gary.

I want to smile and tell him everything's okay but I can't seem to manage it.

● ● ●

In Belgium and France I am *la petite souris*. The little mouse. In Scotland I am a white rat and I buy your teeth from you with golden coins. Or elsewhere a rat that will exchange them for a gift. And still other places, you must throw your tooth toward the sun and I will catch it and your next tooth will grow in straight and true.

● ● ●

Sometime later I find myself standing in front of the mirror with night's dark pressing against the bathroom window. I don't know how much time has passed. How long I've been standing there holding a cigarette.

Ash is scattered in the sink. I've burned my fingers.

● ● ●

We call her Baby Jill but really she's three years old.

● ● ●

I feel like I've watched the footage of Baby Jill's rescue for centuries, like I've strode down history's backbone with her memory wrapped around me like a blanket. But it's only been a few weeks, I think.

Someone tried to kill Harlan Fero in jail. Another inmate.

Everything here is coming untethered.

• • •

Do you want these? the cashier says.

What?

He holds out the pack of cigarettes. He's wearing a Save Baby Jill shirt.

You just blanked out, he says. You were just standing there.

Sorry, I say. I put the cigarettes in my purse. Sorry about that.

• • •

On Wednesday Gary comes and it's like nothing has happened, but things clearly have. I can see traceries of veins in his papery cheeks and the lightning bolts on his fingers now are clouds or maybe just pressings of color. His T-shirt has holes in the seams of the shoulders. In the driveway there's a truck shaped like a hot dog, and I smile when I see it.

Six bins? he says from the doorway of the bedroom. That's it, Carol? What have you been *doing*?

That look he gives me, I know it. That's real fear, what's in his eyes.

• • •

The next day is the day Baby Jill dies.

Too much trauma, doctors say. She fought so hard. A tragedy.

And this is me, sitting in front of my computer, crying and crying. Lighting cigarettes and putting them out. Watching the video of the fireman saving her again and again, letting her live over and over, letting her be saved, watching him pull her little body from the flaming door.

• • •

That night I appear in a child's room and from the dim wash of the nightlight I see there's a man in the bed too. He yells when he sees me, scrabbles to pull up his sweatpants and I bid the child sleep and forgetfulness and then unfurl into a particular form I've long known myself capable of but have never partaken in. I think I'm still crying, maybe, thinking about Baby Jill and also because I know what this man was doing. How have I not happened upon something like this before? What kind of rules are these? I am filled with a kind of blank, thrumming savagery toward him.

Don't touch me, he says. Oh, don't you touch me. He tries to crawl under the bed.

And then we go up to the roof and the first thing that happens is I take out all of his teeth.

• • •

You're done, Gary says the next day. He stands coughing in the doorway. One of his eyes is pink and heavy with blood. It's a beautiful day outside. This juxtaposition: Gary, and the houses across the street framed by the searing blue sky.

He earned it, I say. Didn't you see? How was I supposed to stand there?

Gary shakes his head. He's carrying a duffel bag over his shoulder that's rigid with right angles.

You just can't, Carol. It's not in the workings of things.

It's not right, I say.

For the first time ever, I hear Gary laugh. It sounds terrible, like someone hammering cement. Carol, there's no room for right here, he says. Right and wrong's in a whole different building.

By repetition or familiarity, we've both walked back to the spare bedroom. Gary's put his hat in his back pocket and I see gatherings of stitches in his head, unlovely highways of scalp where they had to shave him. Children's teeth are gathered like clouds on the floor, small islands of them—but there's so much blue carpet in there as well. There's so much room left. A two-binner at best, I think.

Well, why? I say. Tell me why. I'm listening, Gary. Tell me.

THEIR SOULS CLIMB THE ROOM

Another hog came down the line, hung up and bucking against the chain wound around its rear leg. Nolan Tice let it go right past him, didn't try to stick it—the guy running the scald tank could deal with it. This was the fifth still-conscious hog to come down the line in as many minutes. Blaswell was operating the stunner; he was supposed to be subduing them before they got to Nolan, and he was doing a shit job of it. The next hog came down the line, forelegs twitching all dreamy amid the cataclysmic roar of the place, the reek of offal, the animal's dark and bottomless eye, and Nolan stuck it quick in the throat, loosing a fire engine-red torrent of blood that jetted against his apron and splashed against his boots and then pulsed into the trough set into the floor, as it moved on down the line. He stuck the next one and the next one and the next. Hogs came down the line every five seconds, twenty-four hours a day, stunned or not. Shackled by that rear leg, screaming and thrashing if Blaswell had skipped stunning them with the paddle, or if the foreman turned the juice down too low to do any good.

He was a felon, Nolan, and had gotten the job at Good Acres Foods the year before because the sticker before him had lost a thumb from a hog kicking the blade back against his hand. Good Acres was about the only place in the county that'd hire anyone with a record, and Nolan made twelve dollars an hour killing roughly five thousand animals a shift, five shifts a week. At night he could feel the souls of all the dead hogs pressing on his chest, pressing down on his ribcage like something real. A near-tangible weight that he could nearly touch. All those souls pinning him to the mattress, pressing down on the animal meat of his heart. There were times where he'd be drinking at Fischer's and he could convince himself they were ghosts that haunted him, that he could practically feel the smoke-like and vaporous souls that climbed the ceiling and hung there above him.

The line kept going. He seethed, stuck, kept track. He counted forty-six still-kicking hogs on the chain by lunchtime.

Even in the lunchroom the sound of the saws and the hogs screaming over them never entirely went away. The pneumatics of the guns, the power-washers that pushed the blood into the drains. The cavernous quality of the place. Nolan found Blaswell eating lunch at a table with a couple other guys. He was a sad-looking, heavyset man with an overbite and a propensity for nervously hoisting his pants over his gut every minute or so. Nolan went up to his table and leaned on it with his knuckles.

"Forty-six," Nolan said.

Blaswell stopped chewing, looked up at him with those wet eyes. "Forty-six what?"

"Forty-six pigs kicking at me, goddammit. Half a shift, I got forty-six pigs still jumping at me? The hell are you doing out there, man?"

The other men traded glances. Blaswell licked his lips. "Reynolds lowered the voltage on the stunner. Said we were getting too much bloodsplash."

Reynolds was the foreman, and Nolan realized right away that Blaswell was probably right. He was just doing the best he could. If the foreman turned the stunner down so low, there wasn't much Blaswell could do about it. Still, Nolan was in a feeling, and the man's admission did absolutely zero to belay his anger. "I don't give a shit about bloodsplash," he spat. "I don't want my own fucking knife kicked into my face."

"I'm just saying. Take it up with Reynolds."

Nine months clean and the fury just unspooled within him sometimes, just came unzipped, like a cartoon of a guy stepping out of his skin-suit and there was just a whirling red cloud inside. "Fuck you," Nolan said.

Blaswell shrugged, looked down at the table as he scooped some crumbs into his palm. Quietly, he said, "Fuck you too, Nolan, jeez."

Nolan started around the table and Blaswell pushed his chair back with a screech. Nolan had a weight bench in his trailer, went running when he wasn't too hungover, and the flesh around Blaswell's neck quailed like putty, but he had to hand it to the guy—Blaswell didn't back down. All the souls whirled inside Nolan like some sad and lonely cyclone. He imagined the soft give of Blaswell's stomach beneath the sticking knife, imagined the man hung up in the stick pit by a chain. This was what the place did to you. He was about to feint toward Blaswell's gut and get down to it—job be damned, who was or wasn't right be damned, that rage just begging him to take over the show—when he felt a hand grip his bicep and squeeze.

Behind him, Manny said, "Not worth it, man. Keep your paycheck."

Everyone spent a minute huffing around the table, standing there. Nolan finally exhaled hard and offering a hand to Blaswell, saying something about how he'd take it up with Reynolds. Saying he was sorry that things got heated.

All bullshit, but Manny was right. He needed the paycheck.

• • •

After lunch he stuck and stuck and stuck. The math said that he had killed nearly a million animals in ten months at Good Acres, and the weight of that number bound him to the kill floor as if he were rooted there with wire. He imagined the souls of the hogs migrating from their bodies and writhing against the ceiling, wending fog-things that followed him home like a red cloud, that fell like leaves in his hair. Souls that clung to his shirt like cigarette smoke, that writhed there like butterflies.

• • •

He and Manny were drinking at Fischer's after their shift. Nolan felt bleary and tired, and even after showering in the changing room he could smell nothing but blood and hogshit, the greasy, brutal press of animal flesh. The whole bar stank of it. Every one of them did. It suffused the whole town.

"One of these days some pig is gonna kick that knife right into my throat," he said. He picked at his eyebrow with a nail. "It's gonna happen."

"You gotta stick and move, man." Manny grinned, ducking his shoulders like a boxer, his fists to his chin.

Manny had been at Good Acres for twelve years, which made him an ancient, doddering old man by slaughterhouse standards, though he was hardly over thirty. He'd started working the chutes, corralling the hogs, but he was a utility man now. Utility men could do any of the jobs in the plant: driver, stunner, shackler, sticker, gutter. He'd worked the scald tank, had scooped entrails and congealed blood from the pit troughs. Twelve years at a slaughterhouse had turned him into a stooped-over little man with an endless thirst and a pair of eyes that didn't quite work in tandem anymore, the result of countless drunken fistfights. Sober he was fine, but drinking always brought him to some turning point where he became something else. He ordered the two of them another round and told Nolan he was stupid for getting into shit with Blaswell.

"I mean, he's got a point," Manny said.

"I know he does."

If the current was set too high on the stunner, it could burst capillaries in the hog's body, leave dark spots on the flesh that had to be cut away. It hardly ever happened, but less meat meant less money, and policy was policy. So the foreman would set the paddles low enough that you'd sometimes have to stun a hog seven, eight, twelve times before they buckled. And with the chain running a new animal every five seconds, nobody had time for that. You slowed the line, you got written up. You *stopped* the line, you got canned. So there wasn't much choice but to let the hog through, stunned or not.

"It's Reynolds you should be mad at, you know?"

"Yeah," Nolan said. "I hear you."

Manny was getting that far away, glassy-eyed look that always sparked a bad feeling in Nolan; he'd seen a drunken Manny pull a switchblade on a guy in the parking lot a few months back, and he'd had that same sleepy, bemused look on his face that he had now.

"I gotta get out of here," Nolan said, scrubbing his face.

"You can always quit," Manny said, gazing up at the television hung above the bar. "What'd you do before this again?"

"Sawmill," Nolan said. "Worked a planer."

"That's right. They shitcan you?"

Nolan shrugged. "Mill went under. Same thing everywhere."

"Yeah."

This, of course, was a severely edited version of the story. It was true the mill had begun piecemealing shifts out, a lot of guys getting laid off, so that Nolan and everyone else he knew was left fighting for scraps, hardly anyone full time, but what was more true was that the same time he'd gotten his hours cut was when he'd met Deb and started falling down the rabbit hole of meth—first snorting it, then smoking it, then eventually shooting it. He'd never shied away from narcotics before, but meth had opened up new avenues of need inside him. Quickly enough it had dissected any love between them into distinct categories of obligation: there was dope and there was everything else. After his inevitable firing from the mill, desperate and hungry, with the two of them always on that trembling line between kicking and not, he'd done some strong-arm work for the local chapter of the Crooked Wheel club. He'd twice been the lookout when they'd broken into pharmacies, and they'd paid him in dope. He and Deb had lost their place, and then he got busted with twenty grams in his truck and landed an Intent to Sell conviction that got him four years in Salem. He served two, his PO landing him the job at Good Acres. Deb was long gone by then, locked in the arms of her own trip. It's not like she'd waited for him or he'd expected her to; she was already enmeshed in the thing before he'd met her. He'd gone willingly along. It had been a nine-month white-knuckle ride since getting out, and he still ached for dope sometimes with an almost electric bitterness in the back of his mouth. He still didn't know if he was lucky or not.

He'd seen Deb six months ago, and she'd looked like something exhumed from a grave and propped up against a wall. It was hard to believe she was the same person—that a couple years could carve that much from a body and still let them stay upright.

"The work's not for everyone," Manny said, bringing him back. "It's tough work. It wears on you."

He opened his mouth to tell Manny about the souls of the hogs, how he thought of them all the time, how real they seemed. But then he imagined how he'd feel in the morning, knowing that he'd told Manny about it, and changed his mind.

"You ever think about quitting?" he asked.

Manny laughed. He wore a gaudy silver watch that he took off during his shifts but now he shook it on his wrist. "Man, I got cousins in the cartels back home, you know? The things they have to do make this look nice."

Nolan lifted his glass. "Shit, you imagine that? If this is as good as it gets?"

It was a measured, crafty gaze, the one that Manny gave him. Sleepiness and cunning in equal bounty. That same laconic air that he'd had in the parking lot when he'd slipped his switchblade out, almost like he was sleepwalking. Nolan saw that look now and thought, Ah, here we go.

"If you need money," Manny said, "I can get you money."

"I don't need money. I need to stop killing pigs every day."

"It's easy work."

"Easy and legal?"

Manny laughed and shook his wrist.

"Yeah," Nolan said. "That's what I thought."

• • •

He dropped Manny off at his apartment and had just settled onto the couch with a beer when there was a knock at the door. His trailer was small and the sound reverberated through the place.

Barefoot, in his shorts and a T-shirt, the narrow living room was awash in the dim light of the table lamp and the TV when he opened the door. Deb was standing at the foot of the steps next to Bo, a big Viking-looking motherfucker who Nolan had sometimes worked with during his meth days. The porch light was harsh and unforgiving, carving Deb up into harsh planes, darkening the hollows of her eyes, lighting the constellation of tiny scabs cratering her cheeks.

Seeing the both of them was like falling into quicksand. Deb had withered even further. Bo was in his club leathers, his graying hair tied back in a ponytail. They clomped up the porch steps and Nolan could feel the give in the floor.

"What's up, my man?" Bo rumbled, his eyes glittering. Without looking at her, he told Deb to sit down.

Nolan said, "What is this?" and shut the door behind them. Deb was wearing jeans dirty at the knees and a sleeveless green blouse that showed the scattershot range of bruises on her arms. Skeletal, her neck thin as a branch.

Bo hooked a thumb at her. "This slag's into us for four grand."

"Fuck off," Deb rasped.

"Shut the fuck up," Bo said. He turned his gaze back to Nolan. "If we hook her out, it's gonna take forever for her to pay it off. I mean, look at her."

"Fuck you, asshole," Deb said. She lit a cigarette with shaking hands and worried a sore on the back of her hand. Nolan felt the souls of the hogs fill the room.

"Say it again," Bo said, smiling, peering down at her. His teeth were big and tilting and yellow, and it gave him an almost childlike quality. "Say one more word and see what happens."

Nolan walked to the fridge and took out beers. His heart hammered in his chest. "What do you want me to do about it? Me and her aren't together anymore."

Bo cracked his beer and drank, wiped foam from his beard. "She said you could swing a down payment for her."

Nolan looked at Deb. "She said that, huh?"

"She did."

"We split before I went to Salem. You know that."

Deb snorted.

"Listen," Bo said. "It's cool that you didn't fold on anyone, that's good. The pharmacy jobs, all that. You could have flipped and you didn't. That's respected. But if we don't get something from her, you know what's gonna happen. The guys'll just take it out on her for a while and then sink one in the back of her head and throw her in a trunk somewhere."

Deb had turned her face away, was looking at the wall. Somewhere there was a buried ghost of this person he knew. They'd fallen down that hole together, hadn't they? They had slept together likes sacks of flung bones, exhausted, entrenched in a shared war. It was never love, but it was something. She put a ragged thumbnail to her teeth, the quick rimed in dried blood.

Nolan looked at Bo. "How much time can you give me?"

Bo shrugged, sniffed. "I mean, not much, honestly."

• • •

The next day during break, he and Manny went out back and smoked on the dock. The cries and bellows of the animals drifted out even there, but Nolan had long since grown inured to it. He looked at the long low-slung buildings that housed the pens beyond and thought of when Deb had first moved into his trailer. She'd hung up a crocheted little thing in the kitchen that said *Bless This Mess,* and had thought it was the funniest thing, saying it made her feel cozy.

Everything just gets winnowed out of a person, he thought. Just carved right out. The way the world takes hold and shakes you in its jaws.

"Tell me about it," he said, and Manny smiled like he'd been waiting.

"About what?"

"You know about what," he said.

They smoked a while longer and then Manny looked around the dock and said, "Reynolds has a car."

"What?"

"He's got a race car."

"Who?"

"Reynolds, man."

"Shit," Nolan said.

"No, man, it's easy. He's got it under a tarp in his fucking carport. He drives the thing around on the weekends. Him and his wife take trips and he goes to racetracks with it. We don't even have to drive it, man. We hook it up to my buddy's truck and pull it out. The engine alone, Tice."

"Never mind. Forget I asked."

"No, come on—"

"Reynolds isn't someone to play with, Manny."

"We take it to my buddy's place and he does whatever he's gonna do. Gets rid of the VIN, sells it. In California or somewhere."

Nolan looked at his face, tried to gauge him. "It sounds pretty thin."

"It's four thousand dollars, man," Manny said, laughing. He slapped Nolan on the shoulder with the back of his hand. "Two grand a piece. Just like that. Just hook it up and go."

Back in the stick pit, Nolan wondered if he had it in him. He'd been rabbit-scared the whole time parked outside the pharmacies, Bo and another Crooked Wheel rifling through the place, throwing everything into big garbage bags. Nolan sick and sore in his bones, his heart clanging every time a car passed by. Prison had turned something in him. He didn't want to go back, but he knew that Bo was telling the truth about what would happen to Deb.

A hog came down the line then, whiskered and bellowing, and just as he went to stick it in the throat it kicked out at him, its flank smashing against him in a collision of heat and muscle, a riotous stench of shit and fear, and Nolan's blade kicked up and zippered across his forehead. It didn't even hurt, just felt like someone had poured warm water on him, but he knew it was bad. He dropped the blade and slapped the red button at his station that brought the line to a halt. The trouble light in its cage above his station began to pulse, everything buried in a warble of sirens.

Reynolds came barreling up. He was a big man with a shorn scalp and razor burn on his throat. "Ah, damn," he said right away. "Go to the nurse's station."

He used his key to turn off the siren and then went to the rotary phone mounted next on the alarm. Nolan heard him order a utility man to come and work the stick pit. When Reynolds looked back over his shoulder, he saw Nolan looking at him.

"Get fucking moving," he said.

• • •

"Well, you need stitches, is what," the nurse said.

Nolan had a towel pressed to his skull. "Okay."

"I can't give you stitches. You gotta go to the ER."

Reynolds thundered into the room, frowned at Nolan with his arms crossed. "How we doing?" he boomed.

The nurse said, "He needs stitches." She was an older bottle-blond woman in rayon pants and a floral print blouse. Talc from her rubber gloves dusted her wrists white. Nolan had seen her working the video poker machine at Fischer's, but they'd never exchanged more than a nod before today.

Reynolds stood there with his hands on his hips, his tongue probing his cheek. "Can't we just bandage him up, send him back out there?"

"This ain't a boxing match," she said.

"I got a skeleton crew out there as it is, Vicki. Give me a break."

"He's bleeding like a stuck pig," Vicki said, and Nolan laughed. They both looked at him. "He needs to get to the hospital," she said.

Reynolds tried to fix Nolan with a smile. "How 'bout it, bud? Slap some gauze on there, send you back out? Take one for the team? I got a crew that's as thin as a bride's nightie out there. You'd really be helping me out, Nick."

"It's Nolan."

Reynolds didn't even flinch. "Nolan, right." His eyes cut to Vicki and back, and he sucked at his teeth and seemed to make some decision. "Nolan, you've got a record, is that right? Your PO set this up, didn't he?"

Nolan's face grew hot. "Yeah."

"Vicki," Reynolds said, "can you give us a sec?"

Vicki vanished like smoke, and Reynolds leaned against the counter and frowned down at his tie. "I'm not gonna lie to you, Nolan. District manager has my ass in a sling. We're way short on our quota this quarter."

"Okay."

Nolan could tell that Reynolds pictured himself as a man doing what needed to be done, a man with his back against the wall. A man with a family and a mortgage and all the rest. A man in a bind, doing the best he could.

"You know where this is going, right?"

"I think I do, yeah."

"Finish your shift or empty out your locker."

"What if I call my PO? Tell him you're strong-arming me?"

Reynolds shrugged. "You can do that, sure. But really, when you think about it, why would he believe you? And even if he did, why would he care?"

• • •

He came home to Deb sitting on his porch smoking a cigarette. She was wearing a puffy orange coat that almost enveloped her, that she got lost in. It was filthy, the hood fringed in matted fur. There'd been hardly anything in his locker to take home, and what was there was suffused with the stink of the slaughterhouse, so he'd simply shut it and left. Driven home one-handed, the towel pressed against his head, unsure of what else to do. Wasn't like he could cover an ER visit.

He stepped out of the truck and Deb's eyes grew big. She stood up and flicked her cigarette into the yard.

"What happened?" She pushed her hood down.

"Knife kicked back up on me."

She came down the steps and reached for his face. It was midday and the bones of her wrists looked like stones wrapped in skin.

"Jesus. Come on," she said, and took him by the sleeve, walking him up the steps.

"What're you doing here, Deborah?"

"I come to see how you are."

She led him to the bathroom and turned on the faucet. Took the bloodied towel away and found a clean washcloth in the closet, ran it under the water.

"If they're letting you run around, Deb, why don't you just take off?"

"And go where?"

"I can't believe you stuck me with this. You know? I can't believe it."

She cleaned the wound gently. Her hair had grown thin; he could see her pale scalp beneath. Souls hung thick in the room, writhed against the walls. "You want me to stitch this up?"

"Depends. Are you spun right now?"

Her laugh was brittle, exhausted. "That cross you're on is mighty high." She found a sewing needle and a little cardboard wrapper of thread in a drawer and held them in her palm like an offering. When he looked in the mirror, the wound was like an open mouth.

"What do I owe you, Deborah?"

She set the needle and thread down and pressed herself to the wall. She hugged her elbows, tiny hands poking from the sleeves.

"I just don't know what else to do," she said. They looked at each other in the mirror. It was easier to do it that way. "He wasn't making none of that up. You know they'll do it."

"I know it."

"I got nothing else."

"Just run, Deb."

"Where?"

"I don't know."

He knew she was right. Crooked Wheel knew people who knew people, and the kind of people that Deborah would walk among just to stay alive were of a type that would make finding her easy. The world was small, and the need she was saddled with would just make her world smaller still. She was trapped, and so was he.

• • •

Two nights later, he and Manny sat in the truck across the street from Reynolds's house, drinking gas station coffee and making sure the lights stayed off for a long while before they did anything. It was a neat split-level house, set far back on a county road. They could see the carport set a good distance from the house; the gray shape of the car under the tarp was barely visible in the gloom. Manny wanted to give Reynolds and his wife time to go to sleep. He'd taught Nolan how to use the winch that was fastened into the bed of the truck, and Nolan was worried it would be too loud.

"Do they have a dog?" Nolan had asked earlier that night. They'd been sitting at Manny's kitchen table; Manny's wife was making hamburgers, and the three of them were drinking beers. Nolan had been over there before and had heard Manny's wife speak maybe twenty words the entire time he'd known her.

"I don't know," Manny admitted.

"It's gonna suck if they have a dog."

"Don't worry about it."

"A dog that hears that winch is going to bark its head off."

Manny stood up and went over to the sink and grinned. "You know what happens after that," he said, and picked up a knife that was lying in the sink, jabbed it in the air.

"Stop," his wife said, and touched his arm. She was smiling. Manny put the knife back in the sink.

Now they were waiting in the truck. Nolan's head hurt. He had a big bandage on his head, something from a movie. Rent was due in a week and a half; not even counting what he'd need to give to Bo. Maybe, he thought, I'm the one who should run.

"You really think we can do this?" he asked. The window was cool against his cheek.

"I think we are doing it," said Manny. "I think we need to."

The souls of the hogs pressed against Nolan's heart. "He's going to hear us," he said. "It's a fucking winch, man."

"He's not going to hear us."

"But what if he does?"

"You can spend your whole life thinking about what might happen," Manny said, "and never move a foot."

A half an hour later Manny drove the truck in reverse up to the carport, the headlights dark, Nolan creeping on the grass alongside, ready to hook up the winch.

• • •

Later, he would scramble into his trailer and slam the door shut, crumple against it. Somewhere distant a dog would bark, and in the darkness the souls of dead hogs would hang on the ceiling like Christmas lights. His breath would come in hitches that were fast and small, like a rabbit breathing. His side would be hot but the rest of his body would feel numbed and cold, like God had reached down and punched him right there. He would rise up and slap at the light and look down and see that blood already slicked the floor, that his hands were shiny with it, and he would let out a keening animal noise and slap the light off. The souls of the hogs would be quiet and watchful on the ceiling, hung there like bats. Like someone opening a door or coughing: that was how quickly it had all gone wrong.

He would crawl over to the recliner and pull himself into it and sit there with his knees pressed tightly together, his cold hands clasped between them. He would weep for a little bit and feel small, like a speck of dust in a storm.

Headlights would wash across the wall and then stop.

He would cry out and stand up, staggering from object to object like a man at sea. The headlights would stay there, illuminating the room. He would make it to the back door of his trailer and open it and lurch out onto the beaten swath of ground that was his backyard. The moon would hang overhead, the night salted with stars.

He would walk away. Barbed wire would snag at his shirt and he would gingerly peel the fabric away and then fall over as he tried to step beneath a strand of it. He would cry out again and spend a minute on his hands and knees, gasping. He would rise and stagger on until he came to a small brackish pond, ringed in blackberry bushes and chokeweed. The water would be cold; mud would grasp at his shoes. The pong of the greenery around him would be heavy with rot. Water would rise to his thighs, the topography beneath his feet uneven and strange.

All the souls. All the souls of all the dead hogs would gather inside him, their executioner, the one who remembered them, the one who sanctified them. A million souls! And the way the water touched his wound, enveloped it. He kept walking into the water.

Perhaps he could hear the voices of men behind him. Perhaps it was a singular voice.

Perhaps, really, it was something else, and not a voice at all.

HOSPITALITY

THE PARKING LOT

The orca is a monolith crafted in plaster. It rises from the roof of the motel, twenty-seven feet from base to snout, its flesh ridged and bumped, the paint flaking to show its psoriatic underpinnings. Spattered in birdshit new and old, it has become the physical embodiment of all of Sam's worries and loathing. It is as if the Orca Motor Inn were some sea which the beast was dissatisfied with. Its once-white belly is now yellowed and cracked, its fins sun-bleached gray, it looks less majestic—what his father had presumably been hoping for when he'd built the motel forty years ago—than Mesozoic, something ancient and wraithlike and more than a little scary.

The Orca Motor Inn is L-shaped, two stories tall, and made up of twenty-four units. Between the building and the parking lot is a gated pool with a small slide at the deep end. You can see the orca from the Strip.

The building inspector, doubling in this case as an assessor for the bank, spends approximately ninety seconds on the roof looking at the whale before coming back down and ruining Sam's life. He is a small, dapper man who looks fussy enough to polish agates up his ass.

"It needs to come down, Mr. Akers," the inspector says. They are standing in the parking lot as the April wind whips a dank mist in their faces. Sam's ladder still leans against the lip of the roof. There are a grand total of three cars in the parking lot, including his and the inspector's. Sam, wearing a T-shirt and darkly hungover, shivers in the cold.

"What do you mean?" he says, his teeth chattering. "The whole thing? Like, the whole animal?"

The inspector nods, looking up at the orca and then writing something in his clipboard. "The whole thing, oh yes. Absolutely. It's compromising the structure of the building."

"What does that mean? Compromising? What do you mean by that?" Sam feels idiotic, simply parroting everything the man says. It is ten-thirty in the morning and he wishes at that moment to have taken any other path in his life than this one.

"It means," the inspector says, "there's a serious health risk here. As you can see, the majority of the weight is resting on the base of the structure, which is significantly more slender than the rest. The whole building is aging, and the statue is simply too top-heavy, Mr. Akers. It's dangerous." He has Sam sign a sheet and then hands him a copy of it.

"It's fun," Sam says helplessly. "It's supposed to be a fun thing."

The inspector shakes his head. "You've got thirty days to have the structure professionally removed, or the city will fine you and have it removed at your expense." The man drives a white Honda Civic with the city's crest on the door, and Sam is not surprised to see him smooth his tie before sitting in the driver's seat. Sam feels a sudden desire, so strong it brings a flush to his cheeks, to shut the door on the man's head.

He runs his hand over the stubble on his face. "But this is a family place," he says. He practically sputters it. "Where am I supposed to get the money? And what about my loan? I'm buying boxes of ramen with my credit card here, man."

The inspector turns the ignition and smooth jazz diffuses throughout the car like a fart.

"My loyalty's to the city first, Mr. Akers. Get rid of the whale and we can reschedule the rest of the loan assessment. In the meantime," and here he points to the roof, where the diseased whale's snout is just visible, "the statue is your priority."

The inspector's car eases into the rain-slicked street. Above Sam, the sky looks like a dirty shirt. He has never felt more alone in his life.

ROOM 119

When it comes down to it, and Carlos knows this, you preface anything with "accidental" and it doesn't mean shit. It doesn't. Because the end result is the same: Gravity still reaches the same terrible velocity. The breadth between negligence and malice becomes irrelevant when people get seriously hurt. Carlos knows this, he isn't dumb. Well, no, he *is* dumb, clearly, he's dumb as a bag of shit, but he knows there are plenty of people sitting in prison that will claim that whatever act had brought them there had been an accident. But putting "accidental" in front of it doesn't negate anything. So that's it, he deserves everything he's getting, all the panic. Whatever comes to him, he deserves it. He knew he shouldn't have let all of those dudes get on the ride—the Safety and Operations Manual had been explicit about that, clear as day—and he'd done it anyway. Because he wanted Kelly to think he was casual and aloof and *cool,* man, that he didn't care about anything, and because it was only the third week in April and his feet were already getting fucked up from standing in the chlorinated water all day, and because the dudes had been a little drunk at nine in the morning and bigger than him. It was an accident birthed of negligence and not ill intentions, but so what? They had not looked right, those dudes, not on the Safety Camera that showed the end of the ride, as Kelly started yelling when they came tumbling out of the bottom of the tube, their Flotation Pod rolling lazily out after them, empty, and now, Jesus Christ, what was he going to do now?

Carlos wants more than anything to call his mom, but his phone is dead. He is afraid of the motel phone, afraid that the manager will be able to listen in to his conversation. His car in the parking lot seems to blaze hot with criminality, flaring like neon. He can't even enjoy his first solo hotel room. He wonders if the Safari So Good managers have put an APB out on him, if the cops are actively out *combing the streets.* It seems entirely possible— maybe one of those guys died or broke their necks as they careened down the winding, darkened waterslide. And there's a police station right across the street. Carlos sits on the bed, absently flicking through TV channels and trying not to cry. The motel manager is standing out in the parking lot with some guy and Carlos winces every time the ladder they're using clangs against the lip of the roof. It's as if the world has thrown some net around him and is slowly cinching it tighter. Soon he'll rise from the shallow pool they've corralled him in, thrashing and bleating. He'll be caught. Of course he'll be caught. He shouldn't have run in the first place. But he is chubby and eighteen and brutally, mercilessly in love with Kelly Klaamden, his fellow Ride Operator of the Whirlwind Water Slide at the Safari So Good Waterpark and Resort. This is his first post-high school summer job after laying about sloth-like and aimless in his room for the past nine months, smoking weed practically every day while his mom was at work, and he'd just had this *moment,* watching those bodies slide broken and thrashing out of the bottom of the Whirlwind's yawing mouth, grainy on the Safety Monitor but unmistakably *hurt,* where he saw his entire future flare and then blacken like a stone flung into deep space—there and gone. There's nothing left to sustain it now, it's over. His life is done.

So he'd run.

"It was an accident," Carlos says, a sob like a sudden hot stitch in his throat. "Dude, it was an accident and I'm *sorry.*"

There is an infomercial on TV, some guy showing how finely a brick of meat can be sliced with these particular knives, and it shows a close-up of the silver blade cutting through the red side of flesh marbled with white fat and that, that is it, Carlos feels exactly like that. Carlos, *exactly,* is that side of meat. The man looks so happy to be where he is, cutting the brick of meat with those knives, and Carlos lays back on the bed and puts a pillow over his face and starts to cry.

ROOM 201

Sara's jeans are worn the color of seafoam in places and her wrist when she reaches for the handle of the motel lobby door is thin and pale enough to show the blued veins beneath her sleeve and just a flash of an ugly green bruise on the inside of her arm. Sara wears her hair in a ponytail threaded with gray and jeweled with tiny droplets of mist and her eyes are like chips of gathered flint. She coughs while filling out the form, small, delicate coughs in which she presses the back of her hand to her lips. She pays in cash and signs the forms under a name not her own, lists a license plate number not hers, and the manager gives her the room directly above his office. He's intoxicated to some degree and needs a shave, and when he hands over her room key tells her it's the quietest room in the hotel. She is not sure what differentiates a hotel and a motel, but this is clearly of the latter variety. The manager looks at her with red-rimmed eyes and seems a man lost, grasping at any passing thing, and in this manner she feels a kinship with him.

(Still, she can't help it: a cataloging of the man's exploitable vulnerabilities as he stands there staring at her with his wet, mournful eyes, holding out her tasseled keyring—larynx, eyes, nasal cartilage, vertebrae, tongue, fingers, wrists.)

She takes the key and thanks him and heads out to her car to get her suitcase. She and the executive will be having dinner at seven that evening, and Sara needs to sleep. Small red flecks of blood color the back of her hand.

THE TOWNSHIP PROPER

Wisconsin Dells is a city in south-central Wisconsin. Spread throughout four counties (Adams, Columbia, Juneau, and Sauk), it takes its name from the dells of the Wisconsin River, a glacially formed gorge scattered with stunning sandstone formations along its banks. Together with nearby towns Lake Delton and Gaston, the city forms an area known as "the Dells," a popular Midwestern tourist destination.

The Dells has an estimated five million annual visitors, due mostly to its plethora of indoor and outdoor waterparks. It has proclaimed itself the Waterpark Capital of the World, and is home to the largest outdoor waterpark in the U.S. (Noah's Ark), the largest indoor waterpark resort (Kalahari Resort), and America's largest water and theme park resort (Mt. Olympus Water & Theme Park). Other attractions in the Dells include the Dells Boat Tours, numerous golf courses, mini golf, go-kart tracks, horseback riding, Ricky Gimmlett's Wilderness Show, the Green Pines Amusement Alley, the Delton Lake Casino and many other places of interest. Most attractions are located on "the Strip," otherwise known as the Wisconsin Dells Parkway. Accommodations range from economical motels to RV parks to chain hotels and smaller themed resorts featuring their own, admittedly less extravagant waterparks and amenities.

The Orca Motor Inn is located on Highway 12—or Wisconsin Dells Parkway South. It's reasonably far south from places like Noah's Ark, at least in comparison to other motels, and worse, is directly across the street from the Gaston Police Department, a squat, unlovely cement building with a parking lot and a few scattered police cruisers. Sam Akers's father had been of the opinion that being so close to the police would be reassuring to travelers. Sam, his own optimism long since evaporated like liquor held captive too long in a bottle, believes its proximity further scares people away.

THE MANAGER'S OFFICE

Sam is ensnared in a sleeping bag behind the desk in his office. He looks at the splinters of light on the ceiling, all that illumination aching to get in beyond the shade and kill him dead. His head is full of a flat blank murder, the orbs of his eyes burning as they ratchet about in his skull, and when he turns his head (the air mattress beneath him sullenly squeaking), he spies the discarded whiskey bottle and bile leaps gleefully to his throat. It takes all of his strength to quell it.

He has been sleeping in the office for over a month now. It seems to have happened in slow-motion, really. Sleeping behind his desk on an inflatable mattress and a sleeping bag, boxes of his belongings stacked around him, their flaps hastily scrawled with things like KITCH. PLATES and BILLS. While his tenancy is technically not legal due to zoning issues, fuck it, he owns the motherfucking building. At least until the orca falls and crushes them all to death.

Hard times abound. The motel is at full capacity, with all twenty-four units occupied, two months out of the year. Maybe three. At times, like now, even though the busy season is less than a month away, it's at more like ten percent. He blames, to varying degrees: the Gaston Police station right across the goddamn street, the state of Wisconsin, monolithic megaparks like Noah's Ark and Safari So Good, the entire tourism industry, capitalism itself, surfing, Hawaii, his father, Fate, God. He has become inured to this litany. As the megaparks have become more self-contained, places like the Orca have become increasingly irrelevant. It is easy enough to cast blame outward most days, but on his more humble, aching mornings, where his brain feels too large and inflamed for his skull and his beating heart pounds away like a terrible pendulum in his ribs, Sam blames Pabst Blue Ribbon and Paramount whiskey and his own weaknesses. This rarely lasts, however.

It had been a question this year of paying taxes on the building or paying rent on his one-bedroom apartment in Lake Delton. The fact that at thirty-seven years old this question is one that Sam must contemplate brings about a bitterness that is almost unquenchable, one that flares to life at a moment's notice and can send him on a crying jag, or growling with rage and pacing about the room. So he ditched the apartment, left most of his belongings there and scrawled a note to the manager to have fun with his deposit. The bank has tentatively approved him for a loan, something he can coast on for a while, but this is reliant on a new assessment of the property. Hence a visit from various assessors, including the smooth-jazz-loving building inspector. The state of his loan seems doubtful now, though it seems an easy enough thing to clear up. Just hire someone to knock the fucking whale down and then call the bank.

Still, Sam's frequent quandary: it feels like the skull under his face is comprised of broken pieces of glass and the day is just too *sad* out there. How did he get here? How did the world become so infused with this kind of brutal *leadenness*?

Sam lies in his mummy bag, looking at the splinters of light above him. Bile forced back down to its appropriate quarters, he clears his throat. "My heart," he rasps. "My heart is breaking right inside me." This feels right somehow.

As if in answer, he hears the brittle *ting ting* of the bell at the reception desk and groans in disbelief. Withdrawing himself from his mummy bag proves difficult, and leaning against his desk and putting his shoes on brings about another dangerous bout of nausea. His head is being squeezed by a pair of gigantic pliers, the sort employed by a demon, most likely, one of a fully realized evil. He will die momentarily, he knows: no one can live through a hangover like this. He steps from his office and sees one of the two current guests standing there, the fat Latino boy. He is reading a map of local attractions, his hand hovering above the bell once more. Sam swears a hideous and graphic death upon him should his hand drop.

INTERDEPARTMENTAL EMAIL ISSUED TO ALL ACTIVE REGLITE ARMS MANUFACTURING (RAM) MIDWESTERN SUB-REGIONAL VICE PRESIDENTS (SRVPS), SUB-REGIONAL PRESIDENTS (SRPS) AND INTERDEPARTMENTAL LIAISONS (ILS), DISTRICTS 12 THROUGH 19, REGARDING RECENT SUCCESSES AND MANDATORY TEAM-BUILDING PROTOCOL

TO: ACTIVE SRVPs, SRPs, ILs, DIST. 12-19, US DIVISION
FROM: GERALD DEVENEAUX, REGLITE VP, US DIVISION
RE: SUCCESS & TEAM BUILDING! BRING YOUR SUNBLOCK!

Ladies and gentlemen, well done.
Incredibly well done.

It's been a good year at Reglite. A very good year. Because of *you.*

I'd like to personally thank you all for your dedication and ingenuity to the long and sometimes rocky road that has been the Barker 9mm Handgun account. Safe to say, it's been a success. In countless ways, *innumerable* ways, from manufacture and design to marketing and promotion, you and your teams have worked tirelessly to make the Barker one of the most accessible, affordable, economically successful, reliable and safe home defense handguns in the country. The numbers don't lie, and I thank you for it. Our CEO, Dr. James Lerner, thanks you for it. Our stockholders thank you for it. Most importantly, the American people thank you for it.

Since the release of the Barker least year, RAM stock prices have risen *eleven percent,* unheard of even in our industry. The Barker itself, in its three models, has generated over *$250 million dollars profit* for RAM within the last fiscal two quarters alone.

It's safe to say, ladies and gentlemen, the *Barking Dog* campaign has been a "roaring" success. Reglite has, since its inception in 1922, always been on the cutting edge of arms manufacturing. With team members like you, because of your dedication and sacrifice, I feel confident in saying we've not only met the challenge of our competitors, we're poised to surpass them.

I know many of you have sacrificed much during the past two years of the Barker campaign. I know you've lost time with your families, missed opportunities within your communities. As a token of the company's gratitude, we've assigned you all to spend a week—staggered throughout the next quarter (there's a lot of you!)—relaxing at various luxury family resorts within our lovely Wisconsin

Dells area. We believe it's important to reward hard work, as well as build strong economic ties within our communities.

Bring your families. We know they've missed you. This is paid time, of course, non-vacation, with a few hours out of the day scheduled for team-building exercises, strategy planning, strength assessments. The rest of the day, spend with your families. Have dinner with your wives and husbands. Spend the afternoon swimming with your children.

More details shall be forthcoming from your Regional Liaisons, but in the meantime, prepare yourself to take a break. You deserve it.

Sincerely,
G. Devereaux, Vice President, US Division
Reglite Arms Manufacturing, Milwaukee, Wisconsin, USA

THE LOBBY

The manager zombie-stomps from his office with the tail of his shirt hanging out and the sweet stink of alcohol around him like a fog. He clips a filing cabinet and then walks full bore into a plastic palm tree on his way to the counter and Carlos is mildly impressed when the man doesn't even blink. The plant topples, spraying a fan of real dirt on the floor, as the manager reaches the counter and braces himself against it as if it were a kind of life raft. Carlos smiles wanly and takes a step back.

"What can I do for you, sir?" The manager's voice sounds as if some vital inner workings have recently become lathered in gravel.

Carlos says, "Uh, I wanted to pay for another day? And I was wondering if you had phone chargers or something like that? For sale?" Something Carlos has loathed about himself for years, but especially since Kelly pointed it out to him: how he phrases everything as a question, as if seeking permission and allowance for the simplest of things. And here, then, a testament to Kelly's transmutative powers: even this brief thought of her lends some iron to his spine.

The manager lowers his head and looks at Carlos through hooded eyes. Dude needs a shave, to put it bluntly. His mouth is slack and he looks for all the world like a man being taken over by something otherworldly; a possession of some kind. He stares at Carlos like this for ten seconds, fifteen. Finally he shakes his head like some dog casting water off its back, and says, "What? A phone charger?"

"And another night?" Stay strong, Carlos. "And another night."

The manager puts his hands over his face. He names a price for the room through his cupped hands. "But a phone charger I don't have. This isn't a Radio Shack. Or a fucking, I don't know, a Walmart. I don't know if they still have Radio Shacks."

Carlos fishes out his wallet and says quietly, "Well, your sign said you have amenities, so I was just wondering."

Still talking through his hands, the manager says, "I make a pot of Yuban at seven in the morning and keep it here on the counter until ten, along with some Styrofoam cups. Those are the amenities."

Carlos hands him exact change and is surprised to see the man put it directly into his wallet.

The manager catches his look. "What," he says, "you don't need a receipt, do you?"

Carlos thinks of Kelly, stands up a little straighter. "I do need a receipt, actually."

Looking as if he might begin weeping, the manager pulls out a pad and begins writing.

EXCERPT FROM THE *SAFARI SO GOOD EMPLOYEE SAFETY AND OPERATIONS MANUAL*

Operator shall utilize Weight Meter (located directly under the Safety Monitor) for all riders. There are no exemptions allowed; clients must always utilize the Weight Meter before being gained admittance to Safari So Good Waterpark Amusement Ride: (Whirlwind)™. *No single riders allowed on ride. Total weight of riders shall not exceed 650 lbs. Total number of riders shall not exceed four (4). Weight disparity between individual riders shall not exceed 250 lbs. Riders must use Flotation Pod. Ride operator shall not allow new riders on* Safari So Good Waterpark Amusement Ride: (Whirlwind)™ *until operator has visual confirmation via Safety Monitor that previous passengers have disembarked from end of ride. Ride operator shall keep in radio contact with fellow operator stationed at completion of ride. If necessary, operator will seek verbal affirmation of passenger completion and readiness from fellow operator. Operator shall stay posted in six (6) hour shifts, with ten-minute breaks allotted every two (2) hours. In case of emergency, operator shall notify fellow operator of emergency situation, and also contact appropriate* Safari So Good Emergency Contact Units *stationed throughout premises. Operator must stay stationed at his/her posting throughout emergency. In case of breaks, operator must wait for relief operator; operator may not leave* Safari So Good Waterpark Amusement Ride: (Whirlwind)™ *unattended for any reason.*

A RESTAURANT WITHIN A NEARBY
WATERPARK RESORT

Here is Sara's car, discreet and featureless amid a sea of them, the parking lot itself nearly an acre. See how the gray hands of twilight, the diffusion of the air, seems to mute the sound of the waterpark within its fences beyond. A massive place, the resort. Thousands of people cocooned within those fenced borders, acres and acres of brightly colored buildings, dozens of them, waterpark slides jutting from them randomly like strange appendages. The kinesis of children at play, of parents harried or relaxed, teenagers ensconced in clumsy, joyous flirtations. Such boundless energy.

See Sara at a table in a dimly lit restaurant within the resort. See her in a dress a touch too regal for the setting. See the waiter with a sunburned nose arrive with a fresh bottle of wine; see Sara smile as her hands arch across the mouth of her wineglass, politely refusing a refill. See the bruise on her arm covered with makeup. See how she carries something electric about her in spite of her collarbones so pronounced. The curving ladder of her spine pearled with translucence, her skin so pale as to be papered with blue-green veins when her skin is made taut by movement. And still the man across from her mistakes this electricity, her imperious *will*, for passion. She has been looking for him for some time now. See his cocksure stature; he is practically throwing his arm over the back of his chair. His eyes glitter like coals over the flickering candles and somewhere in the cavernous room, as their plates are brought to them, a small band of roving musicians, each of them with ukuleles and a headpiece denoting a different wild animal, begin singing "Happy Birthday" to someone.

Somewhere in the din, a child begins crying, and that is part of the curse, isn't it, Sara?

"To tell you the truth," the man says, his teeth so big and white, the hairs on his wrists glittering like wire in the candlelight. He is tan and wears a graying, impenetrable pompadour. He is old enough to be Sarah's father. "To tell you the truth, my wife thinks I'm at a business dinner. This whole week"—he waves his hand dismissively, signifying the restaurant, the waterpark, the entire resort, possibly Wisconsin—"is just a way for the company to get a nice write off. They're throwing us a bone, you know?"

Great machinations have been brought into play to bring her to this moment. It is a crux in Sara's life, or rather the apex of a catalyst this man and those like him have brought about. Sara has been vastly transformed from the woman she was even six months ago. This man is a cog in a great and terrible machine; his intentions may not have been malicious, but this means little to Sara now.

It means, actually, less than nothing. All things have brought her here to this moment.

She hears the child crying nearby and still she smiles because hearing children cry, of course, that's just something that happens. The world, the world is full of children that are not Sara's. Hearing children cry after your own child is no longer, after the unknowable trajectory of one errant bullet, after your own child has been culled from the earth like a stalk of wheat, that's just part of it now, isn't it? Just part of what follows the act of waking up, of this merciless business of living?

The child cries and cries.

"I'm glad you could make the time for me," she says over her glass.

The man smirks. "I am too."

Their food arrives. Her wine tastes like fuel, something rancid, but she drinks for its effect. The man looks archly at her and, oblivious, motions to the waiter for another bottle.

ROOM 119

Carlos parks his car around the corner of the motel so as not to be visible from the police station. He is afraid to drive and so that evening walks to a Walgreen's a mile down the parkway, cars screaming past and occasionally blaring their horns at him. He buys a charger for his phone, some bottled water. He buys a loaf of bread, some peanut butter and jelly. He cleans them out of their bananas at the register. He's been living on vending machine candy bars and bags of chips for two days now, water from the bathroom sink. His guts have cinched tight in riot against him.

When he returns to his room, he plugs the charger in and turns his phone on. There are messages from his mother, texts from Kelly and his manager at Safari So Good that he is afraid to look at. His heart flooding with relief, his mother picks up on the first ring.

"Hey, Mom," he says, his voice heavy.

There is a momentary pause. Her voice is harsh, banked with anger. *"Hey, Mom? This is a joke, Carlos? Ai, where you been? I called all your friends, the hospitals, the police! I thought you were dead!"*

He turns the TV back on but thinks he catches a glimpse of the man with the meat-cutting knife and turns if back off.

"I messed up, momma," he says.

"I know it, *tio.*" He'd had such plans for this summer. It was going to be so different. His first job away from the family's restaurant, his first *real* job. He would lose weight, make some money. He would move out at the end of summer, get his own apartment. He thought of Kelly, how she would text him when he had a day off, just little things, about some kid crying in line, something she'd hear people scream as they flew down the darkened tube of the Whirlwind. His tears came then, long blubbering sobs that threatened to rend some vital part of him in two.

"Hush now," his mom says. "Carlos, stop it. Knock it off, okay?"

He breathes deep, long jagged rips. "They weighed *way* over the weight limit, Mom, these four drunk guys. Big guys. Older than me," he says.

"Okay," she says.

"I shouldn't have let them get on."

"I know, baby. Your boss there, he called me. Said you were in big trouble. One of those men broke their arms."

"Oh God." Carlos has a vision then of making a run for it—he will trade license plates with the other car in the parking lot and just go. Minneapolis maybe, or Chicago. He will run.

And yet. And yet. Just an arm? Was that it?

For just a moment, he thinks, *I could be safe.*

"Carlos," his mother says, "stop. It's okay. He says you need to call him. That you're fired, you know, but they have insurance, all that. He wants you to call him."

"Dude, no way. Mom, I can't."

Her voice gains an edge he knows well enough. "You have his number, Carlos?"

"In my phone, yeah."

"You call him, Carlos."

"Mom."

"You call your boss. A man fixes his problems." Her mantra since his dad's death four years ago.

But I'm not a man, Carlos wants to scream. I'm fat! I'm only eighteen! I can't even drink yet! I haven't even had sex!

"Where are you?"

"A motel. I don't know. On the parkway. There's a whale on top."

"This isn't going to go away, Carlos. Call your boss and come home."

He breathes. "Okay, Mom."

"I mean it, now. No joke."

Something thunders on the roof then, a booming, thunderous clang that makes the cheap sconces on the wall jitter.

"Okay, Mom," Carlos says. "I will. I love you."

"Get your butt home, Carlos. I love you too."

There is another boom on the roof. The joists of the entire building seem to shudder with it. Carlos lifts up a wedge of blind and looks outside and sees nothing but a fat pallid moon shrouded with wisps of cloud. The thin jewels of traffic on the parkway. There is another boom and he sees the window glass shiver. Carlos steps out into the parking lot.

THE ROOF, AGAIN

What *of* children? Their innocence? Where had *his* gone? What happened to *him?* He remembers himself, Sam does, as a boy, but does not remember the wonder with which he'd presumedly trodden through the world. His father had built the hotel after coming home from Vietnam; stationed in the Mekong Delta, he had somehow fallen in love with surfing, of all things, with Hawaii and Fred Hemmings and Greg Noll. He did his tour and had come back home and married and put everything he had into this place, had the orca built, festooned the lobby with longboards, those ridiculous potted palm trees, the whole garish aesthetic, but it had *worked,* people had come, they loved the wonder of it. His father had installed a wet bar beside the pool and served people drinks in coconut halves, and Sam remembers this. He does. He remembers the surface of the swimming pool cut into a thousand diamonds of reflected sunlight, the gleeful screams and caws of other children at play, his own sense of safety. His father, grizzled and happy in a patterned shirt and cutoffs, was a man who could rend or salvage the entire world at his choosing. Sam had loved his life as a boy.

Where had that feeling gone?

His head is heavy with whiskey. The ladder wobbles beneath him. Some material in the roof shingles make them sparkle under the moonlight. The sledgehammer, long forgotten in a storage closet, is a comforting weight in his hand. Sam stands on the roof and pulls a flask from his pocket, momentarily mesmerized by the view: the resorts further north on the parkway glitter in the distance like small cities, the traffic threaded beside them like glowing tributaries. It is possibly one of the most beautiful things Sam has ever seen in his life.

He nearly stumbles off the roof with his first swing. The sledgehammer glances off the side of the statue and Sam skitters to regain his footing. He can feel the shudder of the building in his feet. He steadies himself, carefully places his flask in the pocket of his shorts, and swings again. This time there is a satisfying crunch, and forty-year-old plaster crumbles like ash, dusting the hair on his legs. He swings again. Again.

Down below, a voice calls out. "Uh, mister?"

"I'm renovating," Sam calls out without turning around. "I'm doing renovations." Sam's blood is singing. He should have done this years ago.

He turns to look down only when he hears someone below him squealing like an animal.

THE PARKING LOT, FOR THE LAST TIME

The man with the gray pompadour bursts from Sara's room above the manager's office, wailing. He is naked save for a pair of white briefs. His pale legs are bound together with tape, his hands tied in front of him. His back is crisscrossed with a dozen deep cuts, so much so that his underwear is colored a bright, racecar red back there. He hops delicately down the stairs one at a time, still keening under the dimestore moon as Carlos and Sam stare on, slackjawed and mute. The man's eyes are crazed, his mouth stuffed with fabric of some kind and taped shut, and still he hops delicately down the stairs on his bound legs.

Sara steps from the doorway of her room holding a pistol. A Reglite Barker 9mm, all sleek black plastic and steel. Sara is limned in moonlight and so achingly thin, something is clearly wrong with her. She is sick with something, ill, but she is also thrumming with a deadly kind of surety. She takes one step down the stairs, two, and as the man finally hops to the landing of the ground floor, the light of victory in his eyes clearly visible, she leans over the railing and shoots him once through the top of his head. He topples to the pavement, all vitality leached away in a moment. His head thuds sickeningly on a yellow parking block.

They stand there, the three of them.

A police cruiser slowly pulls into the parking lot across the street.

For just a moment, no one moves.

THIS WORLD OR THE NEXT

Sissy limps before the stragglers, the last few locals who shyly drop in her basket their sweat-dampened dollars, their fistfuls of change. It gives Sissy a seaward lean, her limp; she can't use her walker and hold the collection basket both, so her steps are careful, halting, intentional things. They stand in a rented room in a community center in Macon, Georgia, and most of the remaining audience—women in Walmart blouses and men who favor trucker caps, the frayed bills bent in a half-moon—pull back from her even as they drop money in her basket. There is still foam at the corners of Sissy's lips. Blood dots the blue tarp spread out beside the lectern. The room is still electric with unease.

Branson says, "Dig deep, friends."

He says, "We thank you, and the good lord thanks you."

He says, chuckling, "Every bit helps. It's a long way to Tuscaloosa."

He has long grown deft at talking the audience back from the edge of the thing.

He catches Emma's eye and winks. She smiles in return. The blood has run in strings down her arms and she presses bandages to her hands. She knows to show them the blood, to turn so they can see it.

It's why they're here, these stragglers. This is why they drop the money in—this proximity to God, and to Emma's willingness to do this to her body.

She feels a stirring of the old love for herself, for the world. It is a brief moment, but galvanizing; she is shipwrecked within God's cupped hand. His light is hung bright in her bones. She has called Him forth tonight—they all have, all four of them, petitioned Him to show mercy, to save them all—and in this moment she feels that He has answered.

Emma watches a local, her face creased with fatigue, mouth like a knife-slash, reach into her purse as Sissy approaches. The woman holds a soda cup as big as a mortar shell in her other hand and drops a small sheaf of bills into Sissy's basket. The man next to her—bearded, in a camouflage T-shirt, a Skoal ring worn white in his jeans pocket—leans over and hisses in her ear.

She quiets him with a single smoking glance, her jowls quailing. And Sissy is already gone, having done a lap around the room, heading back toward the lectern, toward the blue tarp.

The show is over.

• • •

Sissy sits on a folding chair in the corner of the room and counts their take, her walker unfolded before her. Clyde has bandaged himself and Emma and now they fold the chairs and clean the coffee pot, careful of their hands. Branson vacuums, tidies the room; they have a system down. They need their deposit back.

When they step into the parking lot, the humid Georgia night is like a fist. Branson is careful to make sure the glass door is locked behind them before he slides the keys through the mail slot. The sky is speckled with stars, the air rich with the smell of warm pavement. Katydids clamor in the trees.

Branson has slid open the side door of the van when someone yells "Hey!" and the four of them turn toward the sound. The big man in the camouflage T-shirt steps from a truck swathed in piecemeal sections of primer gray; the springs groan in protest when his boots hit the pavement.

"Well, hell," Clyde says quietly, sounding amused. He stretches like a cat, his arms raised. His old life, Emma knows, was built on a different foundation than this one, but every so often Branson must call on him to revisit it. For now, Branson lays a hand on Clyde's arm and steps forward in his place.

He says, "What can I help you with, friend?"

"Y'all took my sister's money," the man says, his fists on his thighs. His face is hooded beneath the brim of his hat.

Branson pushes his dreadlocks off his shoulder. "And we're grateful to her, honestly. And to you. Thank you for coming tonight."

"You're not hearing me. She's got kids to feed."

"The good lord has a tendency to return that which is passed on. It's one of the great gifts that—"

"Y'all aren't understanding. I'm taking her money back."

"I'm sorry," Branson says mournfully. "That won't be happening." Then he reaches into the maw of the van and turns back with a pamphlet. It is a printed pamphlet outlining the precepts of the Hand of Light; they leave them in rest stops, on community bulletin boards. Sissy titters, clutching her walker, her gray hair obscuring much of her face.

The man makes no motion to take it. He turns his head and spits. "That crazy horseshit that went on in there? I ought to call the cops, is what I ought to do." He looks down at Emma's bandaged hands and sneers. "The fucking Health Department."

Branson sighs. He steps back, touches Clyde's elbow. Clyde claps his hands together softly and steps toward the man. Sissy giggles again. Streetlight glints off Clyde's teeth. He is happy. He is doing a thing that he loves.

Emma gets in the van, in the very back seat, telling herself they are filled with Light, the four of them, that they are good. They are envoys. God is leaning through the veil to touch them.

The sounds of combat begin outside the van.

Emma lies down and prays. *God's hand is the hand that cradles us.*

• • •

They spend the night in a condo outside of town. It seems that Branson has no shortage of friends or acolytes spread across the country, though they are now down to only four people, the smallest the group has ever been in her year and a half traveling with the Hand of Light. They are people reliant on the goodwill of others, on God's grace. The GPS on Branson's phone leads them to a duplex on a suburban street heavy with pecan trees and Priuses in driveways. The key is under the mat, as instructed, and Branson, Sissy, and Emma gather their backpacks and sleeping bags and shuffle inside. Clyde will sleep in the van, as he always does.

The place is sparsely furnished. There is a single plant on a wooden cube beneath a window that looks out into a manicured side yard. The two bedrooms are adorned with paintings from the same series—a single slash of gray drawn across a rough white canvas. The kitchen is brushed steel and marble; on the island there is a note, and Emma watches Branson frown and crumple it up and drop it in the garbage. He presses a palm against the horseshoe-shaped scar on his forehead and she knows enough to retreat to a bedroom. The door locks, and Emma is grateful for the privacy. She undresses and spends a moment staring at herself in the bathroom mirror. She slowly unrolls the bandages wrapped around her hands. She looks at the cuts along her lifelines and then washes her hands in the sink until the water runs clear. She prays for patience and clarity. She showers, wraps her hands in fresh bandages, crawls naked into bed. Falls asleep beneath that jagged gray slash of paint. At some point in the night she thinks she hears Branson cry out.

• • •

There's a dream that Emma often has. She's trying to find her husband, Brad, while the two of them travel throughout the same house, continually in different rooms. Calling out to each other, hearing each other's footfalls. She'll see his shadow on the hallway floor and then go to the hallway and he's gone. When he calls her name, his voice is hoarse. It's a fitful and anguished dream. She has it often.

• • •

Emma awakens to the smell of coffee, of Clyde laughing somewhere in the house. The world comes to her in slow increments. She gets on her knees and prays, her hands clasped on the bed. Her incantations: For God to pierce the skin of the world, for sight beyond the veil. For clarity and patience. The prayers clang hollow within her, a stone thrown down a well. The hollowness itself has become a part of the routine.

In the kitchen, Branson is cooking eggs and buttering toast. At the kitchen table, where Clyde and Sissy sit drinking coffee, a grapefruit sits halved on a plate, a spoon jabbed in its meat. Clyde is worrying a tooth that was loosened the night before. Emma, wearing a bathrobe she found in the bedroom closet, pours herself a cup of coffee and sits down. This trinity: her and Clyde and Sissy, all that is left now. The last supplicants of the Hand of Light, the last of Branson's charges.

A plate of eggs is set before her, a slab of butter marooned on a piece of charred toast. The same rests before Sissy and Clyde. Branson will feed himself last. Emma stirs the eggs with her fork; eating has long become an obligation. She asks Branson how he slept.

Back at the stove, Branson frowns, considering. "I had a lot of dreams, Emma. But I couldn't quite make out what they were."

"I heard you yell out sometime last night."

He nods. "I'm sorry for waking you."

Clyde says, "No visions, then, boss?"

"No, buddy, I'm sorry."

Clyde chews his food—carefully, because of the state of his mouth—and stares down at his plate. His hands are bandaged also, but Emma knows he has a blurry tattoo of a swastika in the webbing between his thumb and forefinger; he has told her that the Hand of Light has shown him that some men have illumination spilling out of them and some are as lightless as a cave undersea. *Skin don't matter none, Emma.* He's told her that his hate has been scoured from him, that he is cradled in God's hand. "Well, shit," he says.

"No potty-mouth at the table," says Sissy with a gap-toothed smile. Clyde looks up and laughs, delighted. Sissy owns two dresses; she hand-washes one while she wears the other. Today is the blue one, sleeves to her wrists. Her gray hair is plaited and pinned above her neck. It's rare for her to speak, rarer still for her to joke, and Emma tells herself it's a good omen.

Branson asks how Emma's hands are doing.

"They're fine," she says.

"You sure?"

She turns to him and flexes her fingers. They make starfish shapes above the bandages.

• • •

They pack up, and Emma pretends she forgot something inside. They wait for her in the van. She runs to the kitchen, fishes through the garbage. Beneath eggshells and grapefruit rinds, she finds the note that Branson had thrown there. It is wet, browned with coffee grounds.

You're running out of running room, the note says.

• • •

A year and a half she has been with the Hand of Light. Eighteen months she's allowed Branson's visions to dictate the course of her life. No, that's not true, she tells herself. God is the shepherd, not Branson. She'd gone to a meeting on a whim with her brother, who'd heard it was something akin to old-time revivalist meetings; religion with a dramatic, doomsday bent. She remembered being curious, ironically detached, hoping to be entertained. There had been many more congregants then; the bloodletting had been a true spectacle. Her brother had left horrified, nauseated. But it had seized something in her, something vital. She had truly felt God's hand there in a rented retail space out in Tigard, had felt the hand of God touch her, standing in that sad commercial space with butcher paper over the windows, industrial carpet on the floor. It had awakened some faith inside of her, some feverish purity. The congregation had stayed in town for a while—Branson's visions were coming to him daily then—and soon she was attending every meeting, talking to the members for hours afterwards. She'd left Brad—another note on another countertop—and joined the caravan when they headed down south to California. She remembers those early, delirious days of faith.

But Branson's visions have slowly faded in the past six months. His clarity is gone. His headaches have worsened. The group has awoken over the months to find members disappeared, their cars gone. Some of them have the grace to apologize to Branson to his face; most leave in the middle of the night. Now it's just the four of them, and Emma's faith, once so galvanizing, has diminished with every mile, every roadside stop.

• • •

Clyde drives the minivan while Branson answers emails on his laptop in the passenger seat. Emma and Sissy sit in the back. Sissy sits with her hands folded in the blue lap of her dress; she has always seemed content with the silence within herself, fine with watching the highway unspool outside the windows. Emma misses her phone sometimes—the Hand of Light disavows such things, the physical trappings of the world, though Branson uses his laptop and phone for administrative and business needs—but she is often grateful to be far away from the internet, from the constant, relentless barrage of information and noise, the furious deluge of people and their rage, their endless clamor. She'd been a wife, a professional, a woman long wearied by the parry and thrust of people's response to her childlessness, how she and Brad were oftentimes viewed as diminutive—or intrinsically damaged—for not wanting children. And now? Now, she tells herself, as the telephone poles and car dealerships and fast-food outlets whip past, now she is free. An envoy of light.

• • •

Except the event in Tuscaloosa does not go well. The shows have not been going well for some time; Branson's visions are only colorless blurs now, snippets of strange films spied through the gauze of his dreams. The world beside this one— the main precept of the Hand of Light, that there is a world next to this one, so similar to ours—has pulled away from him. The skin of the next world over is blighted, thickened. It seems that God is perhaps turning His face away from Branson, and Branson is weary because of it. The promoter of the revival (Branson insists on the term *revivals* to harken back to the early days of canvas tents and snake-handling, of faith-healing and possibility) has done a poor job of flyering and outreach. Emma is dismayed to see that hecklers outnumber the potential attendants. Clyde makes short work of them with a hushed voice, a gripped bicep, a clear willingness to commit violence, but when the room is cleared, there are only a half-dozen people in the audience. A man in a chambray work shirt and a Brylcreemed pompadour, and five old women clustered together like hens. The rest of the folding chairs are empty. The promoter himself has claimed a personal emergency and failed to appear. Regardless, Branson plunges forth.

Even as his visions have dimmed and his headaches have intensified, he remains a steadfast showman. He begins slowly, talking about his early college days as a partier, navigating the world via staid poli-sci courses at school, the quiet pride of his parents. Then the motorcycle accident, the lack of a helmet, how God had seemed to peel his skull back and shout His light inside. The peace Branson felt as he lay dying in the road. The sudden understanding—in a bomb blast of clarity—that infinite worlds lay spread out before this one. That God lived in the space between these worlds.

His voice by this point has risen, and he begins to pace and strut the confines of the room. Emma sees the community center building manager walk past the doorway, looking uneasy and concerned. Branson's eyes are crazed, he pivots quickly, his dreadlocks flipping over his shoulders. "God's hand *cradled* me, friends, held me there in place. God's hand kept me safe until the paramedics arrived on that long and lonely stretch of roadside. Lifeblood spilling out, but I heard that voice. And that plate in my skull, friends, affords me a gift: God's voice in my ear. God, thundering forth, consoling me through my rehabilitation. Consoling me *still*, okay? Filling me with the knowledge that there are other worlds than this one, worlds right next door, but only one God. The holy God, the God of Light. One God for all the worlds." He is shouting by now, and Emma sees one of the old ladies clutching her purse and nodding along and Emma feels the familiar shiver of being a part of something that encompasses more than just her.

God's light, Branson insists, is not free. To pierce the skin of the world requires tribute, he says, a tribute based in love, in fealty, and it is here that Sissy rises, her eyes peeled back to the whites, and begins a shimmering dance of nonsense words, her hair a whirling halo, her body jittering as if a current runs through her. The man with the pompadour sits with his arms folded. The old ladies lean back, eyes owlish and alarmed behind their glasses. Sissy vibrates, raises her arms, a thick noise at the back of her throat. God roves through her, Branson says. He bellows of the need for ablution, the willingness of the blood as a salve, as currency of faith, and here Emma rises, trying to feel the Light, trying to summon Him, and Clyde does the same, the pair of them rising from their chairs in the front row, both of them guttural and beseeching the paneled ceiling of the community center, and it is here that Emma and Clyde draw knives across their palms, drip blood on the tarp laid at their feet. The ladies gasp. Even in her fervor she tries to find a spot on her lacerated palms that she hasn't cut recently, tries to place a new cut away from half-healed ones, puffy and raw, and God is here, she tells herself, God is here with me and all is not lost, and the women are horrified, the women are enrapt, Branson booms through the room that God is knocking to get in, and Sissy falls to the ground, foam frothing from her lips, locked in a seizure, locked in her petition to God and Emma raises her bloody hand toward the ceiling as appeal, as offering, as a sign of her love.

• • •

Emma doesn't know how much the old ladies give them when Sissy passes the basket that night, but Clyde is unhappy. In the bathroom, after he has cleaned her wound, he pulls Emma's bandage too tight. She winces, and he winces in return. "Sorry, hon," he says.

"Are you worried?" she asks him as he rinses watery blood from the countertop with paper towels and throws them in a garbage can that is already close to overflowing. "You seem worried."

"Nah. No. We're good. We are cradled by the good lord."

Back in the room, the old ladies are gone. But the man with the pompadour is still there, talking quietly to Branson while he stacks chairs. A cloud walks across Clyde's face and he stalks toward them, elbows pumping. The man with the pompadour sees him and grins, throwing out his arms as if to be crucified. "What? What're you gonna do?"

For a moment Emma thinks that Clyde will hoist a chair and swing it into the man's face, but Branson puts out a calming hand. "We can handle this," he says. "We can work this out."

The man's eyes don't leave Clyde, who stands behind Branson now. Sissy leans on her walker and cries, big honking sobs, her hair like a curtain. Emma's dread is slowly being pulled up from the depths inside her, a dread that she hasn't felt since before her days in The Hand. The old, ugly dread, the stilling kind, the kind that left her in bed all day, immobile and mostly speechless. The dread she'd tried so hard to leave behind.

The man with the pompadour sneers at Branson. "Don't give me that shit," he says. "There's exactly one way to work this out, and you know what it is."

• • •

Branson is wracked with another migraine after that, so Emma sits up front as Clyde drives. Clyde plays country music CDs at a volume she can hardly hear, songs where the outlaws seem to cherish their heartbreak. Outside, the world is demarked by islands of light off the highway, by road signs that glow briefly in the headlights and disappear. Branson lies with his head in Sissy's lap in the backseat, a towel over his face. Emma envies him his darkness. The glow from the dashboard carves Clyde's face into harsh planes of darkness and light. At rest stops and gas stations, he smokes furiously, pitching his cigarettes to the pavement in a shower of orange sparks, cursing openly. Branson is diminished enough that he says nothing about this.

At some point Clyde pulls into another gas station and looks in the backseat. Branson is asleep, or dead, or, Emma thinks, hiding from them. Sissy leans against the window, sleeping. Clyde sighs and hoists his hips up, digs his wallet out of his back pocket. He hands Emma a credit card, tells her to pay for the gas and grab them some coffee. "Looks like it's you and me on this ride."

They are in Wyoming, and even though it is the middle of the night, the summer heat throbs up from the asphalt like something alive and ill-tempered. The inside of the store is cool and garishly bright. The woman behind the register looks young enough to be Emma's daughter, if she had one, and in that moment she feels tremendously lost. She wanders the aisles, gathers pastries wrapped in cellophane, potato chips seasoned with unnatural dusts, sports drinks the color of irradiation. The cashier wordlessly rings it up and when Emma tells her their pump number she gets a single nod in response. Emma wants something more—some recognition that she is here, at a gas station outside of Cheyenne with a van full of strangers tethered by something that right now feels very, very far away. She pushes a five-dollar bill over the counter and asks for quarters, and this garners an eye roll, at least. The coins are a weight in her pocket, as meaningful as a weapon. Clyde has moved the van into a parking spot; she sees him through the dirty windshield. He leans his head against the steering wheel. It's either prayer or exhaustion that bows him.

She had noticed a pair of payphones at the side of the building. Clyde and Branson are allowed to handle money—since her first bloodletting, she truly has tried per the precepts of the Hand of Light to disavow the earthly trappings of capitalism, of *need*, but a stone-edged, prudent part of her has always known this was a possibility. She has kept a small amount of money tucked away, and feels a momentary starburst of shame at her lack of faith.

The phone number rises from her memory, easier than she'd thought. She sets her sack of groceries on top of the phone booth. Sweat rolls down her ribcage.

Brad hasn't changed the outgoing message. After a year and a half of being gone, she hears her own voice telling her to leave a message. Emma pauses after the beep, a litany of nonsensical messages whirling through her mind. In the end she simply hangs up. She thinks of him checking the answering machine—older than her, Brad had been adamant that they retain a landline—and wonders what he will hear. The dim growl of the highway? The thunder of her own heart?

She walks back to the van; everyone is awake and upright now, even Branson, though he looks pale and drawn. She hands Clyde his credit card. He nods and roots through the bag, selects a doughnut covered in cracked chocolate icing. She gets in the passenger seat and they make their way toward the on-ramp. They are heading west, back to Oregon. It's a dwindling down of some kind, she can feel it.

"I forgot the coffees," she says. "Sorry."

Clyde shrugs. "Fuck it."

• • •

Highway 80, and they tuck through a corner of Utah. It's beautiful. Marbled foothills are studded with green trees that line the road, verdant and thriving even under the punishing sun. Branson seems to have shrunken further into himself. Clyde has driven through the night and his face is hollowed out with sleeplessness. The van has taken on the warm fug and press of bodies. Sissy snores.

Hours later, night is once again bluing the foothills and Clyde pulls into a rest area. He looks into the rearview mirror. "You want to drive, boss? I need to sleep, or I'm gonna run us off the road."

Branson peers out at the parking lot with his haunted eyes. His stubble is coming in and this somehow makes him look even younger. He and Sissy are holding hands. "I don't think so, Clyde." His voice is quiet, neutered. His voice has been robbed.

Clyde's eyes flick to Emma's and then back to the mirror. "How about we get some rooms, then? I think everyone needs some rest."

Branson shrugs, nods.

They find a motel off the highway. Clyde books the rooms while the three of them sit in the van and listen to the engine tick and cool.

She and Sissy get a room; Clyde leads Branson into the other one. The last thing she hears is Branson saying that he might need to go to the hospital, and this fills her with an inexplicable mix of fear and rage. How often has she heard him rail against those who would usurp God's hand, the grace and healing of His touch?

She has given up everything, and now the young man she has napalmed her life for—this twenty-six-year-old boy who heard God's voice and has almost daily urged Emma to loosen her blood as petition to Him—is buckling under a headache.

Their room has a pair of beds, a small desk, a bathroom with a toilet ringed in hard-water stains. Sissy sits on a bed and Emma lays down on the other. "We'll be okay," she says, but Sissy does not respond.

Emma stands and finds the television remote. She turns the TV on and sits on the edge of her bed. For a moment she and Sissy are twinned like that. A woman is crying on the screen; her face is tinged green. Sissy lies down and grabs an edge of the comforter, wordlessly pulls it over herself like a cocoon.

• • •

She dreams again of Brad searching for her, and wakes covered in sweat. She puts on her clothes and walks out into the parking lot. Gingerly closing the door behind her, she shuts out the sound of Sissy's musical, childlike snores. The highway is over there, a river of light and sound.

The interior light of the van is on. Someone is rooting through it. She walks over and sees Clyde's ass leaning over the backseat. She says his name and he slowly, awkwardly extricates himself. He sits on the floorboard, his feet on the pavement. He isn't wearing shoes.

"He's gone," Clyde says. He thumps a pack of cigarettes on the back of his hand. Crickets chirr in the field between the motel and the highway.

"What do you mean?"

Clyde smiles around his cigarette. "I mean, he's gone, sweets. Someone called him an hour ago, and I watched him walk right out the fucking door."

"Someone called him?" She seems incapable of doing more than repeating what she hears.

"Remember that country bumpkin motherfucker that rolled up in Tuscaloosa? One with the Elvis hair?"

She does.

Clyde yawns, scratches an eyelid. "You know what a wolf ticket is, Emma?"

"No."

"Well, Bran's been selling wolf tickets."

Emma looks back at the open door of Clyde's room, as if Branson will walk out of it.

"He's broke, is what I mean." The cherry of Clyde's cigarette glows orange. "He's borrowed money from folks, and now they're looking to collect."

Emma's confusion must be obvious, because Clyde grins around his cigarette. "You think we can pull all this off on twenty bucks in donations a night? Driving across the country? Motels and truck stops and shit?"

She thinks of the note she found in the condo. "Are they following us?"

Clyde stares down at his white feet, blows smoke at them. When he looks up at her again, she can see his fear, and that's when she realizes that his fear has always been there. "I don't know," he says. "But they found us in Alabama, right?" He grins that crooked grin of his. "I mean, I'm doubting it was his momma that called just now."

"What do we do?" she says, meaning *What do I do?*

"It wasn't all show, hon." Clyde rolls his head on his shoulders like an old prizefighter. "He seen things, that kid. I know it. Was a gift laid upon him. I believe it when he says he sees the good lord walking strong in the world next to this one."

Yes, she thinks, *but we need Him here, don't we? Who cares about the world next to this one?*

Emma walks back into her room and grabs her bag. She has brought painfully little of herself along. She has a fistful of quarters, another small sheaf of bills in her backpack. Bandages and rubbing alcohol for her hands. Bags of junk food. Sissy doesn't stop snoring.

Clyde is standing against the van, still smoking. He seems unsurprised to see her carrying her backpack. He lifts his chin toward her door, raises his eyebrows.

"She's still sleeping," Emma says.

He nods. "Don't suppose I could interest you in waiting it out. Seeing if he comes back."

"Do you think he's coming back?" Emma says.

Clyde spits. "No." When he looks at her, the fear is so bright and clear on his face that she wonders how she ever missed it.

"Godspeed, my dear," he says. "It was good running with you."

She walks across the road into an overgrown field that will take her to the highway. The grass is dry; she feels crickets jump against her legs. She turns and sees a pair of trucks pull into the parking lot, their headlights washing across the face of the motel. Clyde is still smoking next to the van. She sees the headlights run across him and stop, illuminating him. Spearing him with light. She sees him raise his hand to shield his eyes.

GIFTS

The conflict shrinks ever inward and summer, finally, brings skirmishes that ring the city. Rumors abound: rations will be lessened, insurgents' boots can be felt in the ground like an approaching train, they've turned our incantations against us. There will be a curfew, evacuations. At night the sound of far-off mortars drift through the open windows and in daylight the gutters are dense with flies roving mounds of rotting garbage, sheets of flies that tremble like green-black skins.

The days are filled with a still, joyless heat, where grit gathers like a film on the skin. The television is on, of course—it's mandatory—but soundless, and the day is so quiet that footfalls can be heard on the sidewalk below. Footfalls on cement, and beneath the soles shell casings and glass shards rasp like bitter stones.

Upstairs in my apartment, Jinx and I have sex for the last time while the neighbor moves out next door.

"I want to get out," the neighbor says to his friends as they drag something heavy along the floor, "before some motherfucker *makes* me get out, you know?"

Jinx and I, our hips notched together, the skyline outside the window immutable, thumbed with smoke. Jinx's bones are like pipes socked in felt. Drops of sweat fall from my nose to the notched valley of her breastbone, and it's not love, whatever's left between us. It's something sad and faded and winding down.

My trembling arms, our hips thocking together hard enough to ache, hard enough to leave bruises tomorrow. We go from chair to floor to couch, this panicked routine, this sadness, bits of detritus sticking to the pale awkward moons of her ass, the jutting bird-wings of her shoulder blades, the palms of my reddened hands. The air smells of plastic and outside uncoils a long and faraway stutter of weapons fire, discordant and arrhythmic. The neighbor and his friends thump and bang their way down the stairwell to his freedom, to his death, to some other place than this.

"Don't stop," Jinx says, her face turned away from me.

"I won't," I say.

When were we the closest to love, she and I? The very closest to it?

We end joylessly, silently, not looking at each other. Jinx covers her hands across her breasts and I rise up. She believes that there is somewhere better than here, somewhere we can go besides this place. She believes in the Lottery; that some blessed citizens are given access and means to leave, gifted with a place void of conflict. It's the same wall we have run up against over and over, she and I. The same argument for months and months, and today she is going. Jinx is leaving, and what was meant to be a quick stop to say goodbye—a severing as painless as possible—has turned into this, a prolonged ache. And the separateness I feel right now is like its own thing, like some third thing in the room that we've given birth to. I pull on pants and, gutted, pretend interest in the television while Jinx gets dressed.

You can hear the rustlings in the walls, constant now.

On the screen are tanned, hugely muscled, well-fed men in ridiculous costumes slamming into each other. The television won't go off for another four, five hours, and now it's Sports—wrestling—and after that will be News and then Incantations and then Lottery and then the screen will wink out like a dim star, leaving us to the cadence of war outside the windows. Onscreen, they pan the stadium's crowd and a cavalcade of hollow-eyed people like Jinx and I are raging back at me, gaunt and blood-mad. A Great and Terrible Wraith, my favorite guy if only for his colors, petitions the crowd, raises his massive arms up and waves his hands and struts in a rooster circle, bringing the people to a frenzy. His orange and green singlet gleams with reflected light, the ragged bubblegum-pink scars uncurling beneath the neck of his mask. The image of the hatchet buried in a skull on the back of his costume, his sigil, surrounded by the logos of corporate sponsors. Another wrestler—Vim and Vigor, maybe, or the Ceaselessness, or Name Me Terror—writhes around on the mat behind him, ensconced in a false agony. The death-tally of the insurgents runs in a yellow ticker at the bottom of the screen, ever growing. It's ageless, this entertainment of watching men hurt each other. We've done this for centuries, we'll do this until we're dust.

"I should go home," Jinx says. "Should finish packing."

I appreciate the distraction of these men, the supposed sport of it, but mostly I just think about all the calories ingested, how much the fuckers must get to eat to stay huge like that.

• • •

Jinx lights a cigarette and I sit at the kitchen table and sneak glances at the blued backs of her knees, at her little feet as she puts on one sock and then one shoe, the way she yanks hard on her belt. She catches me looking and I quickly turn my head and watch the last dirty swath of sunlight move across the wall. The wall is creased here and there in ways it wasn't a month ago.

"What is that?" Jinx says. "That noise."

"Kind of a rustling sound?"

"Yeah."

I say, "Kind of a *writhing ululation?* A—I don't know—a *papery oscillation,* maybe?"

"Jay," she says, sounding tired.

I point to the wall, the wrinkles there like bad paper-mâché. "It's just the building," I say. "Just whatever's happening to the building. To the city. I don't know, Jinx."

I walk her downstairs. There is some part of me that knows this is for the best, that we tried, that it hasn't worked for a year, maybe more than a year— that eventually we found each other lacking in some integral way, some way that I will probably not be able to name for a while. But another larger part of me is desperate to stop it. Is already steeped in loss from it, and delirious, and halved. We were together since the war was a distant thing, back when time could be measured in clearly defined increments: When we could travel freely. When we could get fruit. Gasoline. When convoys didn't fill the street with dust and menace and blank-faced boys bristling with weaponry. When we did not perform spells on the bodies of our dead or the dead of our enemies. I can tell Jinx and I are finished by the way she walks ahead of me and I walk behind her, even though the stairwell is wide enough for both of us. I keep wanting to reach out and lightly touch her arm, to be someone different than who I am. She's leaving, I think, she's leaving.

When we get outside the heat is like being smothered with a smoldering garbage bag, suffocating, and Hooper is standing on the sidewalk in front of my building. He is *always* standing on the sidewalk in front of my building, the shithead, and today he sucks his teeth and nods at us as we pass by him. Beneath his vest and helmet, Hooper is all sweat and Adam's apple and wrist bones. His uniform is sweat-salted white at the armpits and he's missing a button on his shirtsleeve, right there above where his hand rests on the grip of his rifle. This man ostensibly charged with protecting us, he stares at Jinx's ass as she walks down the street.

"Listen," I say to him, acidic with sarcasm, "I just wanted to let you know that I appreciate all you do. I think it's really valuable," and I walk backward a few steps and Hooper, oblivious, actually touches his fingers to his helmet's visor and salutes me. I'm full of what's happening between Jinx and I, I'm sick with it, and his gaze on her like that, and the feeling in my heart, it makes me want to spit blood in the guy's eyes, knock him down and put my knees on his arms and yank his helmet off and bray laughter into that implacable, smug, half-starved face. I want to ask him if it's worth it, what he's doing, when he's still as practically as hungry as we are. Instead I turn and Jinx is walking far ahead of me, *mad*, her legs knifing the ground, her hands gripping her elbows. I have to run to catch up.

"I couldn't help myself," I say, singsonging it.

"Of course you couldn't." She won't look at me. "When can you, Jay?"

"He's an asshole."

"Whatever."

We reach her car, which is covered in a skin of ash. She turns to face me, the car door between us.

"I'm never going to see you again, am I?" It comes out of my mouth as pathetic as it sounds, as pathetic as it feels.

Her face softens and she looks away and for just a bit my heart lifts, like *maybe*. But then she says, very quietly, "I don't think so," and when she looks back at me I can see her assuredness tighten like a fist around her whole body. I'm a little awed by it. Tiny bits of ash already dot her shoulders, hang like flakes of snow in her hair. And it's still so goddamned hot out. We've been outside for a minute? Two minutes?

So much of everything seems a slow dismantlement.

"I don't want you to go."

She shakes her head, pulls a strand of hair from her mouth. "Not everything makes it, Jay, you know? Wrong place, wrong time? Too different? Who knows. We've just talked it to death." She shrugs. "I'm sick of it here," she says, and as if in response comes the crumple of an explosion, some doom-spell uncoiling over toward Industrytown. Neither of us flinch anymore.

I look down my street. All the buildings with their windows boarded, cars humped in silt. Numbers slashed in chalk on brick walls, symbols: street-side magicians plying their own chickenshit spells against the dark, against the insurgency. Hooper, and other guys like Hooper, stand in clusters with their guns, stocky with body armor, their faces rimed in dirt except where they're sweating. Garbage, piles of bricks.

"I just feel like we can change," I say. "Like nothing's too late."

"If we could have, we would have," Jinx says. "It's poison here, Jay." She gets into her car and gently, careful of my fingers, shuts the door.

I'm stunned with the finality of it—*we did it, we split for good*—and I'm crossing the street back to my building when someone picks me up and throws me from behind, flings me into the air, when my ears fill with this tidal roar, something animalistic, like I'm being pressed down to the bottom of the ocean. Then the street rises to meet me and I skid on pavement like it's iced, like it's choreographed, and things begin to tumble and flower down around me in slow arcs that are almost beautiful, and I stare in wonder as something metal and edged in char is sticking out of my wrist and I can't feel it, I can't feel a thing, there's just a roar, this bright, singular roar.

• • •

"It's not like there's words for it," Harrison says. His hand tries to divine the tabletop for his beer bottle. "It's not like there's a statute on loss. Anybody who says so is wrong. There's no other way to say it. Fuck 'em."

"I know, man. I hear you. I appreciate it."

We're sitting in my kitchen nursing a twelve-pack of Harrison's black-market beers while any number of fans creak and push hot air around the apartment. It's quiet save for the fans and the skittering in the walls and the occasional rattle of a convoy down below. This is our most recent tradition, born from my mourning: beer and bullshitting. Blind Harrison, Black Market Harrison, who lives in the apartment above me and has been my friend almost as long as I knew Jinx, brings me boxes of beer and listens to me sloppily recount any number of tales. The minutiae of she and I. Our greatest hits. My cavalcade of shortcomings and regrets. (How the stick-and-poke tattoos we gave each other—each other's initials, Jesus Christ, so corny—got infected and soon enough were little more than gray-green blurs on our arms. The crooked incisor she had, and how for the first year we were together she covered her mouth whenever she laughed. The way she went sock-shoe, sock-shoe when she got dressed. How we would lie in bed and she would drape her hair over my face while I talked; how that was the best darkness. And how it felt like I was flying when the car bomb went off, how the street seemed to be moving toward me instead of the other way around, and how I shook afterwards for two days, sick with adrenaline and shock. Flaming shrapnel raining down on me, Hooper pulling me by the collar into the doorway. Some weary doctor working outside of a ration center pulling the shrapnel from my wrist, stitching me up, giving me half a dozen pain pills, all they could afford.)

I talk and Harrison sits oblivious of the afternoon light and listens.

He's a bad man, according to the neighborhood. Housebound Harrison, the man who never leaves the building, the shot-caller. Harrison handles booze, dope, commodities. Food. There's a price for it all, but when isn't there a price? What's ever free? It makes me wonder, sometimes—will there be a price for this? For our palaver? I find it hard to match, the man they claim him to be and the man he is in my kitchen, listening to me stutter and weep. Grayed flattop, his cane folded in his lap. Mostly it's the eyes that moor you, those eyes marbled with blue and gray cataracts—thirty years ago, a single operation could've saved his sight, but the world's a far cry from how it was thirty years ago. They look, I think, like the chilled and resolute center of an iceberg. They search my face when I talk.

"I just miss her," I say dumbly—that's why we're here, isn't it? "She didn't even want to be with me, and still, it's just this leveling."

"If I ever find 'em, Jay," Harrison says, and finds his beer bottle, and tilts it to his mouth. "I ever find the sergies that planted that thing, I'll come get you." He swipes his hand down his face, wicks the sweat away. "They'll know they been got, I promise you that. You know? They'll regret it."

Do I want that? I open my mouth and then I close it.

She was leaving anyway. We were done.

But I do want that. I do. Because really—there's a part of me? There's a part of me that's like, had she lived? Had Jinx just driven away? We could have fixed it in the long run. I could have found her. We could have salvaged it, this thing we had. I don't know if that's true. But among other things, Harrison traffics in vengeance, and I surprise myself by wanting just that.

We've got a signal, he and I—three taps on his floor or my ceiling—and if he's home, he's knocking at my door a few minutes later. Blind man of the neighborhood, a dangerous man, and I've never seen him outside the building. But it's true, his name runs in threads all along the streets here, all through the brickwork, falls hushed from people's mouths. He says *I got my finger on the pulse of the nation, Jay,* when I ask how he does everything, how he makes it work. He says that to me, and then he winks one of those marbled eyes.

"Hey," he says now, and I watch as he puts his hand on the table and an insect—a cream-colored moth with dust-heavy wings, big as a half-dollar—falls from a crease in the wall and trundles toward his tented fingers and then away from them. This is what the sounds in the walls are, the movement of these things. They've only recently begun burrowing out (this is the first one I've seen in daytime) and revulsion rises in me, my hands go slick with sweat. "Hold on," I manage, "there's a bug right by your hand—"

"I know," he says. "I can hear it. Leave it."

"It's nasty, Harrison. It's one of the ones from the walls."

Harrison nods. "You hear about your new neighbor?"

At first I think he's talking about the moth, which lays on the table, stunted and confused. "No." I can't take my eyes from it. It's vibrating like something electric.

Harrison nods. "It's that guy," he says. "It's that guy you like."

"Oh, what? You mean next door?"

"Yeah. The wrestler."

The moth's wings flutter, spotted with flakes of plaster.

"What? Who?"

Harrison lifts his head toward the ceiling. "What's the guy's name? A List of Partial Demands? A Half-Hearted Vengeance? Something long like that."

"It's not A Great and Terrible Wraith, is it?"

Harrison slowly begins unfolding his cane. "That's it. That's exactly who it is."

"He lives *here*? How the hell do you know that?"

"Because I ran into him."

"You ran into him."

"I literally ran into him. Walking down the hall and he was carrying a bunch of boxes and didn't see me. Guy's just beastly, Jay. Just a huge man."

"So he just introduced himself? 'Hi, I'm A Great and Terrible Wraith, maybe you've heard of me?'"

"That's pretty much how it happened, actually."

I say, "Maybe it's just somebody bullshitting you."

Harrison shrugs, and on the table, I think the moth is maybe dying. When it walks, there's these clicking noises that get buried in your ear somewhere. Watching it move is like watching the skin get peeled from a skull.

"That guy's *sponsored*, Harrison. Why would he move into this building?"

Harrison's lips pull back and he brings his cane down on the table. He's so fast. There's a loud crack and our beer bottles jump and one rolls onto the floor. He turns those beautiful marbled eyes toward me.

"I get him?"

The moth skitters to the edge of the table, tests it in a panic.

"Not even close," I say.

"Damn." Harrison smiles, folding his cane back up. "I was hoping for some real ninja shit there." I knock the moth to the floor with a bottle and then step on it. There's a brittle crunch beneath my shoe, like autumn leaves.

Harrison says, "Anyway, Jay, I don't know if you noticed or not. But here's about as good as anywhere else these days."

• • •

The heat breaks, and power rationing comes with the autumn rains. Sections of the city flood and are abandoned to the insurgents. Home Protection sends a covert group of magicians and numbers men into an insurgent camp on the outskirts of Industrytown and their heads are sent back with their own incantations stuffed in their mouths. The rainfall is so heavy the streets below seem to warp like something spied through antique and untrustworthy glass. Mold slicks the walls of my apartment. I cough at night, and if I ever believed in magic, I don't anymore. The moths continue to lace their way throughout the building, the city. Come morning the floor is littered with their carapaces, pale as finger bones.

I write Jinx letters with the hiss of rain outside my windows, letters in which all is resolved, in which our lives are retold, in which I have wooed her back to living. I put the letters in envelopes and seal them and put them in my desk. I try my best not to cry out when a moth tumbles to the floor.

Occasionally I hear someone through our shared wall. Scrapes and murmurs. If it really is A Great and Terrible Wraith, I have yet to see him.

• • •

We're gifted with electricity today and I'm down in the basement, breathing through my mouth. Slime slicks the basement floor, but the washer and dryer still work, and even as the building slowly empties of tenants, as we sneak away in the night, or pretend some grave errand and try to make our way in daylight, I remain indebted to these small luxuries. I crave them, their normalcy, the repetition of these actions.

Today I pull my clothes from the dryer and among them is a mask. An orange and green mask with worn stitching and frayed eyelets. I put the mask in my laundry basket, stuff it beneath my clothes. I walk quickly up the stairs, expecting to meet him on the way, some scar-riddled behemoth, some huge motherfucker who can read the theft on my face like a birthmark, like a tremor.

In my apartment, I hold the mask on my hand, tented on my fingers. Every light in the apartment burns and the fabric almost glows incandescent.

I put it on, still warm: and you, Jinx, become a sudden ghost like a knife blade down the furrow of my skull. You bloom like fire, the heat of your life and your death inside me, at play relentlessly behind my eyes. Your voice runs a wooden cup down my spine like a xylophone. I see you, I see your life, your sorrow, your triumph, I see you as you saw yourself, and how I saw you as well.

This is wraith, this deathlessness, this haunting: how much you cared about us even as we ended it, even as you prepared to leave, and how you were afraid of so many things I never knew about, and how little you trusted to tell me.

You wanted me to come with you. I was blind to it.

And I yank the mask from my skull and my breath comes in shuddering gasps, and I'm loosing these sputtering, jagged sobs. And already, seconds later, curse stacked on curse—the shutter-stop epiphanies from beneath the mask begin to fade like smoke. As soon as I know it, I forget it.

• • •

Jinx had an uncle who was an analyst for Home Protection. He was relatively high up, and she was always getting extra stuff on her ration card because of it—cigarettes, vegetables. Extra fill-ups, stuff like that.

Once he gave her a day pass outside the checkpoints. It was right after I met him at a get-together at Jinx's parents' place. The uncle was a small, dapper man who carried his power around like an expensive coat, like plumed wings. He looked, you know, like someone's uncle, but also like a man who had the surety and mercilessness to call in a drone strike on a tenement building with children inside. The three of us talked, drank wine that I would never have been able to afford on my own, and at the end of the night he gripped me around the elbow, a little drunk, and said, "You two fit well, Jay. I'm a fan." And I'll be honest; I was a little flattered.

So he sent Jinx a day pass and we drove through a checkpoint, and some HP kid gave us a map that showed sergie hotspots and places to avoid. We drove through the gate and marveled at the ruination. There was wreckage everywhere: blackened convoy trucks, blocks of buildings that were now just arcs of rubble amid clotted weeds.

But it was springtime, and things were blooming, and I remember both Jinx and I were silent with something approaching awe when we came across the cherry orchard. It was beyond a fence, a leaning fence laced and woven in vines—just hundreds of these blooming cherry trees, all of them stretched for acres on this one unblemished hillside. Pink blooms heavy on the branches, bursting like just-lit fireworks. We pulled to a stop on the side of the road and gingerly, with my sleeves wrapped around my hands, I lifted the barbed-wire fencing and Jinx slipped through and then she did the same for me. We ate a picnic there beneath one of the trees. The scent of it, the way a breeze would send blossoms down to get caught in Jinx's hair. The way she would laugh, chewing something, and thread the blossoms out with her fingers. That memory. Sometimes I think if I could just live in that, you know?

I don't know what happened to the uncle, it's been years, but tonight on the News I sat and watched footage of the orchard, the trees skeletal now but unmistakably aligned on that rising hillside beyond the fence. The sergies had just torched it, and the smoke lay black and roiling against the gunmetal sky, flaming trees bent against the wind.

Above me, Harrison taps three times: *You want to hang out?*

I don't answer.

I just sit there, the mask in my lap, wondering, wondering.

• • •

Winter now. Frost rimes the windows, ghostly as Harrison's eyes. Eventually, grudgingly, the radiator will clang to life, if only for a while. Magicians wend through frozen, windblown streets, shouting curses and clacking rhythms with their dice and charred bones until the police, breathing air into their cupped hands, roll their eyes and tell them to move on.

I lay awake in the scant light of evening, too cold to sleep. No power today. Just one fluttering candle, blankets to my chin. I'm wearing a jacket, a sweater, two pairs of socks. My wrist is long healed but aches in this weather. I'm hungry, and I listen to the wind sneak fingers through chinks in the brickwork outside. Somehow the insects survive the cold and continue their machinations in the walls. I don't understand it. I watch as one tunnels its way through the plaster across the room; the shadows its wings lay upon the wall are terrible, alien.

I rise and gather a glass jar from the kitchen and when I walk back, the moth—they've grown nearly as big as my palm now, and sometimes the images on their wings look like men killing other men, or a child curled in a corner, or Jinx with her hair in her eyes, or the look on my mother's face the day I left home—lays there dazed on the floor, unmoving. It panics when I get near with the jar. I scoop it in, screw the lid, punch holes in the top with scissors.

I hold the candle flame next to the jar and the moth beats beats beats its wings. "That's right," I say, sneering.

And beneath my window is a muffled cough of breaking glass, and then noises bloom from the street and up the stairwell, footfalls thunderous and quick-paced and when lights flutter madly beneath the seam of my door, I lick my fingers and snuff the candle flame. I set the jar down on the floor and tiptoe to the door and press my ear against it. When I open the door, a half-dozen police line the hallway—everything's this strange ballet. They have lights attached to their weapons and details swim out of the lurching murk: a bandolier of ammunition across a chest, a faceplate with a silver crack down the center, dust motes whirling madly in the air.

They have a man pressed up against the wall, his hands zip-tied behind his back, his eyes white and searching through the rills of blood running down his forehead. I don't recognize him.

"Please," the man says. He's crying. "I don't understand," he says. They pull a hood over his head.

The police are yelling at me now, one of them, no, two of them, yelling at me to get back, get the fuck back inside, the bores of their guns are huge, planet-huge, their breath fogging their visors, clouding them, obscuring their faces, and I'm painted in the lights beneath their weapons, blinded, and I squint and raise my hands and gently shut my door, murmuring, "Sorry, sorry."

• • •

The lucidity of a dream, the surety of it, the shape of a man leaning against the wall at the foot of my bed. And he's huge. And it doesn't—it doesn't take a genius to figure out who it is.

But it's a dream, and sometimes bravery's a plentiful commodity when dreaming.

"I guess you're here to kill me," I say. Laconic and slow.

He laughs, crosses his arms. *Now, why would I want to kill you, Jay?* And his laugh is terrible, like scooping something dark out of a drain and then watching it writhe in your hand.

"I don't know," I say, scooting up on my elbows. There's a tilting funhouse quality to the dream. With a levity I'd never have in the waking world, I say, "Probably because I stole your mask from the dryer."

Who says you stole it? He leans in shadows, but he sounds like he's having a great time, like this is all hilarious.

"What, you left it there for me?"

Silence.

I'm supposed to wait him out? What?

"I put it on," I say. "I put the mask on."

Of course you did. What are masks for, genius? Of course you put it on.

And with that, something in me threatens to loosen, and the dream kind of tilts again, and I'm in this panic to talk to him about it, to tell him everything. "This woman, Jinx, okay? I saw—I put the mask on and I saw—"

He shushes me. *That's your problem, Jay. Talking about it isn't going to help. Haven't you been talking about it constantly? Isn't that all you've been doing? Can't you shut your fucking mouth about it? It's like you think you've got the patent on loss or something.*

A sound then like ten thousand moths, a hundred thousand, a million of them, all beating their wings. A million of them veined in the walls, in my fingertips, my balls, the circled bone around my eyes. I think about the moth in the jar, wonder if it hears the armada around it, how close it is to the others, if it knows jack shit beyond the ceaseless curved glass of its jail.

"What's the answer then?" I ask when the sound finally fades, because I have to ask. Because it's a dream, and brave or not, there's things you have to do.

You just live it. You just let the ghost of it all rattle inside you. You owe her that, right? Isn't that what this is all about?

"I don't know," I say. "I don't know what it's all about. I wish I did."

Then you're as dumb as you look, he says.

And then he leans forward and I hear the rasp of a lighter, and he holds the flame to his face.

And it's as bad as people say.

When he opens his mouth, the moths, all of them, they tumble from A Great and Terrible Wraith's ruined mouth. They fall from his jaws like a river of stones.

• • •

I keep writing Jinx letters. There's a selfishness to it, I know. Me, housed in this personal ache as the world continues to rip itself apart. Who's right? Harrison? Or the Wraith? I go with Harrison: time is time. Time doesn't care, time doesn't give a shit. Time moves on whether you are happy or sad or dying an inch at time. Your life is your life.

Maybe, it occurs to me, what the two of them are saying is the same thing.

• • •

I am rolling some of Harrison's gifted tobacco and watching Sports when it ends.

In the ring, A Great And Terrible Wraith picks men up and flings them down like toys. There's a knock on my door, and that's the moment that things change.

I look through the peephole. It's Hooper, skinny as a bad dream, his helmet in his armpit. Scowling in the weak light of the hallway. He looks left and then right. I open the door.

"Come upstairs," he says.

"Why?" I say. *Do I have to?* is what I mean.

"Just do it."

I follow him up the stairs. The walls are studded with holes and plaster grits beneath our feet. A dead moth here and there. How do you tell when a man is tired, or when he is ashamed? Hooper walks like he's both.

I'm only a little surprised when we stop in front of Harrison's door, and Hooper knocks, and from inside the apartment Harrison says, "Yeah." Only a little, because Harrison is the current that runs the neighborhood, isn't he? Of course Hooper works for him.

We go into Harrison's apartment, and Hooper shuts the door.

And it's just the three of us.

The three of us, and the man tied to the chair in the kitchen.

• • •

The Harrison I haven't seen before, he's here now. Full bloom, the bad man of the neighborhood. He stands near the man in the chair. He rests his chin on his hands, which are in turn resting on the top of his white cane. The overhead light carves dark shadows on his face.

The man in the chair is crying. He's held there, I see, by a spool of barbed wire. Blood stipples the linoleum beneath him, runs in dark rills down his little belly, his skinny arms. The man, his eyes are a little too close together, he has a little mouth, he looks like anybody. This is someone you pass on the street and never think about again. Just a naked man tied to a chair with barbed wire, weeping under the butter-yellow light.

"Told you," Harrison says. "Told you I'd get him, bud." It's like a joy inside him, this kindness he's doing me. This gift. The man in the chair sobs, and Harrison reaches out and gently explores the man's face with his hand, gingerly, like a father would a sleeping child. He presses a thumb into the man's eye.

The man shrieks and bucks against the wire.

"Jay, this is Mark. I *think* it's Mark. Is it Mark or Matt?"

"It's Mark," Hooper says quietly.

The man just turns his face away and sobs. Harrison's walls are like mine: peppered in holes, like someone took a shotgun to every room.

"Some other sergies gave this guy up for some pistols, you believe that shit? A couple .22s!" Harrison leans over and slaps him in the face. "You're not going to topple any regime that way! Gotta have *allegiances*. Right, Jay?" He turns to Hooper. "Give him your gun."

And then there's Hooper, with his Adam's apple and his missing button—he's holding his pistol out to me. He won't look me in the eye.

"Do it up," Harrison says, his chin resting on the top of his cane again. "From me to you. You wanted this. You wanted this, Jay, so get him."

• • •

What do you do when all the magic and vengeance, all the ache and hope in the world still won't bring somebody back? How do you make your way? What do you do when the people you thought you knew—Harrison, Jinx—had all these hidden, tucked away lives inside them?

What do you do then?

The heart moves as fast as it wants. Grows when it grows, lies stunted when it doesn't. The heart runs in circles, in mad leaps. Shivers like a dog, comes back again and again to the same wounds until there's enough scar tissue to move on.

What I mean is, the heart's the master, not the other way around.

I drop the pistol on the kitchen floor.

"The fuck are you doing, Jay?" Harrison says.

And I turn around.

Behind me, Harrison says, "Jay? *Jay.*"

My footsteps are loud in the hall and I go down the stairs and the stairs sound hollow, as if everything solid in the building has been hollowed out. I go inside my apartment and I take the jar with the moth and I go down onto the street. I keep waiting for Hooper to come out and do something to me. Shoot me. Take me back upstairs. But I step outside into a night heavy with a salting of stars above the ruined skyline of this city and my breath is yanked away in the wind like torn fabric. It's still cold out, but winter's fading. I unscrew the lid on the jar and I don't even see the moth fly away—I'm afraid to look, I look down the street instead, I look at the spot where Jinx's car was. When I look in the jar again, it's empty.

I take A Great and Terrible Wraith's mask from my pocket and pull it tight over my head and your ghost, Jinx, your ghost runs its hands down my spine again, your life seizes my hair and howls its song through my blood. I stumble off the curb and then right myself and you, you're a siren inside me, Jinx, a clanging bell. Your entire life, your whole life before me.

I take a shambling step, another one.

I start walking.

Haunt me.

COYOTE

Because she is seven days gone and he is so obviously heart-busted, I know it is not a good idea to talk to Tommy right now about Rosa or anything else. About how pointless this is. If it *was* a good time, then yes, I'd have things to say; we've been driving around for a long time. I'd say, "Tommy, I want to go home," or "Dressing like a cowboy doesn't make you one." I'd say, "She is with Danny Lee now. She is probably gone for good, man."

And it's like a bad country song on the radio, what we're doing. Driving around everywhere looking for Rosa like she's missing or wants to be found, which neither is the case. There's scrub and grasslands all yellowed outside the truck window and Two Forks sits like broken toys here, faded boxes of buildings lacing each side of the blacktop. There is always dust on the floorboards and the blue sky is so wide and bright, it's like an ocean flung upside down across my eyes. We have been in Texas five months now, my brother and I.

"Maybe she's at the café," Tommy says, even though we both know that's not true. She hasn't been there since she dumped him a week ago. She's on a bender with Danny Lee and we both know it. She's fired as hell, why would she go back there? But Tommy doesn't know where else to go. We've been all over the county, to all those bars in Marinville and Peyton, and Langston where we should of got groceries at the Shop'N'Save but I didn't say anything because Tommy was in a bad mood already, and now we're back at Two Forks. We've already been to the café earlier today for breakfast, so what I think is that Tommy just wants to be around *normal* people on his day off. Normal people being people besides me. But this time at least I will remember to ask Tami for a little doggie bag for Wanda. Which I guess would really make it a turtle bag. That makes me smile.

We pull in and Tommy squints at me. "What's so funny?" he says.

"Nothing," I say, thinking of Wanda standing on her hind legs, eating food from a takeout bag and drinking a bottle of Lone Star, which is the shit beer here. This is called *anthropomorphism*, which is a word I would pretty much destroy with if I was able to use it in Scrabble.

Tommy says, "She's a good woman, Toby. Don't you be thinking different about her because she's run off to get her bearings for a while." He never talked this way in Portland, all hillbilly. Even most of the people here don't talk like that. It makes me miss my life, like I don't even know him sometimes.

"I don't think that," I say, even though maybe I do.

I liked Rosa. She would bring Wanda food all the time without me even asking her. Plus a hamster wheel for her tank once that Wanda was too fat to use, which was hilarious to watch. And yeah, she is very pretty, beautiful even. Definitely the prettiest of my brother's girlfriends. They seemed to fit well, which makes me wonder what happened, how someone can just want to be there with you and then not.

Past the power poles on each side of the blacktop here, the ground looks like a burned blanket laid down flat. Everything yellow and brown with those canyon walls red and bone-like there in the distance. I'm still not used to how wide everyplace is. I'm not used to feeling this small.

Tami just smiles when she sees us for the second time in one day. She's leaning on the counter talking to a man in a green shirt. She smells like hairspray and is almost as big as me, which is pretty big. My meds make me fat, which is something that Tommy says will change once my body adjusts. Which I know is also bullshit but is still nice of him to say.

"Back again," she says to us as we sit at the counter. I like Tami's face because she has one brown tooth that you can see just a bit of when she smiles; it's like a secret that she's not afraid of telling. She pours us coffee and the first thing I say is, "Remind me to ask you for some vegetables for Wanda before we leave." Tami laughs—not mean—and says, "If I forget to remind you, remind me." And she and I laugh at that and Tommy looks at us glaring like maybe both of us are head-wasted.

I want to say, *Don't look at me like that. I am still older than you,* but we are each other's keepers so I don't. I know he's trying to be more than what's in his nature.

Tommy says, "Just coffee," but even I can see his eyes asking *Have you seen her?* Rosa worked at the café and we would come in here a lot and joke around with her when she was working. Tommy's been here every day since she hooked up with Danny Lee. Tami looks at his cup as she pours, like she is concentrating, but really she's just avoiding his eyes.

I order another breakfast and Tami goes in the back and it's just us and the green-shirted man. Tommy takes his baseball hat off—there's a red stripe running around his forehead—and folds his arms on the table. He looks around the room like he's stuck here.

"What the fuck," Tommy says under his breath but not to me. If his words were solid things, they'd be stones hitting hard and bouncing to the floor. He wears his pain like a shirt, my brother does. Tami comes with my plate and also a paper cup with some corn and green beans and parsley and a baggie of ice on top and underneath, so nice of her, and I say, "Thanks, darlin," and she laughs so hard. The man in the green shirt even smiles. I read my dictionary and Tommy looks at the wall like he's trying to see through it and that is our day.

• • •

We see eyes when we pull up to the trailer that night. They blaze like coins in the headlights and Tommy shuts the truck off and under the moon we see it's a coyote. It is lean and still and grins at us like there's a big joke somewhere right around the corner. It's near my Coop where Wanda is but I'm not worried because it's locked.

"Mother*fucker*," Tommy breathes, yanking the .22 from the rack behind our heads. "Stay in the truck, Toby." He opens his door and the coyote tenses but doesn't run. Tommy fires two shots braced against the doorframe but he's not really trying. He shot a bird with a BB gun once when we were kids. It was in the field behind our uncle's house and we both cried watching its tiny, perfect chest heaving there in the snow, two drops of blood next to its head. We ran away and left it there to die. Tommy's gun is like the way he rolls his shirtsleeves up to his elbows now or how he wears cowboy boots on his days off—he's trying to find a new version of himself, one that makes him feel stronger. He blames himself for what happened to us.

The shots go way over the coyote's head. It bounds away; there is a brief ripple of fur as it turns and runs into the scrub behind the trailer.

• • •

I know for sure that we are each other's anchors, Tommy and me. We are debted to each other, which is how I look at it sometimes when I get sad listening to the coyotes howling up there on the ridge at night. I can't read my dictionary when I hear them, it's too hard to concentrate. Can't even read my comics, which are, the word is, *sequential*.

When I say that Tommy and I are debted, it's just a way of saying that I was twenty-one years old and still living at home with Tommy and Mom and Dad when the call came that he was in jail one night for fighting. This was in Portland and it was three years ago. He had just turned nineteen and was *Heading Down A Bad Road* as our mom said all the time. The call came late at night and the three of us got dressed, and I drove even though I had to work at the pet store the next day. Back then I was in college studying biology and working. I only made it a year and still I've forgotten so much of what I learned. The things I remember, they're like pieces of furniture in a darkened room, like dim outlines. Thinking back to the *me before* is like thinking about someone you've heard of but never met. Someone whose stories get passed down to you.

It was quiet in the car that night. I drove because Mom never learned how— Tommy and I teased her about it a lot, which is one of the things I feel so bad about now—and Dad's eyes were bad at night. They were already pretty old when they had us. I remember being mad at Tommy, and how my mom kept worrying her bracelet with the fingers of her other hand. Me and Tommy were not really friends before the accident, and sometimes I'm not sure if we are now or if it's just the feeling that each other is all we have left.

About Wanda, a very important thing is that certain foods can keep her from absorbing calcium because they contain high amounts of *oxalic acid,* which I forget what that is but I *used* to know. But good ways for her to get calcium, which she needs, is feeding her crushed eggshells or oyster shells or even pieces of plaster, which makes me nervous so I just stick to eggshells. And what happened was we were exiting off I-5 to bail out Tommy, with the sky like the bottom of a river, and a drunk man hit us from behind. He was going over seventy miles an hour the police said later. The only person that didn't die that night in both cars was me. They could see my brain through my skull they said, which actually helped because it swelled up really bad. There's a scar now that runs from the top of my head down to my eyebrow. God, I was fast with my words once.

I know that's what Texas is about to him, to step away from that all. I understand it. But when I think about it and feel sad, I have to play Scrabble with him or read my dictionary or my comics or touch Wanda's shell to go somewhere else. Remembering my old life is like trying to catch water with my hands.

• • •

The Coop is what we call the shed next to the trailer. Tommy fixed it up for me once he and Rosa started seeing each other because they wanted to Get Biblical in private all the time. I don't mind. The trailer is small for two people anyways and can hold the memories of a fart someone kicked out three days before. There's a little door and windows higher up and a hinge for my padlock. It stays mostly cool for Wanda, which is something she needs because she's that kind of turtle, which is a Red Eared Slider. The only problem with the Coop is when you have to go number two.

I can see a little sliver of light under the door of the trailer but I knock to be polite anyway. There's the mad stutter of feet and Tommy opens the door, his hair like corkscrews and a bottle of beer in his hand, and there is such a look in his eyes that I can tell how disappointed he is that it's just me.

"Gotta go number two," I mumble.

Tommy smiles and bows with his arm out. "By all means, my good man. Shit away." He's drunk.

The TV's on. There's trash everywhere. Empty bottles and chip bags and soup cans and I guess I should do the dishes even though I always do mine after I eat. There's a dirt-stiff pair of socks on the small table mounded high with more bottles and Tommy's work pants are slung over the chair.

The bathroom is very small. My knees are pressed hard against the door while I go. I wash my hands at the kitchen sink with Joy while Tommy sits at the table with his beer bottle. Some of Rosa's clothes lay next to him. He has folded them and he sits in front of the TV like he's waiting in an airport.

"Well," I say, my hand on the doorknob, "thanks. See you tomorrow."

He runs his hand down his face with a sound like sandpaper. "You want to go into town tomorrow or you want to stay here?"

"I'll stay here," I say. "Me and Wanda will hold down the fort."

He nods. "You want a beer or anything?"

"No. I just had to go number two."

Howls drift down from the ridge when I step outside and the moon is white and perfectly round. Tommy turns off the TV when I shut the door and the world is dark and silent except for the coyotes.

• • •

A week later we're in the parking lot of the Shop 'N' Save and Tommy sees Danny Lee getting into his truck with a sack of groceries. Tommy has mostly stopped talking about Rosa or looking for her, but he spins the wheel and screeches to a stop and people turn to look. He throws his baseball hat on the seat next to me and jumps out. He runs up to Danny Lee and kind of slaps the bag of groceries out of his hands. The bag falls to the ground and a loaf of bread spills out.

Tommy punches Danny Lee above his eye and then Danny Lee punches my brother twice in the mouth and then grips him by the shoulder and punches him in the stomach. Tommy crumples to the ground. I open my door and Tommy waves his hand at me and shakes his head.

Danny Lee picks his groceries up and puts them in his truck while my brother sits on his knees looking for his breath. A few drops of blood lay on the pavement like red dimes.

Danny Lee looks down at my brother and says, "It just happens like this sometimes. There wasn't any plan or anything like that." Danny Lee looks at me once and nods. This is one of those times where I'm sure I would have known what to do before but I'm frozen in my seat now.

Danny Lee drives away and a woman in big sunglasses and an embroidered shirt looks at us as she stands next to her car.

Tommy stands up and sneers at her. "The fuck are you looking at, honey?"

He gets back in the truck and rucks up his shirt to wipe the blood from his mouth. He puts his hat back on and we drive out of there.

When we make it back to the trailer later that day there are wet marks in the dust. I point to the one in front of the trailer door and Tommy goes back to the truck and gets the rifle. He walks a circle around the two buildings and puts the rifle back in the truck. We go into the trailer and Tommy turns on the TV and walks to the fridge. He says. "Do you want to sleep in here tonight?"

"No. I'm not scared of coyotes. I just don't like how they sound."

He presses a bottle of beer against his split lip. The trailer is hot and airless.

He moves Rosa's clothes to the end of his bed and puts the rest of the stuff on the bench. He takes down Scrabble from the dresser under the table. Scrabble is something all my therapists and doctors said would help me and it's something we do practically every day unless Tommy is real tired after work. The word is *repetition*. Tommy didn't do well in school but playing word games every day has helped us both learn a lot and actually Tommy doesn't cuss as much now.

We start playing and I don't say anything about how we weren't able to get any groceries at the Shop'N'Save because he got his ass kicked instead. After a while, Tommy puts some Rice-A-Roni and a can of green beans on the stove and I tease him about how he's stalling for time. He smiles and uses all of his tiles with the word *penance* and gets fifty extra points and it's the first time he's ever beat me at Scrabble. Seeing him smile like that makes me happier than I think it will.

• • •

The next day I am out in the shadow of the Coop reading comics with Wanda resting in the shade beside me and I see Danny Lee's truck pull off the road in front of our trailer. Tommy is at work in Peyton where he helps make parts for the oilrigs and will be gone for hours. I don't know what to do.

I pick Wanda up as gently as I can and step inside the Coop and put her in her tank. When I come out I try to get ready to fight but I'm already scared. But instead of Danny Lee, Rosa steps out of the truck, dust clouded behind her.

She smiles and says, "Hey, Toby," like nothing has changed. She's wearing a black cowboy shirt with white stitching and very tight jeans and I can see myself in her sunglasses as she walks up to me. Her hair is black like a wing and tied back. She hugs me like nothing is different and I don't hug her back.

"Tommy isn't here," I say.

"I know," she says. "But I left some of my stuff here. You think you could open the trailer up for me?"

"I don't know if I should. Tommy might be mad. Maybe you should call him."

Rosa takes her sunglasses off. She says my name like a sigh.

"Like you guys could get some beers together like before," I say. "Talk it over. He went into the café every day looking for you."

She smiles and shakes her head. "I don't work there anymore."

"No shit," I say, which makes me feel good because I say it as fast as I would have said it before. But then I see the hurt look on her face and I do feel bad.

I say, "You should just call him is all."

Rosa breathes deep and wipes at her eye like it could be a tear there but is probably just dust.

"I can't call him, Toby. You can't just not call someone and then call them. It doesn't work like that."

"It would with Tommy. I know it."

She sighs hard like she does after I've seen her taking shots and then she takes a step backward and says. "You want a ride into town?"

I hold up my comic. "Me and Wanda are reading."

She looks at me and I can't tell what she's thinking. It's mostly like she's putting me in place, filing me away. The brain-damaged fat brother of a guy she went out with for a few months, a guy from out of town. She gets back in the truck.

"You know, I can't believe he leaves you out here all day to . . . to just *rot* all day. It's not right."

"Well, a lot of things are not right," I say. I'm so mad and not sure if I did the right thing, and I want to take it back and *not* take it back but she drives away anyway.

I walk around the other side of the trailer, the sun hot on my shoulders, and when I look up, two coyotes are sitting twenty or thirty feet away from me. They are the color of sand and ash and the only things that move are their tongues. I realize suddenly that I'm crying, and I can feel the scar on my forehead throbbing. I pick up a rock and throw it toward the coyotes but they don't move besides flicking their cold eyes toward me.

"Fuck off," I scream, my voice cracking. "Beat it! Get!"

I throw another rock at them and really try. It falls short but bounces toward one and it yelps and skitters backward and then the two of them turn and lope away. They seem unworried and I stand there and try to catch my breath under the open hand of the sun.

• • •

When Tommy comes home the sunset is running like slow fire against the wall of the canyon. I have a piece of two by four I found leaning against the back of the trailer and I have been walking the *perimeter* of the trailer and the Coop for a long time. My feet are sore and I'm thirsty.

Tommy gets out of the truck smiling. "The hell, Toby? You look like you're guarding Buckingham Palace or some shit."

All my words come in a rush and Tommy's face changes too. He has me sit on the trailer steps and he gets me a glass of water. I tell him about the coyotes and he says they must be hungry to come up that close in the daylight. Then I tell him about Rosa and how I didn't let her in, how I said she should call him first. It looks like he is trying to figure out all the angles of the thing. He looks at his phone, looks hard at it like he's mad and then puts it away.

"You know what," he says. "Fuck it." He sits next to me on the steps and presses his shoulder against mine and it's a comfort. "She wants that redneck, she can have him."

He says he has something for me in the truck and we step out there, our shadows running long in the dust. On the seat is a new dictionary, a red hardcover one, way better than the paperback one I carry around all the time, which doesn't have half the words I'm looking for.

"Bookstore in Peyton," he says and I smile and pat his shoulder because we haven't hugged each other since we were boys.

"Thank you," I say. "It's really nice."

"It's real old, man, look," and he shows me the title page and the date it was published—the math takes me a while—makes it almost fifty years old.

"Now you can get filled in on all kinds of outdated misinformation," he says, smiling.

"It's as old as me and you put together," I say.

"That's right."

I am looking at my book when he says some friends from his work are drinking in Two Forks and he wants to go. We get in the truck, the two of us.

We walk into the bar half an hour later and go over to the table with Tommy's friends. I sit down and put my new dictionary beside me and I listen as Tommy and his friends drink beer and talk and laugh. I drink soda and laugh at some of the jokes—the ones I get—and someone plays country music on the jukebox. They order shots, Tommy and his friends, and get louder. And I see Tommy looking at some girls playing pool over in the corner of the bar and it's a nice time. It's good to see him happy and not like he wants to peel parts of himself away, walking around restless and busted all day and night. It seems to me like time can maybe heal most things. Maybe not all the way and maybe not everything, but just enough.

And then, when his friend Mitch is telling a story about how he got fired from his last job, all that is gone. I realize that we didn't lock up the Coop or the trailer when we left and that I didn't put the top of Wanda's tank on. It is like someone grabbing my throat and squeezing.

I say, "Tommy, we have to go."

Tommy looks at me. His eyes are unfocused and he's drunk and I am mad at myself and afraid for not seeing this before.

"What's the deal, man? Let's stay awhile," he says. He is *slurring* is the word.

"We forgot to lock the trailer. Wanda's lid isn't on."

He thinks about this for a moment, or pretends to. "I'm sure it'll be fine, Toby. We'll go after this round, okay?"

Tommy turns back to his friends and laughs at something Mitch says and yes, all my good feelings are gone just like that.

I grab Tommy's ring of keys and run out to the parking lot. I am trying to find the key to open the door when Tommy, behind me, says, "Door's unlocked, Toby."

He gets in the passenger seat. Drunk, he wears the look of a man surprised, his eyebrows raised and his mouth slack, but he doesn't say anything as I get in and start the truck. I swear it's as if the ghosts of our mom and dad are sitting right there between us.

I back out of the parking lot and Tommy says, almost cheerfully, "This is illegal as shit."

The night stretches from one end of the world to the other, it seems like. I have traveled this road with Tommy a hundred, two hundred times. Driving comes back to me without even thinking and I wend my way through the few stoplights of Two Forks, passing the few random sets of glowing taillights on the way.

"She'll be fine," he says, and I want to believe him but don't. There are so few remnants left of who I was.

We turn off the county road and bounce through the ruts in our driveway. I pull up to the trailer in darkness and brake so hard I hear rocks rattle and clang against the truck's underside.

I hear them before I see them. A half-dozen coyotes are braced around the entrance to the Coop. The door is ajar, the padlock hanging useless, the wedge of night in that place blacker than it is outside. The coyotes' eyes have no light to reflect back at us.

Tommy and I step out of the truck. His hands, I see, are balled into fists. One of the coyotes leans back, its throat exposed, and the howl drifts long and lamenting into the sky.

My brother and I, we run headlong into the pack.

YES, WE ARE DULY CONCERNED WITH CALAMITOUS EVENTS

THE FIRST DEATH

Twenty-three days after the world kind of ends, we all watch as Human Resources Randy strangles the temp with a mouse cord. Right there in the hallway in front of the men's bathroom door. If the tone hadn't been set yet already, well. There you go. Jesus.

We stand there, this wavering ring around the two of them as they writhe on the floor. Someone quietly murmurs his name—Randy's, not the temp's; nobody can actually remember the temp's name, even though he was here for a week before everything happened, and almost all of us are convinced that he's the one that left the shitty, passive-aggressive Post-It note on the copy machine the day that everything went wrong—but that's it. Just a murmured "Jeez, Randy" as the temp (with twenty-three days of sweat around his collar, still wearing his CONTRACTOR lanyard, still with that huge zit right in his septum, which really must hurt like an absolute bastard when you thought about it) lies on his back and claws at the cord cinched around his throat. He knocks over one of the recycling baskets with his madly kicking foot. Human Resources Randy is above him, weeping. The temp's face is so full of trapped blood it's like a painted-on mask. His eyes look like if you found the recipe for "Sheer Animal Terror" and doubled all the ingredients.

The phone starts ringing in reception. Donna stalks toward it with her hand covering her mouth. Jim Bledsoe, staring at the scene playing out on the floor, calls out, "Jesus Christ, Donna, you know what it's going to say." And it's true. We're all very familiar by now with the phenomenon of the ringing phone.

We stand clustered in the hall. We watch Randy strangle the temp.

We cast horrified, pained glances at each other.

We wait for someone to do the right thing.

We've grown accustomed to waiting.

The temp dies with a last wretched click of his throat and the shocking, immediate stench of loosed bowels; shit-stink mingles with the ever-present fug of microwave popcorn like two lovers that are no good for each other. And it's not like we can open the windows. People step back, some of us gagging, while Randy kind of leans, kind of falls over the temp's body. Randy's lips are pulled back to show his big horsey teeth. He's not in good shape, Randy, and he's gasping for air, still crying, his crotch pretty much in the temp's slack face. There's smashed popcorn all over the floor.

Over at her desk, Donna picks up the phone. Her eyes look like dusty glass, vacant and stunned.

"What?" she says into the receiver.

She doesn't write it down, what the voice says.

Twenty-three days after the world ends? We're past taking messages here.

Besides, we've heard it all before.

REGARDING *BRING YOUR CHILD TO WORK DAY*

The world ended, or kind of ended, or was significantly *altered,* twenty-three days ago. On Bring Your Child to Work Day. We used to put stock in this, for maybe the first week—there seemed some importance to it. Part of the riddle. But eventually we decided, no—any given day contains a multitude of alterations. Any given day is fractured with possibility, fraught with it. If it wasn't Bring Your Child to Work Day, we would have placed importance on the pizza someone had brought in (Fridays), or that Donna wore her sports bra underneath her top so she could go straight to her spin class after work (Tuesdays). There would always be some Event in the day, some splintering, some nuance, if we looked hard enough. Some fracturing that the mind ached to lend importance to.

It could drive you crazy if you thought about it.

(We all still thought about it.)

Tricia, the sole team member in Asset Management, which most of us had only a vague understanding of at best, was not the only parent in the office, but she was the only one that either lacked child care or felt obligated enough to participate. Some of us, it was true, would think it a kind of dark irony that Tricia was the one who brought her kid to work. Her daughter Melanie had both *Spondyleopiphyseal dysplasias,* a particularly brutal variety of dwarfism, as well as significant developmental disabilities. Why Tricia? Donna had twin hell-raiser eleven-year-old boys; Jim Bledsoe had a brood of kids from three ex-wives. All girls, the youngest of them a sophomore in high school. But Melanie was the one that was with us. Again, the mind lurches toward solutions, toward answers. We search for keys that fit the locks.

But to be honest, right before the beginning of the end of the world, we had all tried to avoid Tricia's cubicle on Bring Your Child to Work Day because a) who brings their kid to a workplace like ours, how inappropriate is that? And b) honestly, Melanie was only nine but she was also kind of scary and hard to look at. We were ashamed of that, honestly, how unnerved we were to look at her. We felt small by it. We felt shitty. Not even the Mok Brothers made fun of Melanie, or spoke out loud how hard it might be to love her in her shunted, curled little body and pink wheelchair, or how even thinking that—even though we all did, pretty much—almost certainly made us terrible people. We didn't speak of Melanie at all, not before and not after, not in the break room or at the window of the back door where we gazed at the parking lot and the trash field, suddenly made beautiful for its emptiness, its sudden grand expanse. We certainly said nothing to Tricia's face. If anything, we tried to be kinder to her. Even Donna, who had to suffer this new, smaller world without her little boys, without knowing what had happened to them, tried to be kind to Tricia.

WHY OH WHY DID THE TEMP HAVE TO DIE?

Another thing we aren't proud of, that we feel like reflects pretty poorly on the whole, to be honest, was that the fight between Human Resources Randy and the temp started over whose turn it was to clean the microwave.

These things happen, we tell ourselves. Things are being sloughed away. How to smooth over the horror? To sand away our own complicity? Yes, twenty-three days ago such a thing would have been crazy. Insane. But things are vastly different than they were twenty-three days ago.

Some of us feel like that's the point. That's why we're here. An experiment.

A monitored descent into madness. Bugs in a jar, etc.

Human Resources Randy hunches on his knees next to the temp, wiping his big red face and honking his nose with a handkerchief.

"Thanks, Randy. Thanks, man. You happy now, asshole?" says Chris Mok, looking at the temp's body, covering his mouth and nose against the rising stench of the poor kid's bowels. It comes out muffled, almost like a joke.

THE END OF THE WORLD CLUB IS FORMED

A week after the end of the world, after we'd exhausted ourselves, we held a staff meeting. It was decided we would establish a timeline. We would come up with a chronology of events as accurately and with as much consensus as possible. (Human Resources Randy strangling the temp was still a few weeks away; some vestige of civility still held true.) Clues would reside here, we believed, in the documenting of events, and we ached also for the easy cadence of our old lives, for that old numbing ghost suddenly made exotic: routine.

And what could be more routine than a staff meeting?

We went into the conference room. We dissected that day again and again. Jim Bledsoe, our CEO, led the meeting. Donna typed the minutes. (Computers worked fine; every time we tried to log on to our email to send for help, we'd just get rerouted to various other sites—the Arby's homepage, a New Hampshire construction outfit called Anderson Hammer & Nail, the Wikipedia entry for the KGB. But Microsoft Word worked the same as it ever did.) Melanie kind of drew in a coloring book and on the table and herself. Tricia took little hitching sobs and sort of plucked at Melanie's clothes, fussing over her. Abby Brenner clutched her cross pendant and murmured things that were most likely prayers. The Mok Brothers, Chad and Chris, sat scowling with their arms folded and cast surreptitious glances down Donna's blouse, trying to stay mad at what had happened to us. And yet all of us were happy to be there, or at least relieved, grateful for the normalcy of the act. The door to the conference room was a door we could open and close.

"Alright, ladies and gentlemen," said Jim, looking at all of us over the tops of his glasses, his voice stentorian and reassuring. "Let's review. How'd we get into this mess?"

And review we did. It was Bring Your Child To Work Day, but other than that? It could have been any other Wednesday. We'd arrived at the office, hung our coats on the hooked tree next to Donna's desk, or in our offices if we were lucky enough to have offices. We'd turned on computers. We'd grimly picked over that morning's treat selection in the break room (bear claws, discounted, the icing cracked with age.) We drank coffee, Human Resources Randy heating up instant in the microwave because he didn't want to wait for drip. We'd smiled wanly as Vinu, our CFO, greeted us with his daily and morbidly cheerful "Hello to you!" that kind of made us want to strangle him sometimes, honestly. We'd smelled the smell of the copier warming up and kicking out the morning's reports, and noticed that someone had put a Post-It note on the machine's paper tray that said *If it empties on yr print job, u should be the one to fill it back up. Just saying.*

At the staff meeting, Jim Bledsoe asked who'd put the note on the copier. As if it might be some kind of clue. The room fell silent.

"Well, whoever did it," said Van, speaking into the rim of his *Beggin For That Banana* coffee cup, one of our classics, the one with the kind of hippie-ish naked lady wearing the gorilla mask that Van himself had drawn up decades ago, "is a sanctimonious prick." He was the single remaining Visual Artist in the office, and still had major pull with our distributors, many of whom were also older than God, and thusly he was allowed to say things like that when the rest of us were not. The temp, some of us noted, had blushed into his lap.

"What else?" asked Jim.

We'd started our day. Van had a drawing table and a scanner and a pair of double monitors. He shared an office with Stanley, who did the majority of the typesetting and packaging design of our products. "I do the naughty bits," Stanley would always say in staff meetings, in a terrible British accent, which was one of the many reasons we didn't like him very much. Also because he had a penchant for rubbing the skin on his psoriatic elbows while speaking to one of us in the hallway, enough so that we could see little pale flakes snowing down on the carpet, something which Stanley seemed oblivious of, and still another, and probably the biggest thing, was because his lunch almost always consisted of baguettes coupled with various exotic French cheeses—like, almost exclusively, every single day, and he would frequently walk by our offices, or bother us in the break room or, once, even out on the loading dock where Chris Mok was smoking and looking out at the trash field, and Stanley had thrust a clot of *Epoisses* under Chris's nose and said, "Smell that, brother. That's just artistry *distilled* right there," and Chris Mok had purportedly said, "I'm not your fucking brother, dude," and slapped his hand away, and after this, Stanley was soon being called Stankley behind his back by pretty much the vast majority of us, except for Jim Bledsoe, who wasn't in on it, and Tricia, who was just way too nice of a person, and Melanie, who was just a kid, and didn't really talk much anyways.

We'd started work like we always did. The Mok Brothers, with their pastel polo shirts and gelled hair and gym-earned biceps, got on the phone with various distributors and vendors, starting almost every call with a wildly sexist joke when someone picked up on the other end. February was looming, and Jim was adamant that the *Panty Popper* line—Van-illustrated origami penis caricatures that burst from a pair of panties pop-up style when taken out of their packaging—was going to be our Valentine's season boon. The Moks worked on commission and they were hustling hard. We were housed in a small office park out in Tigard, off of Highway 217. Next Door Novelties was a forty-year-old company started by Jim's father; we were a midlevel manufacturer of novelty sex- and gag-gifts. All of our stuff was designed in-house, made in China, shipped back here and then sent to our various distributors through the country. NDN was one of the last holdouts—almost everything was done overseas now. That morning, we'd called people, answered emails. Sent invoices. Stapled and hole-punched. Abby, Jim's niece, wrote copy as best she could. She put her head in Vinu's office—she thought he was one of the only truly kind men in the office—and shyly asked him what rhymed with "pudenda," at which point Vinu just stared at her, blank-faced, his pen above his paperwork. We sent faxes, did a double-take and then hurriedly said hi to Melanie when Tricia pushed her around to all of our desks in her little pink wheelchair, simultaneously pretending distraction and feeling like huge assholes, stunned by the amount of damage a human body could maintain and still survive. The nameless temp worked in the mail room next to Vinu's office, packing samples, sorting mail, and sending "welcome packages" to potential vendors.

It was Wednesday, we said, helpless at our own shoddy answer. We'd gone to work and gazed longingly at the clock. We'd flexed our calves and tongued our molars. We'd clicked the caps on pens and checked our email too many times. We'd watched videos of meowing cats and men suffering horrific injuries on YouTube.

In their shared office that morning, Stanley had said to Van's back, "Got a *Brie de Meaux* today, big man. Gonna knock your socks off."

"Can't wait," Van muttered drily, peering at Photoshop over the rims of his bifocals, coloring in a vagina with the patience of a sixteenth-century monk lettering an illuminated manuscript.

The temp had gazed moonily into the break room refrigerator and told Jim Bledsoe, who liked to snack there because he believed that it kept him in touch with the pulse of the office, that the fog had been super thick that morning, really dense. "And the rain had a weird smell, you know?" the temp had said. "Did you notice that? All metally, kind of?"

"Mmm-hmm," Jim Bledsoe had said, thumbs spidering his phone, bear claw crumbs in his white mustache. (The temp, Jim believed, was a temp, and thusly pulseless in regard to office blood flow.)

Yet that was the only thing that had seemed to denote a possible world-ending: it *had* been a little strange, though, the way the fog roiled so suddenly against the windows that morning. Almost cloudlike in the way it pressed against the glass—at least according to Donna, whose desk faced the front windows. "It was like from a fog machine," she'd said at that staff meeting.

"The fog came in like fog from a fog machine," Chad Mok said, giving her a contemptuous, dead-eyed stare.

"Exactly," Donna said, smiling at him. Mistaking his sarcasm for sincerity, grateful to be understood.

And then around 9:50 in the morning, the power had gone out.

"Power's out," Stanley had informed Van as they sat in the sudden gloom. Van sat with his glasses on his forehead, rubbing the bridge of his nose and staring at his dead monitors. He feared Stanley's cheese, odorous under the best of circumstances, turning in the refrigerator if the power stayed off for any significant amount of time.

"Dude, what?" Chris Mok said in the office he shared with his brother, clicking his mouse, dragging out the last word. "Come on. Seriously?"

"Bro, I think I just rolled into Suck My Dickville," sighed Chad Mok, "and it looks a lot like this place."

Vinu felt his way along the wall of his office and stepped into the hall—the light from the windows was better there. Not by much, but enough. "Hey, buddy," he called out to the temp in the mail room next door. "Just stay where you are. Power should come on in a sec."

Human Resources Randy, whose office flanked the mail room on the other side, agreed. "Yeah, just stay put, pal." The idea of the temp falling in the dark, and the vast potential for ensuing litigation, filled the two men with dread.

Abby Brenner let out a shriek in her office. (Her office was windowless, her door closed.) Her morning's work, copy for thirty or forty incomprehensible greeting cards that she knew Jim would veto anyway for the fact that they weren't dirty enough ("It's okay to say 'pussy' in this business, Abbster, Jesus jumped-up Christ") faded to nothingness as her screen went blank.

That, it was agreed, had been the beginning of the end.

THE DAY THE WORLD KIND OF ENDED, CONTINUED

We were plunged into darkness. Abby's shriek was muffled and hollow.

Melanie, coloring in her mother's office, lifted her head in the dark, as much as she was able, and let out a strangely adult, strangely exultant laugh.

All of the phones in the office rang at the same time.

Donna, seated at her reception desk, was the first to answer. She told us later the line had sounded "ocean-like." Staticky, like a seashell pressed to her ear.

And then came forth the statement we would come to rue, to despise. To fear. The words we would eventually try to divine like cast bones, like a riddle. The words that would turn us, a bunch of sex-novelty dummies, into half-assed, desperate haruspices.

Donna picked up the phone, and on the other end the voice of a little boy said, *"Are you duly concerned with calamitous events?"*

MAYBE A KIND OF PLAN IS FORMED SORT OF

The temp's body lay there in front of the bathroom door.

"Looks like the temp's cooling," Van said as he stood over it with his hands on his hips, and there was a moment of silence before Chad Mok honked mad laughter and swiped at his eyes.

He said, "We're losing it. This is fucked."

"Randy," said Van. "You gotta get up. Gotta get up, buddy."

"I just killed this kid," said Human Resources Randy. "Holy God. Holy God." He pushed himself up off the floor, first one knee and then the other, and stood there with the knuckles of both hands pressed against his mouth. His shirt had come untucked. The entire office smelled of popcorn and shit.

"Let's get him in the bathroom," said Jim Bledsoe.

ARE WE DULY CONCERNED?
DEFINE "DULY"

When Donna had answered the phone that first time, the lights had come back on immediately.

There is a moment when you realize the world has changed, has gone against its own natural order. That moment when the door doesn't open when it should, and keeps not opening, and then stays that way. You want to go outside and the door just does not open. If you both live in that moment for too long and consistently refuse it, you go mad. As simple as that.

And, not surprisingly, that was the moment we lived in. The front door of Next Door Novelties *should* open, the back door *should* open. *The doors should open.* But they didn't.

It was Chris Mok, going out to have a smoke break and look at the trash field, who discovered it. He thought someone, Jim maybe, had simply locked it. He'd gone to the front door then, and that was locked as well. Things were still dim in the fog then.

We gathered in a group at the front door, Jim insisting he had done nothing. His keys turned perfectly in the locks and still did nothing at all.

The phone rang at odd times after that. There seemed no system in place.

Vinu, after the second day, began taking notes of the calls and their times, and events around the office that might correlate.

"If there is a pattern," he said to us later, clearly embarrassed, "I can't discern it."

Day Three: four calls.

Day Four: one call.

Day Five: four calls.

Day Nine: a maddening *twenty-nine* calls, until Chad Mok ripped a phone out of its jack. And yet it still rang, even after he flung it across the room and hit Stanley in the ear with the receiver.

The same question every single time, the same fuzz-boxed, childlike voice: *"Are you duly concerned with calamitous events?"*

"What do you want us to say?" Chad had cried out. "Yes, okay? Yes! We're super fucking concerned!"

Stanley sank to his knees, hissing in pain and rubbing his ear.

We could all hear the boy, hear his terrible incantation still buzzing from the phone on the floor.

THE THINGS WE THINK IT SOUNDS LIKE

Twenty-nine days now. Nearly a month.

The world moves on beyond the windows. The freeway remains clogged with moving cars like slow blood.

Nearly a month! Six days since the temp was put into the men's bathroom.

Human Resources Randy lays supine beneath his desk now, feigns sleep even during the day. We avoid him, we avoid Melanie.

Day and night unfold.

The phone rings until we answer it. We waited, on Day Twenty-Six. "To see what'll happen," said Jim Bledsoe. To win a minute victory—to wait for the caller to exhaust himself and hang up. Instead the phone rang for eight hours and four minutes before Jim sighed "For God's sake," and picked it up. He waited a moment, and then said, "Great. Well, I'm actually more concerned with pillaging your father's asshole and spending your inheritance at the moment," and hung up. An hour later, the phone rang again.

The voice, it's a little boy. We're sure of that. But it's a little boy in tandem with other things. Like those people on true crime shows with their faces blacked out, their voices altered.

It sounds, to some of us, like a cloud of bees made slow and lazy with smoke.

Like someone hurting a cat for no reason.

Like a good, beloved house shrinking from sight as we drive away.

Like a favorite grandmother cursing us as clots of graveyard dirt tumble from her mouth.

Like Chris and Chad's stepfather's pained, squeaking farts as he takes his morning piss, the shared wall between their childhood bedroom and the bathroom thin as a scudded cloud.

Like Melanie's spinal fluid being pulled from her with a needle this big for tests, tests and more tests.

Like a slap to the stomach, the lower back, sharp as a rifle-crack, bruiseless events designed to hurt.

Like that guy in Seattle that night saying *Let me. You better fucking let me. Okay?*

It sounds like we have been placed in some forgotten pocket of the natural world where the machinery has broken down in some intrinsic, vital way.

The doors, they just won't open.

TIME IS NOT OUR FRIEND

So, sure. The world ended, and we entered a forced epoch. A new age. We were encapsulated within the office. We could see the world, but the world could not, or would not, see us. Some rules applied, but which ones we could not discern.

"Screw this," Chris Mok said on the first early evening of the beginning of the end of the world, the time when we would normally be going home. He pushed Donna's desk, a chipped white IKEA affair, toward the glass-faced front door. Outside, it had been a fine, crisp winter evening; the parking lot already so foreign to us it was like a sodium-lit moonscape, another world. The occasional car even trundled down the street. The temp, we remembered, had grabbed the other corner of the desk. They'd pushed it, the two of them, gotten some serious velocity. The desk banged hollowly against the glass, recoiled back against their thighs. His lips pulled back in a snarl, Chris Mok had brought a smart gray oxford up against the window like some blood-maddened showgirl. The glass warbled. Chris and the temp spent a number of minutes trying to break through—at one point, a car even pulled into the parking lot and a man went into Pho G'Dup, the pho place next door. He didn't even look at us as we pressed ourselves against the glass and screamed.

Our cell phones had chirped brainlessly when we dialed 911. We got busy signals when we called our loved ones. Eventually our phones died because no one had a charger.

We tried ordering a pizza online; we begged for help in the comments section. The order seemed to go through—Stanley's Visa was charged—but no pizza came.

VINU RISES

Thirty-three days now. We watch the world brighten and then sieve itself of light. Cars come, cars go. Some of us imagine we can hear the highway. We settle into a loveless rhythm. Odors encroach. The magic of the place happens daily and we become dulled by it. Jim Bledsoe sleeps on the couch in his office. The rest of us sleep on the floor. Jim has an REI sleeping bag in there and one day while he's in the women's restroom (i.e., non-corpse bathroom), he comes back to his office to find his sleeping bag shredded into violent blue tatters.

The magic: A variety of Stankley's cheeses appear in the refrigerator each morning, sometime between 7 and 8 a.m. Same with the cupboards—our bear claws and instant coffee reappear, but only when the cupboards are closed. Stankley eats his cheese listlessly at his own table in the break room, his face snarled with crystalline resentment.

We find solace where we can get it. We try having movie nights in the conference room. Tricia and Van begin a hushed affair, one ostensibly private, but the notion of privacy in the office is a joke. We hear their hushed trysts in the non-corpse bathroom, or the storage closet. Afterward, one or both of them usually cries. (We all do a lot of crying, it's true.) We live on tap water and our magical supply of Campbell's soup, instant coffee, microwave popcorn, bear claws.

One night we wake from our spots on the floor and find Stankley on his knees, screaming into the toilet of the good bathroom, screaming "Help" into the bowl until cords stand rigid on his neck. Over and over again. We watch as he shoves clots of cheese into the toilet. The smell of the temp's remains—the bad bathroom is not far from where we are, nothing is really far—is nearly overwhelming.

"You trying to contact a water sprite, Stanley?" asks Chris, thumbing sleep from his eyes.

"He's channeling the ghost of turds past," says Donna with a strange and unlikely viciousness. We watch as Chris looks at her as if he's misjudged her.

"If you're trying to get help, wouldn't it be more conducive to yell into, say, the air vents, Stankley? Maybe during business hours? How is this going to help us, dear heart?" Van, his arms folded, leans in the doorway. His condescension is as moist and sharp as a block of Blue Stilton.

"Don't call me Stankley, *Van,*" rasps Stanley. Toilet water darkens his shirt up to the shoulder.

"Stankley."

"Don't."

"Stankley, Stankley, Stankley." Van singsongs; fifty years fall off him. A gleeful meanness hangs from him like an extra shirt, makes him young again. Suddenly he is a little, terrible shithead.

And who first takes up the chant with Van? Maybe Tricia, out of loyalty? The Moks? Human Resources Randy? Even Jim Bledsoe, wanting someone else to be on the receiving end of the group's contempt?

Soon we were all yelling it, leering at him, pressing in on him. And oh, it feels good. For just that moment, it does.

Stanley pushes himself up and flings himself at Van. The two of them fly out the doorway and into the hall. They bounce off a partition and topple to the floor in a miasma of dank cheese and the chemical-rich popcorny body odor that has become part of us all. A fake plant topples over, dirt in a dry brown spray on the carpet. Some of us watch the fight while others wonder, still half-asleep, why there is real dirt in a fake potted plant.

Van's hands are hooked around Stanley's throat; Stanley's face is red, his cheeks filigreed with plum-colored veins. Van makes clicking noises in his own throat, growling with effort. One of them farts explosively. One of us brays strained laughter in response.

For the second time, we stand witness. This time, someone tries, if half-heartedly, to intercede. Abby leans forward and puts her hands on Van's shoulders, tries to pull him off. It's a pointless attempt; he outweighs her by eighty pounds, he's furious. With one hand still on Stanley's throat, he flings his other arm and Abby lets go, flinches back into herself.

And then Vinu comes storming out of his office.

He's wheezing, hyperventilating. He's machinegunning words to himself. He wears a pair of stained Jockey shorts and one of our airbrushed *Real Big Backside* T-shirts, huge on his tiny frame, that shows a dinner plate-sized human anus on both the front and back in glistening, minute detail. One of our novelty penis nose-masks, elongated and obscene, hangs off his face like an elephant's trunk. He coughs *"Enough!"* and grabs Van by the hair and buries a pair of industrial scissors halfway into the man's head.

WHAT DO WE LOOK LIKE FROM THE OUTSIDE?

"I just want to know," Donna had said during that first staff meeting of ours, staring at the screen of her laptop, "why no one comes looking for us. Our families. The police. Haven't they reported us missing?"

"And the vendors, bro," said Chris Mok. "That dude Gabe? From Titty Twisters over in Beaverton? Dude comes by *every week* to pick up those joke condoms for his bathroom vending machine. Where's that guy? Where's Titty Twister Gabe?"

"It makes me wonder what we look like from the outside," said Human Resources Randy. "How we seem from the other side of the glass, you know?"

Abby had pressed her cross against her breastbone and muttered something so quiet we couldn't hear it.

"What's that, Abbster?" said Jim Bledsoe.

"I just hope," said Abby, her eyes darting among us and then back to the table, "that this won't make us terrible people. What's happening to us. That we're good to each other."

We had grown tired of Abby mousiness. Her piousness. We had felt, at the time, that her rectitude was cloying. Most of us had rolled our eyes when she'd said that. Some of us had groaned outright. Chad Mok had made a farting noise with his mouth, and his brother cupped his hands around his mouth and said, "Hey, Jesus called, and he wanted me to tell you that you suuuuuck."

"Alright," said Jim, suddenly looking lost and old as his gaze traveled helplessly among the people he was supposed to shepherd. "Alright, now."

SO BEGINS THE PENETRATOR'S REIGN

After he kills Van, things definitely take a turn. Vinu begins referring to himself exclusively in the third person. He calls himself the Penetrator.

"He's gone crazy as heck," whispers Abby. We are huddled over our daily bags of microwave popcorn, Campbell's Vegetable Beef, and Folgers in the break room. We are sick of bear claws.

"Oh, the motherfucker's bananas," agrees Donna, who seems to be embracing a new persona as well. Human Resources Randy eats his popcorn from a paper towel on the floor in the corner. The beard around his mouth has turned butter-yellow from his popcorn intake. The man's eyes now look like something made with a hole-punch and black paper. There are murmurs of concern regarding scurvy. Jim Bledsoe has clearly been usurped and now takes Stanley's old spot at the faraway table.

There are two dead people now, one of them significantly aged, in the bathroom. Sometimes we feel like we're used to it, the sugary shit-stench of decomposition, and then some minute air current assails us and it's all newly terrible. It's not uncommon to hear gags ricochet around the office like a game of Marco Polo.

"Everything's come undone," says Human Resources Randy from the floor.

"This is some odd pocket we're in. Some broken window where the light got out. We've been forgotten."

"Eat your fucking food," says Jim Bledsoe.

"Oh, fuck you, Jim," says Human Resources Randy.

"Silence," says Vinu, striding into the room. He has fashioned a holster out of twine, duct tape, and an old package for Bic pens, and now walks around in the butthole shirt, wearing the scissors on his hip like a gun. We are consistently unnerved. It's not only that we are afraid of him (which we are, very much), but it has occurred to us that if Van can die, if the temp can die, and if Vinu can make the transformation into the Penetrator, a scissor-wielding maniac with a penis for a nose, then anything at all, really, can happen to any of us.

"The Penetrator calls a meeting," says Vinu with his hands on his hips. We all shuffle into the conference room. Stanley has become Vinu's de facto bodyguard, and he pats people down at the doorway for weapons before we're allowed to sit down. We seethe against him: the man's smugness is greatly augmented by the fact that Brie is practically bubbling from his pores.

Nobody wants to sit by Vinu or Stanley and now there's enough room at the conference table where we don't have to. They are flanked by empty seats at each side.

"It'll be a lengthy process," says Vinu, his hands spread out on the tabletop. "To work hard." He speaks in this new, short-circuited way. His eyes are dark and depthless above his penis mask, which bobs when he speaks. The danger in the room is undeniable, a fog that reaches every corner. "But who knows how long we're here for. It's a significant health risk. You'll all take turns. Unpleasant work. Necessary work. For the good of the group. Long-term goal." He grins.

Chris Mok says, "The fuck are you—" and then the look that both Vinu and Stanley give him makes Chris raise his hand, as we've been instructed to do. He quietly says, with a strained smile, "The heck are you talking about, uh, Penetrator?"

"We will remove the bodies," Vinu says.

"Remove the bodies how?"

"We'll cut them up," says Stanley, who stares at Chris until Chris looks away. "Cut them up and flush them."

Abby touches her crucifix. "Oh, God."

"Cut them up with what?" says Chad.

"These will be checked out on a need-to-use basis," says Vinu, and from a plastic Safeway bag, Stanley takes out a pair of items from the kitchen and lays them on the table.

Chad scratches an eyebrow. "You can't be serious, dude."

Vinu smiles beneath his penis. The look of unbridled, boyish joy on his face . . . it's hands down the most terrifying thing most of us have ever seen.

"Does the Penetrator," he says, "look like a man who is not serious?"

He nods, and Stanley puts the bread knife and staple remover back in the bag.

PHONE CALLS

"Are you duly concerned with calamitous events?" the little boy/not-little boy asks.

"Are you duly concerned with calamitous events?
Are you duly concerned with calamitous events?"

And then, speeding up, rhythmic, an incantation:

"Are you duly concerned with mundane events?
Are you duly present for everyday events?
Are you prepared for any eventuality?
Are you moored to the skin of the world?
Are you kind?
Are you good?
Are you the sword or the hand wielding the sword?
Have you accounted for all the wasted hours?
Do you understand the velocity of chance?
Do you believe in the relentlessness of time?
Are you duly concerned with calamitous events?
Are you duly concerned with calamitous events?
Are you duly concerned with calamitous events?
Are you duly concerned with calamitous—"

We hang up and moments later the phone rings again.

THAT ONE BROKEN MOMENT STRETCHED OUT FOREVER

That first night after the end of the world, we'd all sat around the front door and looked at the parking lot. The phones worked but we'd begun to realize they worked in a way that mocked us. Jim Bledsoe's master key still did nothing. The windows buckled but did not give. We sat there in front of the door as if we'd be willing to wait there forever.

Chad Mok's forearms rested on his knees. Outside the glass were fields of darkness, and scatterings of jeweled light. The world was out there, the whole big world.

Chad had said, in a gentle voice, in a voice we would never hear him use again, "It's just a fucking door." He licked his lips. "You don't kick puppies, you don't rob banks, you don't get with a chick and say you're going to use a condo and then not use a condo. You don't do those things. You go around thinking you're a good enough guy. You do that and you just want the world to work the way it's supposed to. That's the trade."

He looked at us, this guy with this searching, naked face, and one by one we had all looked away.

He said, "That's the trade, right? That's how it works."

WINTER, SPRING, WHATEVER HAPPENS AFTER THAT

And there's Brian wearing his Frankenstein mask, standing next to Mrs. Banyard on the sagging steps of her porch. Faith can tell by the way the old woman's hand lies half-curled around the collar of his coat—as if he might run—that he's been fighting again. Faith cinches her scarf around her neck; the air is brittle and sleet falls gritty against her jacket, her footsteps squeaking in the snow.

"Roughhousing again," Mrs. Baynard calls out as soon as Faith sets foot in the yard. "Starting trouble. I won't stand for it, dear." The flesh around her neck quails and shakes as she talks. "I can't." She is wearing her dead husband's hunting cap, a plaid thing with the flaps pulled down around her ears. Brian stands there silently, his hands hanging at his sides, the mask a vivid green in the growing darkness.

"He had to be *separated*," Mrs. Banyard says. "And the language?" She shrugs. "Well. I don't even know what to say."

"I'm really sorry, Mrs. Banyard," she says, and to Brian, "Take it off."

He stands there at the top of the steps, Frankenstein's half-drunk, half-mournful face staring down at her.

"Take it *off*," she says, and finally he does, his hair glued to his forehead in sweaty whorls. Everyone's breath is torn apart by the wind that curls around the side of the house.

They stand there, the three of them, in the deepening gloom of Mrs. Banyard's sleet-swathed lawn. "Did you apologize?" Faith asks, looking up at him from the foot of the steps. Brian nods, looking away. A puffy red scratch runs from his cheek and down into the collar of his coat. He cradles the mask to his chest like a baby.

"Say it again," she says. "Say it so I can hear it, please."

"Sorry," he says, and runs his hand across his nose. He looks up at the old woman and does something with his mouth that is halfway between a wince and a smile. "Really sorry, Mrs. B." His voice trembles.

Mrs. Banyard, a missile silo of a woman, so stoic and resolute, softens. "Oh, hon," she says. Brian has always been capable of this where Faith has not: adults and children alike have always come to his aid, always pardoned him his actions whether he was the instigator or not. "The next time I'll need to talk to your mother, though," Mrs. Banyard finally says, and Faith's breath catches. When her mother is brought up now it's like Faith's heart is this clumsy, questionable thing, like a drunk tumbling down a flight of stairs. She and Brian share a look, there and gone. I shouldn't even be the one doing this, Faith thinks.

Mrs. Banyard says, "But there won't be a next time, will there, dear?" She is smiling now, and pats Brian on the shoulder. She turns to her front door then, wordlessly, to the sound of the television and the outraged cry of another child inside, some other charge Mrs. Banyard and her sister have been appointed to take care of. They have done this for decades, the two sisters, taken care of the neighborhood children; Faith takes some measure of comfort in that—Brian is a handful, but surely nowhere near the worst they've dealt with over the years.

The two of them walk home as night falls and the sleet turns to snow, falling heavy and slow now, flakes whirling in the headlights of passing cars. Faith's wearing a pair of her mother's thin cotton gloves, faux-leather peeling from the palms, and her hands are freezing. Brian has put his mask back on and seems impervious to the cold; he scrapes and kicks his way along the sidewalk, leaving streaks of pale gray pavement in his wake. They pass the Lutheran church, a hulking shape in the dark, and the auto body shop, its edges softened and rimed in snow. Wind rattles the chain-link fence beside them.

"What is your deal, Brian? Seriously."

"She's a fag hag," Brian says bitterly, suddenly furious again, kicking at a mound of snow like a green-faced chorus girl. "And so is Jeff. He started it. They're both fag hag supremes."

Faith covers her mouth and turns, covering her laughter with a cough. This is clearly a term he's learned from Becky. Faith forgets: just because he's quiet doesn't mean he's not listening. "Don't say that," she says. "Don't even get in the habit of saying that."

"Why not?"

Their mother has been gone for eighteen days now, just up and gone, and not only does Faith keep expecting her to return at any second—to find her drinking coffee at the kitchen table, or slowing down beside them in the car, the *thunk* of the passenger door unlocking as she leans over to open it—but Faith has begun to look for signs, in herself and Brian and her father, as to why she left in the first place. And here's Brian with his fag hag comment, and she thinks, *Would I leave? If I were her and I had to deal with that, would I leave? What was it that drove her over the edge?* Faith knows it wasn't a single moment but a collection of them, some internal trigger that went off and her mother said *I've had it.* A word from science class comes to her: catalyst. What final grievance was her mother's catalyst? It's like a tic, she can't let it go.

Faith says, "Because it doesn't make any sense, that's why. And it's mean. I thought you liked Mrs. Banyard."

They keep walking. Faith flexes her hands inside of her coat pockets to try to warm them.

Finally, trailing behind her, Brian calls out, "I do like her. I was just mad."

• • •

They pass the Dousman's house next door to their own and Faith instinctively looks up toward Alex's window on the second floor, but it's dark. It is a massive house that casts their own home in shadow during summer evenings; Alex Dousman's father owns a cleaning company that handles half of the commercial accounts in town. Faith's father has worked for him for years—both of them dour, red-faced men prone to stony silences—and she and Alex share a handful of classes. He's cute enough, and not a douchebag (she's seen him pass up numerous opportunities to be cruel, which seems to her a clearly measurable currency in people her age, boys and girls alike) but Faith worries the quiet heartache she feels toward him is mostly due to his proximity, his closeness.

Becky is sitting in a plastic lawn chair on their darkened front porch. When Faith and Brian walk up, the motion sensor comes on with a click and bathes them all in cold light. Becky's wearing a knit cap but leaves her jacket unbuttoned, a tank top underneath. She's wearing black lipstick, a skirt and black tights with a pattern on them that is couched somewhere between geometric shapes and elven runes. Her legs shine like alabaster underneath. Brian groans when he sees her.

She grins. "Nice to see you too, assmunch."

"Dude, it's *snowing* out," Faith says, motioning at her outfit.

Becky rolls her eyes. "*Dude,* no shit."

"Well, just so you know, you look like a hooker," Faith says, and Becky laughs, clearly pleased.

Becky Tomlinson is exactly twelve pounds heavier than Faith but beyond that is everything that Faith is not. Becky's eyes are ringed in mascara and she wears low-cut shirts that reveal the pale expanse of her cleavage, unabashedly and regardless of the season. She has already had sex, with a lazy-eyed 10th grader named Duane Cosma, who afterward gave her a stick-and-poke trampstamp of a pentagram and unceremoniously dumped her a week later. She and Faith are united—silently—by their weight and the fact that they are, with a few rare and oscillating exceptions of the social strata, each other's only friend. (Faith only knows about the weight issue because she stayed over at Becky's house one night last summer and had seen her quickly get on and off the Tomlinson's bathroom scale—so quickly that it seemed as if the surface of the scale was hot. They were changing into their swimsuits and Faith saw Becky cast a furtive, searching glance at her, wanting to know if she'd seen. It was a look that belied everything else about her and Faith of course pretended not to notice. The next morning, with a feeling that made her feel terrible and savagely happy at the same time, Faith weighed herself. It's like the pettiest gift ever, the twelve pounds, but one she cannot help but pull out and examine sometimes, even if it makes her feel like shit.) It seems like it is the one thing that they've never talked about explicitly. How they're bonded by their low social caste? Totally. How the majority of kids in their school are utter shitheads? Definitely. But their weight is a silent tether. Still, where Faith is quiet, Becky is ferocious—she's been suspended twice for fighting; one of those times was when she punched Lila Tibbetts in the mouth and mashed her braces against her lips. Becky is on her last strike at Piedmont High School, bad news for a freshman. One more "disciplinary event" and she'll probably get expelled from school.

Snow continues to fall and Becky lights a Parliament, crossing her legs. Brian, right on cue, says, "It's bad to smoke, dummy."

Becky blows smoke and looks at him, standing there in his green, stitch-riddled mask. "Thank you, Brian. I'll take that into consideration. Meanwhile, the Wolfman called, and wanted me to tell you that you suck."

Faith unlocks the front door and Brian runs inside. She looks out at the street. A car glides past, silent and ghostly in the snow. "If my dad sees you smoking out here, he'll freak out."

"He's not going to be home for a long time, right? He's unplugging toilets at the Y. Your dad's janitoring it up."

It's true, too, that Becky can be cruel. There's an artfulness to it, an offhandedness that Faith marvels at, even when it cuts.

She looks in the living room window. She can see, down the darkened hall, Brian's bedroom door limned in light. Back to making his monster models, or reading old comic books. He's like some weird throwback to the 1950s, her brother. He is probably the only third grader on earth who claims to admire Boris Karloff.

Becky says, "Did you hear anything from her?"

Faith shakes her head. "No."

(The note her mother left eighteen days ago had been left on the kitchen counter. Next to the coffeepot. Faith had found it. She thought it was a grocery list at first. *I love you all,* it read in her mother's looping cursive, *but I just can't breathe here. I need time. I'll be back soon. I'm so sorry.* Not even her name afterwards. Not even an initial.)

Becky shakes her head. "What a bitch. Who *does* that?"

Faith sighs and squints out at the night. The porch light clicks off and shrouds them in darkness. "Give me a drag of that," she says, and Becky holds out the cigarette.

• • •

Later that evening, after Becky has gone home and her father has come home and started drinking, Faith finds him weeping in front of Brian's bedroom door, wearing only his underwear. He has spent most of the evening on the couch, his coveralls hanging around his waist like a desiccated skin, his T-shirt yellowed at the pits, metronomically hoisting beers and flipping through sitcoms. And now this: a lumbering, loose-limbed man leaning drunk against the doorframe of his son's bedroom. His back is furred, his underwear sagging. He looks like a lunatic's idea of a baby. This used to be her mother's job, calming him, talking him down. It is sometime past midnight and her father wobbles unbalanced in the hallway and Faith feels a familiar flare of anger burst inside her.

"Dad?" she says quietly. "What are you doing?"

Without turning, he says, "I just want to tell him I love him." All the words tumble together, blurred. His hair stands out in jagged tufts. He smells like alcohol and the acrid tang of bleach.

Faith says, "He's sleeping, Dad. You'll scare him."

Her father turns and looks at her. This one red and baleful eye, the purple socket ringed with fatigue and drunkenness. It's a look moored somewhere between contempt and a wretched pity. "Look at you," he sneers. "Jesus, Faith. You're fucking *huge.*" His eyes droop and he braces himself up with a hand against the wall. And then, mawkishly, "You've got to take better care of yourself."

Faith laughs, a quiet little gasp of punched-in hurt, and says, "He's sleeping, Dad. Let him sleep."

His head wobbles on his neck as he tries to focus on her. "Okay," he finally says, nodding. He rasps a hand down the stubble on his cheek. "Okay." He lumbers off to his room, shutting the door with exaggerated care behind him, and Faith wonders if Brian woke up, what he heard.

• • •

Her father had called the police, in spite of the note. "It could have been written under duress," he said to the police officer, who looked, with the crisp creases in his shirtsleeves and the red geography of shaving bumps on his throat, like he'd graduated high school a few hours before.

"It could have," the police officer said, examining both sides of the note as if he expected magic ink to appear. "Okay."

The three of them stood in the kitchen. Brian, oblivious, was in his room reenacting Frankenstein's reanimation; the occasional shriek or maniacal "It's alive!" wafted down the hall.

The officer handed the note back. "Sir, honestly, I'm really sorry. And we'll definitely keep an eye out—"

"What does that mean?"

"—but it doesn't look like there's been any crime committed here."

"She could have been coerced, is what I'm saying."

"People don't just *leave,*" Faith said plaintively. "She can't just *leave,* right?" Her father had looked embarrassed.

The cop asked if Faith's mom had other family. "A lot of times, they can help with an estrangement."

Faith's father had stared at him. "An estrangement? What? I'm talking what if she was kidnapped."

The officer looked at Faith and then at her father. He said quietly, "Honestly, sir. Do you really think that's what happened?"

• • •

This is the part that drives Faith crazy: how their mother's absence seems to have become her greatest trait, the most memorable thing about her. It's fucked up, is what it is. There are the usual timid ghosts batting around the attic of Faith's memory: the marbled quality of her mother's legs when she wore shorts. Her propensity to weep at (in Faith's opinion) nothing, or at least very little—and then to spend twice as long apologizing for it. The pink bathrobe she wore that had grown by the time of her leaving thin and pilled in the arms. Stretches at dinner where Faith and Brian were left to navigate the table's expansive silence by themselves; their father plowing through the meal and their mother staring at the flat wall of night outside the windows, smiling wanly at nothing. Faith's contempt at the wattle of skin around her mother's neck, the shelves of flesh on her upper arms, coupled with her seething awareness that she had her mother beat in the weight department by a mile. The soft-eyed, quivering look that she sometimes got when Faith was mean to her, like the tears would start tumbling at any moment.

But these are just a collection moments, snapshots and instances. It's as if she had been gone, or vanishing, or disappearing in opacity and presence long before she actually did.

Which is terrible, awful, and doesn't do much to alleviate the idea that the three of them have somehow driven her to it, have driven her finally and irrevocably away. That there was no real catalyst at all, not really.

• • •

The day after the incident in the doorway they come home to find their father drinking coffee at the kitchen table, his hair slicked back. It's his day off and he is hungover and still unshaven and they know enough to give him a wide berth. Brian, instead of throwing his backpack on the living room floor and running to the refrigerator, walks stealthily to his room. The house with their father in it has become a series of rooms rife with landmines.

He says Faith's name and looks down at his coffee cup. He runs his knuckles along his chin; she can hear the rasp across the room. It's one of his habits.

"So we're running tight on money," he says. He fixes her with a half-smile. Shrugs.

Faith waits and finally says, "I don't have any cash, Dad. I'm broke."

He shakes his head and looks out the window, the wash of weak light out there hardly seeming to enter the room. Everything—the curling linoleum, the tablecloth, her father's T-shirt—seems bled of its color, washed out.

"I'm not asking you for money, Faith. We've got a long, shitty road ahead of us before that ever happens. I'm just saying things are tight right now, with your mother hauling ass around who knows where. We're going to have to get a little creative. As far as meals go. Pace the bills out. Button down. That's all I'm saying."

She wants to say something—maybe about the cases of beer that sit stacked thigh-high in the garage—but she doesn't. Instead she says, "Okay."

"I'll see if I can pick up extra shifts this week. A few guys are out sick. It's possible."

He looks at her and smiles. It's a sad smile but a kind one, and seeing it she's sure he has no memory of what he said to her the night before.

He says, "It's up to us. We're going to have to save each other here, okay?" And just like that, she feels this warm rush of love toward him, and is angry at herself for it. Is this all it takes? A smile from him? She feels unbalanced, unmoored.

"We have to pay Mrs. Banyard, too."

His father winces and takes a sip of coffee. "That's done for now. Not enough money for it."

"What are we supposed to do? I can't take him to work with me. Royce'll shit a brick."

"He's just going to have to come home after school. I'll get him a key. And enough with the language."

"He's *eight,* Dad. He'll burn the house down."

Her father looks outside again and sighs. He stands up with his coffee cup. "She'll be back. She's done it before."

It's true, and she'd taken Brian, just a baby then, with her. Faith had been around Brian's age when it happened, and she remembers it as a time punctuated, like now, with an eerie silence. Gone was the squalling infant—the impetus, it had seemed to her then, for her parents to fight. She remembers that silence and the harried, strange dinners her father made for the two of them: canned chili, a bright orange square of cheese laid over its surface, thin slivers of watermelon next to it. Pale, tasteless Kool-Aid, bologna sandwiches, a pair of saltines still enshrouded in their plastic. It's hard to remember specific instances, but that's what times does, it blurs everything. They fought and fought and then she was gone with Brian and by Christmas they were back and things seemed better for a time.

"It's not you," he says, his back to her as he rinses his cup at the sink.

"What isn't?" she says.

"You and Brian. She didn't leave because of you."

"I know that," Faith says, bitterly. "It's her *asthma.* The poor lady just can't *breathe* around all of us."

Her father barks surprised laughter, and Faith finds herself laughing too, and the noise is such that Brian comes out of his room. He peers into the kitchen wearing his werewolf mask, his blue eyes blinking inside its hollows, his fingers hooked around the doorframe. Staring at the two of them like some beast, silently testing the air for danger.

• • •

Winter gives way grudgingly to spring. There's an ache involved in it this time, the changes incremental and buried, like the growing of bones. Just slow enough as to be unnameable. Their nights deepen into a fuller silence; their mother does not return and they begin to grow accustomed to it. The deadened purl of snowfall begins to give way to the occasional sizzle of rain on the roof. Her father begins drinking in his room, the door opened a few inches, enough for Faith to see the unmade bed, mounds of work coveralls laying on the dirty carpet as she passes down the hall to the bathroom. He works swing shift and so is asleep, his snores wet and terrible, while Faith and Brian get ready for school. Faith brings Mrs. Baynard her last check; the old woman bids the children farewell with a look on her face that says she knows no good will come of it. Brian is ecstatic. He receives his house key and instructions from their father with an attempt at solemnity that makes the man crack a rare smile. For two weeks, Becky goes out with a nineteen-year-old who works at the video game outlet in the mall. "He's got a dick like a corkscrew," she tells Faith with a mock shiver, and is heartbroken when he breaks up with her two weeks later after finding out how old she really is. The two girls steal a twelve-pack from the stack in Faith's garage and sneak out, drinking in the tiny cemetery behind the church, freezing their asses off. Becky throws up.

Faith gives Brian a mummy mask for his birthday—an expensive one, where beneath the bandages the exposed swaths of green skin are laden with gel-filled pustules—and he refuses to take it off at school until her father is called away from work to speak to the principal. At home, all of his masks are taken away and Brian screams and screams and is spanked. Some paternal guilt then incites their father to have Brian come outside and play catch. Brian begins hurling the baseball at his father until the window to the laundry room is broken, and Brian is slapped across the face and all of his toys are taken away. That night Faith hears both of them weeping in their rooms and wants to scream with frustration.

One night their father goes to a bar and comes home and collapses part of their fence when he clips it with the bumper of his truck. He begins missing some days, calling in sick in the early afternoon, finding someone to cover for him, walking the house in a morose silence, or leaving them alone for longer and longer stretches.

And always, no matter the day and as long as he is home, his first beer is uncapped a) promptly at dusk or b) as soon as his shift is over, whichever comes first. This is their metronome, the clock by which their family's blood runs.

No word arrives from their mother, and still Faith vacillates between *Would I do the same?* and *What did we do?*

• • •

She comes home one evening after her shift to find their father not there, something that has been happening with more and more frequency. A burr of dread snags her this time when she opens the front door and sees, through the living room, Brian's darkened doorway. She wonders for a moment if he's fallen asleep this early and feels something like panic, alongside a sharp heart's-tug of sadness that he should be subjected to this, all these hours by himself.

She sees then the sliver of light in their father's room—it's become his room by now, his alone—and finds Brian sitting on the bed, his hands clasped primly in front of him. He's left the overhead light off and instead turned on their father's reading lamp; it casts an interrogative air around the room, bathing the side of his face in harsh light. The room smells closed in. Stale socks and disinfectant and the contents of half-full beer bottles long turned sour.

"Hi," Brian says, his lips already trembling, sensing his demise.

"What are you doing in here?"

"Nothing," he says.

"Seriously."

His chin notches into his breastbone and he says through pursed lips, "Looking for my masks."

Faith feels another tug. She can see the blue archeology of veins in the skin of his arms. It's fucking heartless, is what it is, that he comes home to an empty house when she's not here. This quiet, withdrawn, undeniably weird kid who quotes from Lon Chaney films. This lonely boy, her brother, a kid who, those rare times when Faith offers to play with him, immediately perks up and says, "Okay. I'll be Nosferatu."

"Get up," she says. "We'll make some dinner."

He looks up at her with his head still tucked down. "You first," he says, almost a whisper.

"What? Get up, Brian."

His lips quivers. He shakes his head, a tear already tumbling from one blue eye.

She grabs him by the shoulder and pulls him up and there sits their father's pistol, a squat black revolver like something out of an old detective show.

"Oh my God," Faith says, drawing it out long and slow, and that's when the dam breaks and Brian begins blubbering. Half-formed words and his hands shoved into his armpits as he slumps against the wall, the scene made all the more garish by the adjustable lamp centered on them, like some interrogation.

"I just was looking for my mummy mask," he says, stressing each word between sobs, and Faith doesn't know if it's the fact that he then drops to the carpet, slapping his palms against the floor in a motion both submissive and woefully theatrical, or the fact that *mummy* sounds like *mommy* and she realizes that both have in essence been taken away from him, but she says quietly, "Get up. Go get the mac and cheese out. And the milk."

Brian peers up at her like one who has been led to the gallows only to find that no one has brought a rope. "Are you going to tell?" he asks, his voice still hitching like a motor trying to start.

She points at the pistol. "Are you *ever* going to touch this again? *Ever?*"

"No," Brian says fiercely. He sits up on his knees. *"Never. I swear."*

"Dad would ground you for*ever* if he knew. He would seriously flip the fuck out, dude."

He nods reverently, gratitude washing over his face.

Hours later they are both in their rooms when their father comes home. She has become accustomed to measuring the length of time it takes him to go through his rounds—jacket on chair, keys on coffee table, refrigerator for beer—in relation to his drunkenness. Tonight is one of those rare nights where he is so drunk, or defeated, that he simply goes to bed, his feet dull and thunderous in the hallway.

• • •

She works three afternoons a week at the Burger Palace—even the name stirs in her a kind of eye-rolling contempt that would sometimes make her mother laugh. The manager, Royce, drives them all insane with a staunch commitment to Burger Palace's credo of service, a commitment that suggests previous employment in some elite faction of the military. Royce is twenty-one, maybe twenty-two, and wears a ponytail and pencil-thin mustache. He is infamous for being cloyingly nice to the pretty girls on staff and a tyrannical shit to the rest of them. He will, everyone is convinced, die a manager of the Burger Palace, lowered into his grave with a spatula in hand.

On the first day of nice spring weather, with wide blue skies and clouds scattered like something flung from a painter's brush, the whole town seems to bare its pale arms and legs and step outside. The place has been slammed all afternoon and is finally slowing down when Alex Dousman steps up to the counter as Faith is working the register. She closes her eyes for just a moment and he is unfortunately still there when she opens them. She is wearing a hat that is the top half of a hamburger bun and she can feel the grease and general effluvia of the franchise settled on her like a second skin.

"Hey," she says, as casually as she can manage, and then, sure that Royce is right behind her, "Welcome to Burger Palace. What can I get for you today?"

He smiles at her, lightning-quick, a look so dense with an unspoken empathy that it immediately validates every shitty hour she has spent there. That's Alex, right there: a glance from him, that one crooked tooth stepped over the other, and all seems well. It almost pisses her off. He orders and she takes special care not to touch his hand when she gives him his change.

"Thanks," he says, pushing his hair out of his eyes.

"No problem," Faith says.

Alex walks outside with his bag and sits down at a table with some other boys. Marissa, a ghostly-pale junior with a cluster of angry-looking pimples on each cheek, looks out the window and nods her approval. "He's hot," she says.

Faith sprays sanitizer on the plastic surface of the register and wipes it down with a towel. She can feel coins of heat burning on her cheeks. "He's not that hot," she says.

"I don't know," Marissa says sagely. "I'd do him." She touches a pimple on her chin while she looks out the window. She sounds wizened, like a woman thirty years her senior. "I'd give him a ride."

"My dear ladies," Royce calls out, shaking the fry basket so ferociously it's as if he were flipping omelets, "back to freaking work, please."

● ● ●

It is the first day of June when Mrs. Banyard's sister dies. News travels fast, and it turns out the majority of the staff at Burger Palace—Royce included—have been privy as children to the Banyard sisters' strict regimen of PBS-only television and grain-encrusted peanut butter and preserve sandwiches. It is soon rumored that Mr. Banyard, thirty years in the grave now, was the spearhead of an illicit love triangle. "He was banging them *both*," Marissa says. "In the same *house*."

"Where do you people get this shit?" Royce scoffs, shuddering. "You remember what the Banyard sisters looked like, right? I've met shapelier truckers at rest stops."

"I bet you have," Marissa mutters.

The funeral is held two days later. Her father wakes up early and Faith and Brian are allowed to take the day off school. Faith wears a dark skirt and a black sweater, her hair pinned back. Brian in his little black suit looks as if he spent the previous night sleeping fitfully in a drawer somewhere. His eyes keep drooping, his chin tilting toward the tie that Faith can't figure out. "You have to keep your head up," she says. Finally, her father, his hair combed, clean-shaven and almost handsome in his own dark suit, comes in and ties it for him. "You look nice," he says to Faith, and she looks at the floor.

The day is overcast and muggy. Mrs. Banyard stands at the front of the concession. She looks tiny, shrunken, but she's flanked by a line of other old women who press silk handkerchiefs to their veiled faces and reach over at various moments to pat her on the back or rub her arm. Faith has never before thought of her having friends. Brian spends the funeral with his face pressed against Faith's side. When the coffin is slowly winched into the ground, he starts weeping, these quiet, barking little sobs. People turn and give rueful, sad little smiles. Their father leans down and puts his hand on Brian's shoulder. "Stop," he whispers. Brian cries louder.

"Hey," her father says, and Faith can see his hand tighten on Brian's shoulder, the knuckles tightening against the skin. He shakes him, Brian's jaw clicking audibly.

"Dad," she says loudly, and she can see people really turn to examine them then, this family. Everyone by now knows about their mother being gone—it's been months now, after all. Her father softens, chastised, and Brian eventually slows to the occasional hiccup, his face still pressed against her.

And like some augury, then: when they return home, there's a postcard. Her father stands in front of the mailbox, squinting, his jaw opening and closing as if he's trying to pop his ears. When he looks up, he seems punch-drunk, dazed.

Faith takes the postcard from him. It's a black and white picture of a field of wheat, a dilapidated barn in the foreground, crisp with ruination, paint peeling from its sides in jagged swaths. The postmark says it was mailed from Montpelier, Vermont four days before. Brian, knowing little but at the mercy of everything, sees the look on their faces and picks up a handful of gravel and flings it against the truck.

On the back of the postcard it says, *I'm so sorry.*

• • •

It is the last day of school and she and Becky walk on the sun-dappled sidewalk, Brian kicking a pinecone behind them, wearing his mummy mask. Faith has survived her freshman year of high school and *feels* like she has—like she has trodden some nearly immeasurable distance and there is some isle there on the horizon, some chance or luck finally made visible. At the very least, summer looms large ahead of her.

"I swear, my drunk to sober ratio is going to climb like a thousand percent," Becky says.

"Totally," Faith says, smiling.

And again, as they turn the corner onto their street, she looks up toward Alex's window and then immediately down, toward the Dousmans' front door, because her father is standing there. It takes a moment for this to register, but it's him. He's wearing his work clothes and Faith can tell by his posture alone that he is drunk. She can see Alex's stricken face over her father's shoulder.

Her father is holding his pistol, pointing it toward the ground.

"Holy fuck," Becky whispers.

"Take Brian home," she says, and calls out to her father. She crosses the street. Her heart thunders in her chest. Fear is an electric, battery taste in her mouth.

She calls out to him again and he turns. His eye is threaded with red veins, a lock of hair tumbling down. "I was just seeing if his dad was home," he slurs.

Alex looks from her back to her father. Alex's little brother, younger even than Brian, tries to look past his elbow and Alex pushes him back.

"Dad," Faith says. She puts her hand on his elbow. "Let's go home."

"We are a having a discussion," he says. "Me and him. Do you know why?"

"No," Faith says.

"His dad here just fired me," her father says, his face etched in drunken indignation. "Just today. Too many write-ups, he says. Late too many times, he says. Sick." He turns to Alex and cries out cheerfully, "You believe that shit?" Alex flinches.

"Dad, let's go."

Her father points a finger at Alex, the pistol dangling from his other hand. "When he gets home," he says with exaggerated slowness, "you tell him I need to talk to him. You understand? We need to have words, me and him."

Alex slowly closes the door.

"Man to man," her father calls out.

• • •

Fifteen minutes later, Faith is not at all surprised to see that it's the same young policeman who steps into their yard and drops to one knee on their walkway, his pistol out and drawn toward her father, who sits sagged over on their concrete steps, his hair hanging in his eyes. The pistol sits on the pavement between his feet and a tendril of spit dangles between his knees as he looses hard, wracking sobs. The policeman's partner, a heavyset woman with a blonde ponytail and a leathery tan, advances toward her father, her own sidearm drawn. She says something into the radio on her shoulder. Her pistol wavers from Faith to her father and back.

"Don't," Faith says. "It's okay." She steps away from him onto the lawn.

"Put your hands up," the man calls out. "Put your hands up and get on the ground. Now."

"Get on your knees," the woman says. "Do it."

Her father gets to his knees and the woman steps behind him and takes his wrists. She lays him on the ground and leans on his neck with one knee as she handcuffs him. Her father groans. Faith can't see his face.

"You're hurting him," Faith says.

And then she turns and sees Brian in the doorway in his mummy mask, with its gel-filled sores and tinted red cups over the eyeholes. Becky stands behind him, the two of them couched in the shadows of the living room, her face so sweetly terrified for him as he steps forward onto the porch. He steps down into the yard, into the sunlight where the policewoman leans on their father's neck, and the other cop pivots, his pistol pivots to take in this new movement, and Brian pulls off his mask. Faith sees his face blanched white save for the red coins of his cheeks and the fervent ice-blue of his eyes, and this is it, she recognizes it, a catalyst, some catalyst, and here is Brian reaching for his father, stepping onto the green grass and reaching for him, this is a moment that's too far along for any them to ever entirely turn back from.

FORGIVE ME THIS

You stop at a gas station that glows in the valley like its own miniature city. A cement box of a store, a half-dozen pumps under light as bright as a morgue table. Constellations of moths beat themselves senseless beneath the standing roof.

You are driving—okay, your cousin Lynn is driving—from Portland to Bismarck. You're on 90, somewhere between Coeur D'Alene and Missoula, and the night yawns ahead with nothing but the promise of more darkness, more fields of meager scattered lights on your peripheries. Salsa music ghosting through rips of static on the radio. Evangelical hollering. The same forty classic rock songs over and over again. You've lost your license to a DUI the year before and Lynn is going to drive you all the way there. You're not close, you and Lynn, except you love her, you have loved her for years. It is some vestige of your childhood, some holdover.

You are going home because your father's house burned down yesterday. He is in a Bismarck hospital and it doesn't look good for him. You cannot afford plane fare. (You also can't afford to pay for gas, but Lynn doesn't know this.) Inside your backpack are shirts and underwear, a coverless copy of *Moby Dick* you stole from the back of a friend's toilet, and a glass jar filled with change, a jar that pulls at the straps of your pack, that weight being about the only comfort you have right now, that and the surety that there is at least a further ways to go before you have to move on to the next thing, the next gathering of new rooms and new decisions.

• • •

Halfway there, says Lynn. We're making good time.

Lynn is five years younger than you. She dances at a club. No, she's a stripper. What's the right term? You want to ask her about it, try to seem knowledgeable, worldly, but you're unsure which term she prefers. It seems important, that distinction. It's quite a scandal in the family, Lynn's job, which you think is funny, given how fractured and fucked up the rest of your family is. She is beautiful and tired and covered in an armada of tattoos, and you have loved her since you were both children. She has always been fearless in ways that you are not. When she smokes and releases her cigarettes through the howling wedge of open window, they bounce in the road behind you and you watch the sparks burst in your mirror. Dig, Lynn's son, sweet and myopic and fragile in his huge eyeglasses, sleeps in the backseat but shifts awake when Lynn pulls into the gas station.

I'll get the snacks, you get the gas, you say, turning your face away and peering at the glowing storefront. That sound okay? You try to keep your voice light. You turn and look at her.

Lynn pauses, blinks at you. Sure.

The nozzle notches into the tank and you see Lynn's torso through the window, see the rips of fog from her mouth as she blows into her hands. You turn and wink at Dig as he stares back at you, his eyes owlish and huge behind his lenses. He is five. He doesn't talk very much. Or maybe he talks all the time. You don't really know. You don't really know much of anything.

You want anything, bud?

A pop?

You get out of the car. Lynn is frowning at the gas readout, notching the total in pennies.

Can he have a pop?

Sure, she says without looking at you.

You take your backpack inside, nod at the red-faced woman at the register. Should I leave this up here, you ask.

It's fine, honey.

You wander the aisles, putting things in your pack. Pointless things. You pour two coffees, grab a Coke, a pair of cheap sunglasses for three dollars. You take out the jar, pour out a swath of change on the counter, pay for the drinks and glasses in quarters. It phases the woman not at all. Your backpack is heavy with *contraband*. (An Evil Dan word if ever there was one.) Stupid things—cupcakes, lip balm, WD40. This feels somehow like you are balancing something out.

Lynn has parked the car and is talking to your aunt on her cell phone. Dig holds his pop in two hands when you lean in and hand it to him. Lynn stands there on a yellow parking block in front of the car, flexing her calves and standing on her toes. A man comes out and watches her as he gets into his truck and you look at him until he looks away. You open a Hostess pie and break it in half, lean in and hand it to Dig, then light a cigarette and lean against the door. You eat and smoke and Lynn shakes her head and says into the phone, We'll make it. We're making good time.

What does your heart do when you hear this?

She says, I know. I will.

She says, Okay, Momma.

She smiles and says, I love you too.

• • •

Well, and you are one of those shitty passengers that falls asleep and doesn't keep the driver company. You don't mean to, but you are tired. After Hillila kicked you out you've been couch-surfing and sleep is sometimes a fitful, fleeting thing. When Lynn's mom called you on your cell phone to tell you your dad had fallen asleep with a cigarette, had burned his house down, you were sitting on Evil Dan's couch (you know a lot of Dans: Dan Smith, Wheelchair Dan, Tattoo Dan, Married Dan, Evil Dan) and in the middle of telling him that Hillila's absence was like someone taking an ice cream scoop to your heart and removing the entire thing in one go. Then your phone had buzzed in your pocket. You'd been staring at Evil Dan's boa constrictor when you answered it. The snake was molting, and it looked fake, how symmetrical and lovely the sloughing skin was. Like bubble wrap! you thought. Your eyes when you answered the phone felt like they were coated in cement dust.

You talked for a minute with your aunt. And he's burned real bad, she said. Real bad. All over.

The snake seemed like it was dead maybe.

Okay, you said.

She said, I'm real sorry, hon. And then she waited for you to say something, but what was there to say? How many times had he fallen asleep like that, cocooned in a fog of spent alcohol, only to have the cherry of his smoke burn his stomach, fall between his legs until he awoke bellowing and slapping at his thighs, his glass tumbling and rolling in circles on the floor? How many times throughout your life?

They're not—her voice caught, the way a shirt could get snagged on fence wire—they're not real sure he'll make it, but you should probably come. You should come.

You didn't want to tell your aunt you couldn't drive anymore.

I'm not sure what your vehicle situation is, she said, as if she could read your mind, but Lynn could drive. It's just that they don't know if he'll make it. They don't know.

Okay.

You never learned the snake's name, but when you hung up it turned its head, tongue tasting the air.

• • •

So you fall asleep like a jerk, and you have a dream. Lynn wakes you up in the middle of it and you come awake knowing that you have cried out, made a noise. The radio is playing a song you remember from high school. *You can't take me, but I'll go with you.* It's a bad song. Lights alongside the highway strobe past you, light up your legs and chest and then vanish behind you.

You were dreaming, Lynn says.

Dig says, You yelled. Real loud.

You sounded happy though, Lynn says, smiling. It was weird.

Sorry, you say. You scrub your face and your hands make a rasping noise along your whiskers. You look at the clock and are grateful at how little time has passed. How much further you have to go. You want to stay in this car forever, with the cousin you are in love with and her sweet son with the strap around his glasses. They love you the way family loves you—without reserve, without grace, like drinking a glass of water. The dream is a fading thing; it's like sneaking your fingers under a piece of old wood and lifting, only you don't want to lift it. It's pointless. Nothing good will come from its examination.

• • •

Hillila was someone you met at church. Evil Dan would take you to a Catholic church up in Laurelhurst sometimes for Mass. You liked it. Another Evil Dan word: he called it *interloping*. He combed his hair and took out his pentagram earrings and you'd go on Saturday nights after a few beers. You liked the solemnity, the sense of ritual. The priest with his singsong lamentations, the drifting tendrils of incense he pushed with the backs of his hands as he walked down the aisle, chanting Latin. The choir sang above you, and the ceiling was high and everything was hushed and glowing, and when you leaned over and asked Evil Dan—who in his pastel shirt and tie really did look like a wholly new person (Systems Analyst Dan, maybe)—what that spot was above you where the choir sang, he told you it was actually called the choir.

Oh, you said.

Or the choir stalls, he added. Like a bathroom stall, you said, still a little drunk, and a lady in front of you turned around, frowning. Evil Dan winked at her and you belched behind your fist but it came out louder than you meant, and you heard someone laugh behind *you* and when you turned and looked, there she was. This blonde girl that would turn out to be Hillila, but you of course wouldn't know that until after Mass when everyone was hanging out outside talking and did it really matter anyway? Was that what you wanted to spend your time thinking about? Here, in this car, when you haven't felt safe or good in forever? When you can't help but picture your father curled in a hospital bed, shrunken with heat, a charred collection of sticks in the shape of a man.

• • •

You arrive at a rest stop as dawn blues the tree line. The lawn beside the cement building is waterlogged and dotted with scraps of trash. Skeletal trees. Mist hugs the ground and dead leaves float in gasoline-blurred puddles. Everybody goes to the bathrooms. Dig takes your hand as you walk toward the men's room and something in you tightens as clearly as if someone was working a ratchet inside your ribs.

Will you stand guard? Dig asks as he goes into a stall.

Sure, you say, and a trucker standing at a urinal smiles against the wall.

A minute later you make your way out of the bathroom and you take *Moby Dick* out of your jacket and put it below the pocked and dented steel mirror. Your face in the mirror is funhouse distorted. You only look for a second.

Outside, the sun is burning through the morning clouds. Every blade of grass seems dotted with jewels.

• • •

I can't believe I'm coming back here, Lynn says.

Me neither, you say.

It isn't about the fists of your youth, the lurching zombie-stomp of the man's footfalls as he tried to keep his balance, the blood that sometimes stippled his undershirts. The glassy way his eyes tried to lock on yours while his skull drifted like seaweed in a current. It was not the offhanded dismissiveness after you left home, the yawning silences. Closer perhaps was the casual cruelty of your phone calls, the way he would answer your talk of doing well in this new town with those little chuckles. Those derisive grunts, that way of decimating the conversation. That way of leveling you with just the hum of your shared history.

Don't bullshit a bullshitter, he'd say. You and me are the same animal.

• • •

You are outside of town, onto Highway 94 now and traffic is good, traffic is really light. You are going fast, with the sun truly burning through scudded clouds and it's when you see the cylinders of the Tesoro Refinery out the window, those silver gleaming monoliths rising brutish from the ground—always the waypoint that home is near—that your heart thunders in your chest like God has reached down and squeezed.

Momma, Dig says, I have to go to the bathroom.

We're almost there, bud, Lynn says. Can you hold it?

Dig thinks for a second and then says, Yes, I can hold it.

Telephone poles blur past you. They look like spears driven into the earth.

Stop, you say.

Lynn looks at you.

Stop, you say again.

The wind rips at the door in your hands when you open it.

• • •

Your dream was this:

You dreamt of the hospital, of thin coffee served in flimsy pale cups. There were chairs with fabric seats and wooden arms. A painting of the ocean on the wall. A television was mounted high in the corner of the room and showed something anxiety-inducing—a nature show, or impossibly healthy people in advertisements for home exercise equipment. The nurse was pretty and sleepy—not Hillila, not Lynn—and smiled, really smiled, when she saw you.

You dreamt that you came to the Emergency Room clean-shaven and unworried.

As if it had been a whole different life.

He was in his bed, uninjured, and the light caught the clean lines of the bars caging him there. Keeping him safe. The blue veins in his hands, tubes notched in his elbows.

Machinery surrounded him but did not touch him.

And he smiled at you, he did, as you felt the warm rasp of his hand on the back of yours, and when you bent down and held him, you did it for love and not for duty.

DUNSMUIR

After I did my thirty days of inpatient at St. Joseph's, I got a job at a Bean There, Bun That, way the hell out in Gresham. Best I could do. It wasn't really cooking, more like just heating up flash-frozen burritos and flipping precharred hamburger patties that came packaged in long wax-paper tubes. I had to wear a hat shaped like a lettuce leaf and the menu had items with names like Cheesy Total-Taters and the Taco-the-Town-Wich. But it was work, you know, and Franny and I had the Bump to think about, which is what I called the baby girl that was on the way. The baby that was coming regardless of the fact that I was newly sober and rabbit-scared all the time, that low-level terror constantly thrumming through my day like the background hum of an amplifier left on.

You get those stretches in your life. Stretches where it seems like the voyeur that passes for God just picks up the house you're living in and rattles it around a bit and sets it back down, waiting to see how you'll handle it. We had a month of straight misery, Franny and me, all these terrible things right in a row. First, I drank too much one night and wrapped our pickup around a pole, blowing a .22 when the cops came. That was significant. Thank Christ Franny wasn't with me. I got thirteen stitches in my scalp, spent the weekend in jail, had my license pulled, and lost my job at the restaurant where Franny and I worked. The judge sentenced me to thirty days in St. Joseph's inpatient treatment program. Then we found out that Franny was pregnant, which wasn't a bad thing but came as a shock, you know. The terrible thing, the cosmic rug-pull, came after I'd been in St. Joe's for a couple weeks: Franny's sister Rochelle was killed. Murdered by her boyfriend. I mean, just that word itself, Christ. It was one of those things that you read about in the paper and it makes you think about how terrible the world is for about two seconds, and then you move on to the next thing—until it actually happens to you and the people you know, and then the bottom just drops out of the world. Rochelle, Franny's sister, had lived in Dunsmuir, a little hippie town in Northern California, and Franny had to go identify the body and sign off on it, talk to the police. It was Rochelle's boyfriend Pete who had done it. A drug thing, the Great and Terrible Scourge that was methamphetamines; the police report said he was strung out, incoherent, had been up for days. I'll admit, I took a moral high ground. *I'd* never do *that,* I told myself at the time. Meanwhile, my skull was still scabbed up where I'd headbutted the rearview mirror.

But I wanted to go with her, see. I knew that I needed to.

Ron, my addiction counselor at St. Joe's, gave it a no-go.

We were in his office. "Conditions of your sentence say you can't leave the state, bud," he said.

I picked at the pilled fabric of my seat cushion. "My sister-in-law got murdered, man. Give me a break."

Ron's office had carpet that beautiful singing green of a Heineken bottle where it wasn't worn and threadbare. Water stains that looked like Italy or a flaccid dick on the tiles above his head. A Serenity Prayer poster done in terrible calligraphy hung behind his head, the laminate curling at the corners. Ron was a big ex-biker with a grayed ponytail and some of the worst jailhouse tattoos I'd ever seen in my life. I understood he had lived a life before he landed in the chair before me. He had a voice like gravel in a tin cup and was unapologetically high on the Twelve Steps. It would be a long time before I didn't hate him. I certainly did right then.

He leaned over and squinted at my folder, thumbed through my paperwork. "You guys are married?"

"Well, no," I said.

"This is an *in-house* treatment center, Dave. You get that, right?"

"Come on, man. Seriously."

Ron leaned back. "I'm sorry. It sucks. But unless she's your actual spouse, we're legally bound. You came here through the courts."

"This is bullshit," I said.

"It is," he agreed. Then he leaned forward, all solemn, and said quietly, "Listen. Consider this a prime time for you to start building a relationship with your Higher Power," and I solemnly resolved to shit on his desk before my thirty days were up.

So Franny had to take the train down to Dunsmuir, a sweet little town near Mount Shasta, and go gather her dead sister's remains without me.

I was able to call her later that week. The "community room" at St. Joe's had frayed linoleum floors and a TV that made all the actors look like they had just stepped off the mother ship. There were stacks of faded board games and a few shelves of Jonathan Kellerman and Danielle Steel novels with their covers ripped off. It also had what was probably one of the last working payphones in America. Next to the phone was a sign-in sheet on a clipboard; we were allowed an hour a week of phone time, on the honor system. It was supposed to be an opportunity, Ron said, for us to start telling the truth for the first time in our lives. Cash register honesty, he called it.

We made small talk, and I told her how much I missed her, and then she said, "His mom tried to talk to me at the funeral home."

"Pete's? Jesus."

"Yeah. She heard I was coming somehow. She was waiting outside. She felt so bad, I could see. She's just this little old lady, Dave, all folded over and tiny. She's heartbroken. But I just couldn't talk to her."

"That's okay," I said. "Seriously. That's a reasonable response to a difficult situation."

"What?"

"You were giving yourself necessary space," I said, and rolled my eyes: two weeks in and I was already spitting out rehab-speak. Christ, *I* couldn't even tell if I was being ironic. It was annoying and yet—it was also the longest stretch of unbroken sobriety I'd had since high school. Franny had always had some internal brake inside of her: she could always reach a point and just stop. ("You mean like a normal person," Ron would say to me.) She'd maybe be a little hungover the next day. She'd stop, but then she'd watch me go. She gave up trying to corral me. I was like a car rolling down a cliff where some villain had cut the brake line. I thought *Stop* every once in a while, and the next thing that came was usually *Screw that, what's the point?* It'd been like that since I was fourteen years old. I felt like a living bundle of nerves that day in the community room, and couldn't stop worrying the scab where they'd taken the stitches out. I felt like the enormity of my past mistakes like a guy walking through a dark room, afraid to turn the light on and examine how bad it really was.

Franny rode the train back to Portland with Rochelle's ashes in the box they gave her at the funeral home. There was no other family; their mom had left when they were kids and their dad had died of stomach cancer a while back. It had just been the two of them for so long, and now it was just her. Just Franny. Man. On the train, nobody asked her about the box she kept under her seat; Franny was pretty, but she could be hard too, and had a way of compartmentalizing herself and just shooting out these fuck-off vibes sometimes. She was one of those people who could either fan her wings out and make a lot of noise or curl up and not take up much room in the world.

It was maybe the most useless I'd ever felt, holding that receiver while a bunch of other yelling idiots played Jenga behind me.

"Nobody even asked me about the baby," she said quietly.

"The Bump, you mean." She was five months along by then, and starting to show.

"The baby, Dave. The Bump sounds like you're doing dope. And you're not doing dope, are you?"

"Not me," I said. "Fourteen days sober. High on life. Yoga, meditation."

"Bull."

"Massaging our inner children, Franny. Crystals attuned to our personal frequencies. Today we're doing a colonic session with melon-infused tea. It's good to be alive."

"Funny man over here. Seriously, though. For real."

I looked at the scarred number pad in front of me, touched it with my thumb. "For real, I'm losing it. I'm smoking two packs a day. I drink coffee until my hands vibrate." The wall above the payphone was littered in scrawled pictures, crude and oversized anatomies, misspelled filth. "We talk a lot. We're constantly talking. We go to a lot of meetings, try to one-up each other with war stories."

"Jenga, bitch!" someone behind me bellowed.

"Craig, if you yell that in my face again," someone else said, "I swear to God. If you yell that in my face again, I will saw your head off with this butter knife. No joke, bro. In your sleep. I swear it."

Franny said, "Listen, my break's over. I gotta go. Please, please Dave, don't ever say 'colonic' and 'melon-infused' again," and I could tell she was smiling, and that sadness that had moored us down seemed to lift for just a second. It was one of those rare times where I felt like just maybe I was where I was supposed to be. It was about the best I could hope for, given the circumstances.

• • •

There was a lot of talk about God in St. Joe's, and in my meetings afterward. Ron was a broken record on the matter. Call Him whatever you want, he'd say. Higher Power, God, a doorknob. As long as it isn't you. As long as *you're* not the one in charge. Because look at the mess you've made. Your best thinking put you in that chair.

Maybe before but *definitely* after Rochelle, I couldn't help but look at God as a wing-puller, an anthill-scorcher. Some gleeful little sociopath whose parents were woefully absent, giving him access to an arsenal and the run of the house. I couldn't see that feeling changing any time soon.

"I just had to let go and let God," some guy would inevitably say during group, hands buried in his armpits, jiggling his knee and trying so hard for a feigned nonchalance. Shooting for a wisdom and serenity none of us had. Instead just coming across as a man in the slow burn of a sustained panic attack, usually while wearing bleach-spotted sweatpants and flip-flops. "I just had to admit that I wasn't in charge no more."

Yeah, I'd think. *And look who is.*

• • •

Maybe a month after I got out of treatment, we were in bed and Franny woke me up and said, "I want to take Rochelle's ashes to the waterfall."

I'd drooled all over my pillow and Franny touched my face in the dark and recoiled. "Ew," she said. "Nasty."

"Sorry."

"I'm serious, Dave."

"Okay," I said thickly, trying to wake up. She was still deeply sad, you know, and would fall into these silences I had a hard time pulling her out of, and I figured this was a good thing. This ash-burying thing was movement, you know, and grieving, and part of the process. Two or three times a year, when she was alive, Franny and I would pick Rochelle up and go camping down there near Mount Shasta for a long weekend. It was all national forest out there, you didn't even need a permit. Just pick a road and find a spot to park and hike in. There was a waterfall that we always went to. Franny was right: it would be a good spot. I said, "We need to get a truck or something." Quieter, trying to own up to my mistakes, I said, "I mean, since I wrecked ours."

"Oh," she said, just as suddenly sounding deflated. "Right. I didn't even think of that."

"We'll make it work," I said.

Franny rolled over then and I thought she was asleep until I felt her shuddering just a little bit. Crying right there next to me with her back turned. I rolled over, cinching my arm over her. "Fran? We'll make it work. No problem."

• • •

The Bean There, Bun That was out on Stark Street, four lanes of traffic going heavy all the time. We were next to an auto shop, and I'd sit out back next to the dumpster and smoke while I watched the mechanics go in and out of the bay doors and do paperwork in their little glassed-in office. Rusted engine parts and empty bottles of motor oil lay in the sticker bushes out back by the fence, and they had a line of cars for sale against one side of the building. They were mostly rust-punched pieces of shit that were new when I was in diapers.

I'd sit out there on the little scarred picnic table someone had brought out, my wilted lettuce-hat next to me, and smell the grease, the restaurant garbage turning in the heat. Feel the sun tightening the skin on my scalp. I'd think about drinking and try every way I could imagine how to get it to still work for me. How I could pull drinking off and still keep Franny, who'd dealt with years of my messes by then. Who I knew, since Rochelle's death, had reached a saturation point. She'd leave me, I knew that. The math just didn't work. So I smoked and smoked and white-knuckled it. I'd watch those guys trundling around in those dark loading bays, metallic clangs drifting over in the slow heat of the afternoon. I sat out there and thought about Fran. About Rochelle. The Bump. I even thought about Pete, the killer. I'd been sober for over two months at that point. Miracle-level stuff, even if I lived through skin-crawling anxiety pretty much as soon as I woke up. And I watched Franny weep and rage and suffer over the death of her sister until she finally settled into that silence once again, that stillness she had cultivated so long ago. A long-time mourning. She wouldn't talk about it with me. You want to fix the people you love, take their pain out like extracting a tooth, concise and quick like that, and it just doesn't work that way.

• • •

Like I said, it'd be a blazing untruth to say that I didn't want a drink. I did, often very badly. I'd catch the 20 bus home from work and I'd stink of grease and charred meat and there'd be an undercurrent of chemical stink, the grease cutter we used to clean everything. I'd have a red ring around my skull from my lettuce leaf, and pining for a twelve-pack of beer and some whiskey in an old jam jar was like pining for a girlfriend who had broken your heart, how the ache almost felt good.

One day we were heading home and I saw a kid and an older lady, probably his grandma, playing catch in their little yellow yard. He was probably ten or eleven and as the bus trundled past them, the lady dutifully threw the football. It was pure grandma-style, that throw, and didn't go very far, and the kid dutifully trotted after it. It just about killed me, seeing that. The kid and his grandma playing catch. It felt like someone had put a bag over my heart and knocked it around with a sock full of quarters. Where was the dad? Inside? At work?

Or had he wrapped his truck around a telephone pole? Or driven into some bicyclist in the dark and wound up in prison?

I thought of my mom, who was sixty now and the Bump wasn't even born, trying to roller-skate around with her cruddy hips. Or teaching my kid how to drive, or telling them how shitty dudes could be. All those things I wouldn't be around for.

I was afraid of the world when I wasn't drinking. But I was more afraid now of what would happen if I went back to it. Most days I'd get off the bus from work grateful to not be drunk, as if I'd walked past a lion's open cage but the lion hadn't noticed me.

● ● ●

After Franny talked about taking Rochelle to the falls, I told her I was going to some meetings and I worked extra hours instead. Covered for some people. I pulled out the cash limit allowed on my ATM card for the next few days, and at the end of the week I headed over to the auto shop and talked to one of the guys there. Paid cash, and he signed the car's title over to me just like that. I drove the thing home and parked it up the block from our apartment. It felt scary being behind the wheel again—I felt like I had a neon sign over my head that said *This Guy Is Totally Driving with A Suspended License.* I was worried I had done the wrong thing.

When I went into our apartment, Franny was watching TV and eating a popsicle, her feet up on the coffee table. The shades were drawn and a little fan was pushing all the hot air around. There was a little rind of belly showing between her tank top and her shorts, and her lips were orange from the popsicle, and my heart squeezed so tight seeing her I just about felt like dying. I bent down and kissed her on her sweaty forehead.

She laced a cool hand around my neck and kissed me on the cheek. "You smell like a hamburger," she said.

I said, "That would probably be a Triple TacoBurger, actually. Come outside with me."

She groaned. "Oh, do I have to? It's like a million degrees out there."

"I want to show you something."

So we walked outside and Franny held my hand and ate her popsicle with the other. We walked down the block and I stopped in front of the car and kind of did an arm-spreading gesture, game show-style. Like, *here you go.*

Franny stood there. She stood on one foot and scratched the back of her calf with her flip-flop.

Finally, she said, "What am I looking at, Dave?"

"It's our car. I bought it today."

"You bought it? Like, you drove it home?"

"Yeah."

"Dude, you have a *suspended license.*"

"I thought we could take our trip," I said. "To the falls."

There are moments when someone you love will look at you with such pity as to almost break your heart in pieces. Just cleave it smartly right in two. You will in that moment come to understand the deep workings of your own idiocy, but because they are who they are, you'll be okay with it; you'll be forgiven in the same instant you're chastised. The look Franny gave me as she wiped a lock of sweaty hair from her forehead with the back of her hand was this merging of pity, exasperation, and love. I felt helpless and dumb with it, and I was still okay.

"It's like a camper," I gushed. "We can sleep in the back."

She laughed and said, "God, I thought we'd just borrow a truck from somebody or something. This is a *hearse,* Dave."

"I know it's a hearse, Fran. I'm fully aware of what a hearse is."

She looked at the car—it was an ink-black 1989 Cadillac hearse with a cracked windshield and a smooshed rear fender, a car that had cost me sixteen hundred dollars—and then back at me. She hooked her arm around my neck and I smelled this tang of shampoo and sweat, a scent that canceled out my own smell of char. I put my hand on her stomach and felt the Bump there like a bridge between us, this little thing thrumming with life, this tiny kid who would be our charge, who didn't even know yet that she was banking on us not to be total monstrous assholes and ruin everything. I couldn't look at Fran. "I just don't want you to be sad," I said, almost in a whisper.

"I know," Franny said, still looking at the car. "But sometimes you just have to be sad, is all."

"I know."

She kissed me then, quick, and I felt the ghost of sugar on my lips.

"I like it," she said.

"For real?"

"For real. It's weird as hell, but whatever."

• • •

The day I graduated from St. Joe's, Ron had called me in to his office. There were fifteen of us who'd made it through the month without doing something to get kicked out. Fucking each other, fighting, just walking out the doors. For all I know he gave each of us the same speech. He sat underneath his Serenity

Prayer poster and steepled his hands beneath his little goatee and said, "Dave, you're kind of a fuckup, aren't you?"

I laughed—this was Ron's persona at St. Joe's. Half the time watching him in group was like watching a guy poke a bunch of caged dogs with a stick. The other half of the time, he seemed sincere. A good cop/bad cop routine. I said, "That's great, Ron. That's your Associates Degree in Psychology at work there, huh?"

Ron laughed right back. "That's what I mean, Dave. I don't feel like anyone quite gets through that veneer of bullshit of yours. Nobody did in here, that's for sure. It's like you've kind of just skated by on your aw-shucks jive your whole life."

I said, "Well, I'm a complicated individual, Ron." Even as anxious as I was, I'd been sober for thirty days. Thirty days! I was impervious to harm.

Ron smiled and pointed a blunt finger at me. "Seriously, though. Just tell me one thing, now that you've got a tiny bit of time under your belt. What's one thing Sober Dave's afraid of?"

The moment didn't even stretch out. It was like I'd been waiting for someone to ask me that. Before I even really knew I was going to say it, I said, "My girlfriend's having a kid. I'm afraid I'm going to absolutely ruin all of our lives."

Ron stared at me and nodded once. I could easily picture the man as a hell-raiser, but he seemed totally calm, totally comfortable in own his skin—like he had absolutely no problem being a fifty-year-old sober biker with blurry tattoos of naked ladies stomping swine-headed policemen to death on his forearms. I was jealous of that kind of peace of mind.

He handed me a card from a stack on his desk. "Rule one: don't drink, even if the sky is falling down. Rule two: you get squirrelly, call somebody. Go to a meeting. Your mind, Dave, it's like a bad neighborhood. You don't want to walk around there by yourself."

"Thanks for the vote of confidence, Ron."

"How much time you have?"

"Honestly? I drank the night before I came here, dude."

"Okay. So?"

"Thirty days."

Ron smiled, showing me unfortunate rows of horsey yellow teeth. "Good job," he said.

I just stared at him. He shrugged. "Seriously. There's, what, fifteen of you that made it through the month without getting shitcanned? Without Thirteenth Stepping each other or skipping out or something? You're already ahead of the game, bud."

"Thanks," I said.

He pointed at the card in my hand. "Call me when things go south."

"If, you mean?"

He smiled again, a little sadly this time. "No, bud. When."

• • •

I only met Pete once. This was a few months before everything happened. It was early spring and we'd driven through spats of rain the entire way down to Dunsmuir. I remember Pete only as a skinny little guy in a sleeveless Harley Davidson shirt, his arms freckled and reddened on one side and fish-pale beneath. Blond hair and sunburned cheeks. A little snaggle-toothed man with a furtive, restless air about him. It makes me mad that I can't remember more. But the courtroom image of Pete—contrite, weeping, aged, wearing an orange jumpsuit too big for him—was not the same man I met down in Dunsmuir, I know that much. He and Rochelle were always on and off, for years, like bad habits for each other, and Rochelle tended to only invite us down when they were split, save for this last time.

She lived in a little place right past town with the woods coming up to the back door. It was pretty rundown, but there were flower boxes on the concrete walkway out front. The grass got mowed. She took care of it the best she could. But this last time, Jesus, night and day. Grass shin-high. Yard looking like the shitty castoffs of a flea market or the random scatterings of a tornado. We parked the truck next to an old primer-gray Datsun hatchback with no windows or tires. Beside it sat a rusted metal drum loaded with nail-dense scrap wood. A dented washing machine with a bunch of rakes and brooms sticking out of the top.

"What the fuck," Franny breathed.

"I guess Pete must have moved in," I said, as we sat and listened to the tick of the cooling engine.

Rochelle came out onto the patio, her hand shielding her eyes. She was wearing cutoffs and a man's button-up without the sleeves.

"Jesus," Franny said quietly. "She looks like a skeleton."

We stepped out of the truck and Rochelle came over and hugged Franny hard.

"You look like shit," Franny said into her ear, and Rochelle laughed and pushed her away. She hugged me, and it was like trying to catch hold of a bunch of warm bundled sticks wrapped in fabric. "Looking pretty good, Dave," she said. In spite of it all, her voice had that same lovely warm quality to it, gravel and honey. She sounded just like Franny. She seemed happy to see us.

We walked through the house and went into the kitchen. Rochelle handed us beers. Unlike the yard, the inside of the house was spotless. I knew that Franny was looking at the place like a crime scene investigator, looking for some clues as to what was going on; all three of us had sometimes partied hard for sure, but I'd never seen Rochelle look this bad. You didn't have to be a genius to figure out what was going on. I couldn't help but cast glances at the pale bruised planks of her legs; even in the dim kitchen light she looked worn out, her skin yellow-tinged. We caught up for a bit, our conversation punctuated by the occasional bleat of a chainsaw out back. The air smelled like pitch and Pine-Sol.

At one point Rochelle opened up the back door and said, "Pete, they're here. Come say hi, damn."

Pete came in carrying that pitch-smell with him; he had flecks of sawdust in his hair. He maybe came up to my shoulders. He also, I was dismayed to see, had a smattering of speed-scabs on his cheeks. I imagined the pair of them on their second or third day up, Rochelle scrubbing the kitchen floor yet again, Pete dicking around with his cars out front. There was a guy in St. Joe's who said his favorite thing on earth was to smoke some crank and take apart his VW bug down to the chassis, and then put it all back together again. I looked at Franny; we had this moment where understanding crystallized between us.

If Rochelle was embarrassed at all, I couldn't see it. She pointed with her beer bottle and said, "Pete, this is my sister Fran. That's Dave."

"Charmed," Pete said, sounding anything but. His hand was warm and limp. He seemed feral, a snake hit with a shovel but not quite dead. Honestly, I was a little afraid of him.

"What do you got going on out there?" I said.

Pete shrugged, looked out into their backyard. "You always need firewood, right?"

Franny was so pissed at him, her beer bottle clicked against her teeth when she took a drink. "Isn't that all national forest out there, Pete?"

"Fran," Rochelle said.

Pete shrugged and smiled. "I won't tell if you won't," he said. You look for portents of the future and you can find them, sure. The scabs on his face. Missing teeth. The shit in the yard. But did I for a moment think things would end the way they did? No, of course not. But I also wasn't sad to bid adieu to Pete either as the three of us loaded up in the truck. When Rochelle went in to say her goodbyes and get the last of her stuff, Franny slapped the dashboard and turned to me. "Dude's a fucking poster child for *Faces of Meth*, Dave. Oh my *God*."

"I know it."

"She's so fucking *stupid*. Look at the yard! What is that over there? Is that a *hide-a-bed*?"

It was a tight fit there with the three of us in the truck. Franny sat between us and kept harping on Rochelle for every little thing. I could tell she was scared.

"God, quit *jabbing* me," she said as we got off I-5 and bounced our way up the dirt road toward our usual camp spot. "Your bony little hip's like a knife. I should just fold you up and put you in the glovebox."

"Would you drop it?" Rochelle said, holding onto the door handle.

We drove up the trailhead to our spot and parked the truck. We started unpacking our gear, putting up the tents. Twilight was coming. By then they'd both fallen into a loaded silence. I normally loved this part, settling into the quiet, but that last time, Franny would say, "Dave, can you hand me the mosquito spray?" even though it was right there next to Rochelle. Rochelle would reach into the cooler and ask me if I wanted a beer, but not ask Fran. Like that. We built a fire and wrapped diced onions and potatoes in foil and put them in the coals. I felt like things would get better if I was shitfaced.

We were drinking beers, watching sparks whirl and vanish above the fire. There was just the occasional snap of a branch out in the darkness and nobody had said anything for probably five minutes when Franny, looking into the fire, said, "I just worry about you."

"I know," Rochelle said, without skipping a beat, like they'd been talking the whole time. "I know you do."

"If he ever touches you—" Fran started, and Rochelle chopped her hand through the air, sharp and precise.

"Oh my God, stop. He's never touched me, Fran. He's never going to *touch* me. He weighs about sixty pounds and cries at dog food commercials, okay? I don't need you judging me. You two aren't exactly, like, star material yourselves."

"Whatever," Fran said.

"No," Rochelle said, holding a finger up. "I'm serious. Dave? When's the last time you've been sober, dude? I've known you for years and I have literally never seen you without a drink in your hand."

"Okay," I said, surprised by her anger. I had been feeling pretty good by then. Her face was gaunt and hollowed in the firelight.

"And you? Fran? You've *always* acted like you know what's best for everybody on earth. Me, *Dad*, everybody. So there's some shit in the yard, *so what*." She furiously swiped a hand under each eye.

Very quietly, Franny said, "That's not what I'm talking about, Rochelle."

"Yeah? What are you talking about then?"

"Guys," I said.

"What are you *talking* about, Fran? I'd love to hear it. Let's get specific."

"Never mind," Franny said.

"No, let's go. Tell me—again—just what it is I'm doing wrong. Fill me in. *Please.*"

That night Fran cried for a long time. She slithered around in her sleeping bag like a big worm, every noise telegraphed in that stillness of night, and I couldn't console her. She wouldn't talk. I tried to put my arm around her and she said, "Don't. I'm getting snot everywhere."

"It's okay," I said, and I lay my arm over her and she at least let me do that.

The next morning, it was as if none of it had happened. I walked around the campsite like it was a minefield, but neither of them said a word about it. Rochelle asked how we'd slept and Fran said "Good," all bright like that, like it was something they'd practiced.

We hiked up the trail that morning. We'd been there before, and had named various landmarks over the years. There was the familiar dead tree with its trunk split by lighting and Rochelle said, in her *This is your captain* voice, "Ladies and gentlemen, if you'd care to look out your windows, we'll be passing Camel Toe Point on our left in just a moment." It was the same joke she made every time, but this time I watched Fran raise her head up and bray laughter like it was the first time she'd heard it, and just that moment alone fixed something. Not entirely, but I saw Rochelle grin down at the ground as she readjusted her pack on her shoulders.

We could hear the waterfall long before we saw it, and I felt mist start to settle on my face. When we came to the clearing, the water tumbled and roiled into a pool below us—the faded BLM sign said that the pool was exactly a hundred and twenty-five feet down. I was out of breath, my hangover thudding behind my eyes. I watched as Franny and Rochelle stood there in front of the fence with their hands planted on their hips, their backs turned to me, the falls beyond them.

Franny reached over and put her arm around Rochelle's shoulders and whispered something into her ear. Rochelle shook her head and laughed. It would have made a nice picture, the two of them. Just the briefest moment, but I saw it. At least there was that.

• • •

So we took a few days off after I bought the hearse and headed down I-5 toward the falls again. Probably for the last time, I figured, at least until we got settled with the Bump. The sky was threaded with dark clouds that I tried not to think of as an omen. Franny drove, and as we went through towns, people thought we were heading a procession and would pull over onto the shoulder while I winced and made vague hand gestures of apology and Fran just smiled. Rochelle's ashes sat on the floorboards between my feet. We made it to Dunsmuir by late afternoon and stopped at the little grocery store there in town. It was raining pretty good by then. Franny went to get groceries, and I told her I had to take a leak and instead skulked out to the side of the store and used the payphone. It brought back memories—the stout silver coil of line from the handset to the box, the perforations in the gray mouthpiece. Ron picked up on the third ring, which surprised me, and remembered who I was, which surprised me more.

"What can I do you for, Dave?" he said, which has to be one of the most irritating turns of phrase ever invented.

"You sound so chipper," I said.

"You sober?"

"Yeah," I said.

"How long's it been?"

"Almost four months."

"The fuck shouldn't I be happy for then?"

I watched people walking out to their cars stare long and hard at the hearse as they passed it. I was getting soaked standing there. I said, "You remember my girlfriend's sister. The one that got killed."

"I do," Ron said. "Yeah."

I sighed. "Well, we're about to scatter her ashes, Ron."

"Quietly, he said, "Why you calling me, bud? What's up?"

Past the parking lot was the highway, this dark charcoal line thumbed between bright bursts of dripping, flame-colored trees. Cars sped through rainwater going other places, all this *velocity*.

I said, "I'm just wondering if we can ever actually change at all. Like for the long-term. To the point where it means anything."

He chuckled, like he'd been expecting that exact question. Maybe he had, I don't know. I felt that familiar surge of irritation toward him. "You got about four months, right?"

"About, yeah."

"You know what you get with four months sobriety, Dave?"

"What?"

"Four months of sobriety," he said and laughed again.

"It's cute," I said. "These pearls of wisdom of yours."

"You can't rush things, is what I'm saying. You don't get all the answers. It doesn't work like that. You got four months of not putting a drink in front of you. Nice job. But you don't get a key to the city or a handjob from the stewardess or whatever. It's just life, man. There are storms sometimes, and sometimes it's nice."

"Okay," I said.

"Don't try so hard. Just put one foot in front of the other. Do what's in front of you. Time takes time."

"*Okay,*" I said. "Got it."

Ron laughed. "Well, shit, Dave, thanks for calling."

"It's good to hear you," I said, and meant it.

"Oh, you too, bud. Believe me."

• • •

That night we slept in the hearse. It bottomed out on the trail long before we made it to our usual spot, and it was raining like hell besides. We just parked; we'd have to hike in the next morning. Things had changed since we'd last been there. Odd encampments had sprung up, and familiar places seemed mired in bad vibes, spooky. One spot we passed hosted a few soiled mattresses and what looked like some very dirty underwear stuffed inside of a television with an imploded screen, like bandages stoppering a wound. "Who brings a TV out here?" Franny said, which wasn't necessarily the question I would have asked. Another clearing looked like it had been host to a gigantic bonfire comprised entirely of clothes, as if a bunch of nudists had gone buck-wild; sodden shirtsleeves lay in charred ruins outside a circle of blackened ash. We didn't even have a fire, just ate dinner in the front seat and then climbed into the back with our sleeping bags.

Neither of us could sleep. "It's so weird to think that probably a whole bunch of dead people have been right where we are," Franny whispered. It was true; it felt a little claustrophobic, even with the back door open. The sound of rain was really loud on the roof.

"It is kind of creepy," I said. "I should have thought ahead. Are you okay?"

Fran turned to me. She was just a vague contour in the darkness. "Yes," she said. "I'm absolutely okay."

"Did I mess up, do you think?"

"No, Dave." I heard her hand slither out of her sleeping bag and she reached out and tucked a swatch of hair behind my ear. "I'm glad we came."

"Okay. Cool."

"I just can't think of her last hour. That's the worst part. You know? What the last hour of her life would have been like. '*I won't tell if you won't,*'" she said in this high-pitched, acerbic mimicry of Pete.

The next morning, we walked the trail that led to the falls. We passed our usual camping spot. The remains of a small fire lay in a neat circle of stones. Whoever'd made the fire was gone, though, and it made me feel at least a little better, knowing that our spot wasn't host to some underwear/television art project or a bunch of stained mattresses or something. That someone cared enough to keep it clean, or just hadn't cared enough to venture that far.

It had stopped raining in the night and sunlight fell in bright shards though the tree limbs. Steam rose from the ground and you could still hear rainwater dripping from the leaves all around. We took turns carrying the box of ashes and it made me feel indescribably sad and joyous at the same time, that the remains of someone I had known could be distilled down to such a tiny thing. Birds sang to each other above us and we started catching glimpses of the falls.

And then we came to a metal fence—painted incendiary yellow—and a new sign affixed to it that said *Trail Closed for Season. Trespassers Will Be Prosecuted by Order of the National Forest Service.* I'd never seen anything like it out there.

Franny hiked a leg over the fence, didn't even break stride.

"Fran?" I called.

She turned and looked at me, one leg on either side of the fence. I could see the Bump there in stark relief and above it, clutched to her chest, Rochelle's ashes. Franny cocked an eyebrow at me.

"What's up?"

I said, "You still want to keep going, I take it. Over the fence."

She poked her bottom lip out and blew hair off of her forehead. "Listen to me," she said. "I don't want you to drink anymore."

"Okay," I said, my voice suddenly thick.

And what else is there to say? What else can I tell you? We hopped the fence, we let Rochelle's ashes go in the falls. A while later we would go to the Siski-you County Courthouse in Yreka and watch Pete—repentant, weeping Pete, withered as fruit—be sentenced to twenty-six years for First Degree Murder, and all of it, all the pomp and gravity of the proceedings, would clang hollow and pointless inside of me.

I could tell you that I stayed sober through a couple close calls, and that our daughter slept quietly through most of the sentencing but toward the end broke out in quailing howls that rang to me like judgment. That I felt a savage, animal joy at the sound of it, watching her tiny balled fists beating the air. Franny wept next to me, almost in tandem with Pete across the room, and I felt like an animal; I wanted to tear the walls of the world down when I saw that terrible synchronicity. I did.

But that day at the falls? That day at the falls, Franny said, "Okay. Good. Are you coming with me or what?" I walked over and raised a leg over the gate and sat there facing her. We could hear the falls further up the trail, and sunlight fell in a fine and haphazard design that wavered at our feet as the trees shivered in the breeze. A mosquito hovered in front of my face and Franny waved it away.

I said, "Are you listening? Can you hear me?"

Fran smiled. "Yep."

"I'd follow you anywhere, okay?"

HOMECOMING

He had thought perhaps there might be a banner hung along Main Street announcing his return, if not a small but joyful parade. Instead the soldier awoke from troublesome, snow-rimed dreams to find the town even more desolate than it had been before he'd left. No pedestrians on the sidewalks. Few cars. The windows of the beauty parlor now covered in whorls of white soap. The butcher's shop had no door, just a rectangle dark as an open mouth. No parade, no banners or balloons, and as the bus trundled along the street, it seemed to the soldier that each storefront, each threadbare lawn, was instead a place that tugged at some dim vestige of his memory, this litany of places he almost recognized. It was no kind of homecoming.

Carrying his civilian clothes and things in a green duffel bag, the soldier got off the bus and walked along Main Street, trying to recall how he'd felt toward this place before he'd left to join the war. He seemed mostly to have been hollowed out by the things he had seen and done while on the front. He felt that this hollowness was not a thing worth ruminating too deeply upon; it was what it was. War did things to people, he decided. If the town seemed a little odd, seemed like something possibly spied through a dream, so be it. If he himself felt a little odd, that was as it should be, too. He was home now, and alive, and these were the things that mattered. He walked, thumbed sleep from his eyes, tried to shake the last of the dark visions from his head.

He came upon a tavern and decided he didn't want to go home yet. He opened the door and peered inside. He saw tape-covered barstools and slowly spinning ceiling fans, their pull strings furred in dust. The carpet's tread was worn to darkness. The tang of smoke and old beer.

"Come in if you're going to," said the bartender, without looking up from the glass he was cleaning. He sounded cross. "Letting all the damn daylight in."

"Sorry."

The bartender looked up and his face changed, softened. "Oh hell," he said. "I heard you were back in town. You just roll in?"

The soldier was confused. The bartender was thin and sallow, with greasy hanks of hair falling to his shoulders. He wore a beard and a ratty leather vest, and the soldier was sure he didn't recognize him. But this too seemed a minor price to pay for the gift of returning home. "I did," he said. He walked in and sat down at a stool. "Just now."

The bartender drew him a beer and cut the foam with the flat side of a knife. "On the house," he said. "We sure appreciate all that you boys do over there. The sacrifices you've made." The soldier opened his mouth to say something. He himself hardly knew what they were doing over there, but he had learned that it was better to keep quiet about it. He set his bag at his feet. The bar was empty save for the two of them and a man in a far booth, who sat with his face cradled in his hands. He seemed to be weeping, and a cowboy hat sat on the table before him. The beer tasted sharp on the soldier's tongue, like gunmetal.

"So how was it?" The bartender once more began cleaning glasses with a rag. Bent to his work, the soldier could see the thin white line where the man parted his hair.

"How was what?"

"You know. How was it over there?"

He could say many things. It had been bloody, yes. Horrific. Maddening. Heartbreaking. Joyous. Tedious. Ceaseless. He could say *It was like carrying a stone in your mouth for a year.* He could say *It was like holding someone's heart in your hand and just squeezing like this, or like holding someone's heart in your hand and making it keep beating just with your will, just with pure will.* It was, he thought, like a cup being filled and then spilling over and no one caring. It was numbing boredom stuttered with flurries of violence and terror. It was feeling like you were doing something, and then wishing you could be doing anything else. It was laughing with your friend as the two of you sat on a log in the snow after marching for ten hours, your legs thrumming, that tired, welcome feeling of a day's work truly being put to rest, and then watching a dark hole appear in your friend's cheek, a hole that welled with blood, almost delicately, only to have the gunshot drift toward you down the valley afterward.

"It was cold," the soldier said.

The man in the far booth began sobbing.

"What's the matter with him?" asked the soldier quietly.

"Him? Nothing."

"No?"

"He's the sheriff, is all. He gets emotional."

"Why's he crying like that?"

The bartender slapped his rag over his shoulder and gazed at the barroom as if he were assessing something. "I know you just got back," he said, "but trust me. Okay? Trust me when I say there's more than enough to cry about."

• • •

He walked the length of town looking for familiar landmarks. Everything he saw felt vaguely known. He kept expecting to see his house, his boyhood home, but nothing looked quite right. He had left his parents like any young man would: eager to set foot into the world, ready to seize it by the hand and run with it. He had had friends, of course, friends who had stayed in town, friends who had also gone to war. There had even been a girlfriend who had vowed to wait for him. But he had been very concerned about dying while on the front, and he felt like her commitment was a weight that drew danger toward him. He had eventually written her a letter and insisted that she not wait, that she move on. She had written back to him and agreed, her relief stark and obvious. But she had at least offered, and that had warmed him on those long dark nights in the snow, nights spent huddled in strange fields outside of strange towns, nights punctuated with the booms of distant howitzers and other young men scattered around him crying out in their sleep.

He had spent his childhood in this town, he was sure of it. Had fished its ponds and ridden the school bus and caught fly balls on the lush green diamond of the baseball field. Surely he had. But these memories were dim and colorless things, vague events spied through a grim fog. The porch of this house looked familiar, but so did the next one. It was maddening, like an itch he couldn't reach, as if the whole town were a name he couldn't quite place. What was clearer were the visions of marches with his platoon through frozen, mud-hewn fields, passing the darkened windows of strange houses, their eaves hung with blades of ice.

He walked. He noted the few passing cars on the street seemed old and weatherworn, bleating smoke, their fenders wobbling. Was that the bank across the street there? The one that his father had taken him to so he could open a checking account as a young man? And the building next to it—that might have been the library where his mother worked, but it was abandoned now, covered in kudzu, its entranceway soot-stained and scoured with ash. Bombed, perhaps, or given over to some grand accident.

He recognized then that dust coated his boots, bled him of color from the knees down. He walked and walked and found nothing that rang the bell of recognition within him. No place was surely, unequivocally known.

When Main Street finally gave way to thin copses of woods and the undergrowth seemed to make disturbing shapes in the corner of his eye, he turned and walked back to the tavern.

"Figured you'd be back," said the bartender, already pulling him another beer. The bartender was wearing a cowboy shirt with pearls on the pockets and the soldier tried to remember if that had been what he'd been wearing before, or how long it had been since he'd been there last.

"I feel strange," he said. "I can't find anything. My house."

The bartender nodded. "Yeah."

"There's no people here."

The bartender put a hand against his chest, offended.

"I'm not really sure what to do," said the soldier.

From his booth, the sheriff raised his shaggy head from his hands. "What you ought to do," he called, "is find you a house and settle in. Get on with the business of it all." He sounded tremulous and ancient. His voice was like wind yawing through some cold tunnel. It was a terrible thing to behold.

"Just settle in?" asked the soldier, turning around. "Just find a house and settle in?"

Perhaps he would run into someone he knew if he stayed long enough. A friend. His parents. Perhaps the world would become more familiar with time, less laden with dust and colorlessness. Perhaps there would be a sense of homecoming. "What if someone's living there? In one of the houses?"

"Trust me," said the sheriff. "No one will be living there."

• • •

He chose a house at the center of town. It was small and white, with a yard of dead yellow grass and pale flowers beneath the windows. Inside, the house seemed to echo with its own stillness, but that could also be said of the whole town, and besides, this was a thing he was already growing used to.

He lay down in a bedroom and tried to sleep but felt harried again by visions of rifle fire, of the wretched architecture of falling bodies. When he finally stood up and began walking the house, he found Ramon in the bathroom. Ramon was peering into the mirror, looking at the bullet hole in his cheek. The soldier quickly closed the door, afraid. He walked away and in another bedroom. He found a young boy standing there. The boy was bouncing an orange ball against the wall and catching it.

The soldier recognized him, and his heart caught in his throat as surely as if it was some pinned animal.

"I'm sorry," said the soldier, almost blurting it out, and the boy stood with his back to the soldier and thocked the orange ball against the wall and caught it and said nothing.

Next the soldier found his father sitting in a recliner in the living room. His father was eating peanuts as he stared at the dead gray cataract of the television set. He carefully dropped the peanut shells into a blue bowl on his lap. His jaw was dusted in silver bristles.

The soldier stood in front of the television and waved his arms. He yelled. His father kept eating peanuts and dropping the shells in the bowl. The soldier walked back to the bathroom and opened the door and cursed Ramon. He called Ramon names they had only jokingly called each other before Ramon had fallen off the log with the hole in his cheek. But Ramon said nothing. He touched his cheek and watched the blood well and spill.

• • •

The soldier chose a different house. This one was two stories tall and had a red door and a tree in the yard that dropped hard green apples to the ground.

He found his mother in the kitchen drinking a glass of water and when he touched her on the shoulder, it was like touching a wall or a tree or a stone, and she never turned to him.

He discovered the woman, the mother of the boy with the orange ball, sitting on a bed. Her hands lay folded in her lap as if she were waiting in a train station. She was wearing her coat, and snow lay in her hair.

• • •

After that, he slept outside.

• • •

After some time—it was hard to tell, the way night and day worked—he went back to the tavern. The bartender passed the time holding a lighter beneath his palm and pulling it away. Soon the room stank of scorched flesh, but no one told him to stop. No one cared, really. The soldier and the sheriff sat beside each other and got drunk, and even their drunkenness seemed wan and washed out.

"Maybe I'm in the wrong town," the soldier said, frowning into his glass. "Maybe I lived somewhere else."

"You saw your mother," said the sheriff. "You saw your friend." He had told the sheriff and the bartender about some of the things he had seen in the houses. Not all of them, but some.

"You're not in the wrong town," the bartender said, wincing and flapping his hand. He squinted at the blisters on his palm. "This is just the way the world is."

"I've never heard of anything like it before."

"Never?" The bartender winked at the sheriff. "Never in your worst dreams?"

The soldier said, "So is it me or the world that's different?"

"Oh, it's you," said the sheriff. The badge pinned to his shirt was tarnished and green. "*And* the world. But mostly you."

"Am I dead?"

The bartender nodded. "In a manner of speaking."

The sheriff said, "Yes. Mostly. Somewhat."

The soldier finished his beer and a new one was poured for him. "So what do I do?"

Shrugging and smacking his lips, the sheriff said, "You just live. Such as it is."

"I just live?"

The sheriff looked at the bartender, exasperated. "Jesus wept. He just repeats every goddamned thing I say."

"I think," said the soldier, carefully, "that I'd rather be in the war again than be here like this."

"Of course you would," muttered the sheriff. "That's the whole damn point of it all. And still it's better here than out there."

"Out there?"

The sheriff lifted his glass toward the tavern windows. "Outside of town? Go out there alone and you never come back, boy. Lost forever, you go out there by yourself." He cackled and said in that high, pinched voice, "Animals with clouds for heads that whisper poisons at you. Skeletons that walk backward and peel your skin when they glance your way. All kinds of shit. Every bad dream you ever had walks on two legs out there. It's no life, is what I'm saying. This is a half-lit place and everything tastes like piss and rot, yes. *But.*"

"But," agreed the bartender, lifting a finger.

"But," said the sheriff, "it's a life of some kind, however small." He belched into his fist. "Things can always get worse, is what I'm saying."

"You get used to it. That's the thing I always say to folks, is that they can get used to anything."

"Not me," said the soldier.

And some time passed, and they drank, and the bartender seemed poised to burn his hand again and instead smoothed his mustache and cast a look at the other men and said, "You're dead set on leaving, I guess you could go see the old lady."

"Oh Jesus," said the sheriff, as if he'd been expecting it. "I should've known."

• • •

The sheriff led the soldier to a mountain that butted up against the town. It seemed some dim vestige of his old life, this leading the sheriff was doing, this responsibility. As if he truly was charged with the safe passage of citizenry, no matter the odd shape their lives had taken. The soldier had little hope the old woman could help him, but he felt afraid of the way he was growing used to this place, and afraid of how little he was coming to care. Perhaps eventually he would grow to be like Ramon, culled down to a simple mechanism, an automaton.

They followed a switchback road that lay carved into the mountainside. They rose quickly and soon it grew cold enough the soldier could see his breath pluming out before him. It seemed that the sheriff had been exaggerating about the fearsomeness of the land but then he saw that the plumes of their breath made unnerving forms in the air—a sinking ship, a man dangling from a tree, a dead face rising up from a well—and the soldier decided to walk with his head down.

Eventually they came to an outcropping of snow-dusted shale, studded here and there with crooked, hardscrabble trees. The soldier looked down and saw the town laid out before them. It looked pretty enough, but sad too, like something culled from an old magazine long left open in the sun.

"I should remember this," said the soldier. "Even if I can't remember everything that happened before, I should remember this, right now."

The sheriff plugged one nostril and snorted. "Yeah, good luck with that."

• • •

They kept walking. It began to snow in earnest, and the soldier relished the cold. The world around them grew hushed and quiet and white. Once he heard something crackle through the brush beside them and he reached for the rifle on his back, a feeling as natural as someone flinching, and a little orange fox ran across their path. It had a pile of miniature corpses lashed to its back; some of them he recognized, like Ramon and the boy and the boy's mother, and some were strangers to him. And then the fox was gone.

The sheriff laughed so hard he had to lean over with his hands on his knees.

"You really are trying hard to hold on, aren't you?" he gasped, his face red. "Just hanging on tight as you can to the skin of the world. Reaching for your gun! Jesus!"

• • •

Night had fallen when they finally reached the rubble-strewn mouth of the cave. The soldier could make out a tiny pebble of flame in the darkness. They made their way along, their fingers trailing the damp walls, their footsteps rasping on sharp stones. The soldier was holding tight to every sensation now, no matter how fey or unpleasant. The fire grew larger until he could make out the form of a wizened, hunched woman seated before it. Shadows leapt and trembled across her face. Hair pooled upon her crown fine as cobwebs.

"Well, look who it is," crowed the old woman.

"Mother," said the sheriff through gritted teeth.

The soldier said, "This is your mother?"

"It is."

"He didn't tell you that?" The old woman looked at the sheriff. "I'm hurt, I won't lie."

"I was talked into coming here," the sheriff said. "It was no idea of mine."

"You're a sweetheart, aren't you?"

The sheriff ignored her. "He's new," he said, hooking a thumb at the soldier.

She cast an appraising eye upon him. "I can tell by his face that he's fighting the tide, too."

"Oh, that's the truth."

"I don't know what to do," the soldier said. He gestured at the sheriff, who had pulled a flask from his pocket and was lifting it to his mouth. "He says you can send me home."

The sheriff wiped his mouth with his sleeve. "I said no such thing. Other parties suggested you two might want to talk, is all."

The woman eyed them both, patted a hank of gossamer hair behind her ear. To the soldier she said, "He says a lot of things, that one. He told you I killed his daddy, I bet."

"You *did* kill him!" cried the sheriff.

"Hell," said the old woman, "I ventilated him only after I tried charming him, and begging him, and escaping him." She turned to the sheriff. "You yourself watched time and again the things he wrought upon me. Damn selective, your allegiances, and what you've chosen to hold onto."

The sheriff gazed into the fire, muttering.

The soldier wished that he could talk to his own mother, even here, in a place like this. He cleared his throat and said, "I'd just like to go home."

"Well, this is home now," the old woman said. "Believe it. No use letting that part trouble you anymore." Her surety pained the soldier greatly.

She reached into a bag at her side and thumbed a plug of chew behind her lip. She said, softly, almost kindly, "You fought in the war, yeah?"

He nodded.

"Lost friends?"

"Yes."

"Still got your folks, far as you know? Maybe a girl? Lookin' for 'em in town but can't find 'em?"

"All that."

"Looking everywhere, I bet."

"Yes."

"Just you and the two witless wonders in the bar there"—the sheriff scowled and scuffed his boot on the cavern floor—"and all the houses you step in are odd and many-cornered. Everything dust-felted and washed of color. That sound about right?"

"Yes. Look, I—"

"You know you've passed on, right? He at least tell you that much?"

"He said as much."

"Good," said the woman, casting a stony gaze upon her son. "It's his job."

"This just isn't what I thought it'd be like," said the soldier.

This seemed to cheer the woman. She leaned forward. "Oh! What *did* you think death would be like, dear heart?"

The soldier shrugged helplessly. "Less worrisome?"

She cackled and slapped her bony knee. Dark juice spilled from her mouth and she wiped it away with her wrist. "Oooh! Less *worrisome*, says the killer! He doesn't want to *worry*, this one! This shooter of mothers in the snow! This mother-killer! Oh, alright then!"

She spat in the fire and there came the wavering shape of the woman and the young boy, the boy with the orange ball. That snow-heavy street. Ramon had been killed earlier that day, one of four men in their platoon to die by sniper fire, and this coal-edged fury had sat within the soldier, had threatened to devour him all that day. It had sickened him, that rage, as he thought of the slumped shape Ramon had made in the dirty snow beside him. They had retreated, the platoon, and had gone speeding through one of the towns they had already supposedly liberated. There was talk that the townspeople were sympathetic to the snipers, housed and fed them, thought them martyrs.

And the people on the streets watched their convoy pass, all their eyes dark with judgment, he was sure, with smoldering joy at Ramon's death, and the soldier, hardly thinking of it as they sped past, centered the sight of his rifle upon the boy, and the mother had cried out, turned to shield him.

The sound of the shot. The mother falling. Snow tumbling in her open eyes. The truck was around the bend and outside of the city and then it became just a thing that had happened, a thing that lay nested inside him, this withered seed of a thing that threatened to grow if he ever thought of it.

"You lived a long life after that," the woman said. "Home from the war. Children, a wife, business concerns. Do you remember that? Do you understand?"

"No. I came here on the bus."

"You lived a long life. It took shape inside you. Your whole life curled around this single act. Your life grew bones around it, encircled it."

"I came here on the bus."

The old woman nodded. "Sure you did."

"I did."

"Well, this is your reckoning, is what it is."

"So I can't go back?"

"To what?" The old woman lifted her chin toward the fire. "To a time when you could lower the rifle and not try to shoot a young boy in a nation you occupied? And shoot his mother instead? Back to a time when you could save Ramon? Back even further, when you were just a piss-panted lad yowling at your father's knee?"

The soldier was silent.

"What event singularly alters the course of a life, boy? How far back do you need to go? I'd like to know."

Something snapped in the fire, sparks whirled in a funnel. She pressed on. "How far back? Was I wrong for killing that boy's father there, after all he'd done to me? Was I wrong for enjoying it more than a bit? For the sense of *relief* it finally offered me?"

"I don't know."

She nodded. "Nobody does. I don't. You don't. We're all moored here."

The fire dimmed and grew. The wind walked along the walls of the cave.

"I don't know what to tell you," the old woman said. "There's no back, there's no forward. There's diminishment, and loss, and sorrow, and perhaps learning to find some dim purpose through the veil. That's it."

• • •

Eons passed, or rather some abstract and indefinable gathering of nights stacked upon days. And then the tavern door opened, and there stood the limned shape of a figure in the doorway. All heads turned and the bartender, a hand upheld against the daylight, said sourly, "In or out is fine, but standing in the middle won't work for anyone."

The woman stepped in, the door thunking shut behind her. She wore a ragged backpack and cautiously took a seat at the bar, setting the bag at her feet. The bartender pulled a beer and set it before her. She sat there, gauging a great number of things as she studied his face.

"I don't have any money," she said.

"And I don't need any," said the bartender.

She took a sip and set her hands very evenly on each side of the pint glass. She was young and terribly gaunt and in spite of her youth seemed half-shorn of something vital. A badly healed scar zippered its way from the corner of her mouth, behind her ear and into her hairline.

At a far table, a man with a cowboy hat cried out as if in his sleep and the woman flinched at the sound.

"Ignore him," said a man tucked further down the bar. "He does that." He was wearing a dusty uniform, this one, a uniform shrouded in age and misuse. A soldier of some kind, the medals at his breast tarnished and dark.

With her hands still the glass, her eyes roved between the three men. "I was expecting more folks."

The bartender said, "In here, you mean?"

"In the whole town," she said.

"Oh, it's quiet, all right."

"I feel like . . . I think I'm lost."

"Like you've made some mistakes, perhaps," said the bartender, and winked.

"Well, yes."

"Like you've been adrift and then finally arrived somewhere, but not quite the place you were thinking."

"Stop it," said the man in the uniform, and the bartender looked down, good enough to be chastened a little. "You're not lost," the soldier said to her. "You're right where you're supposed to be."

"Meaning," the bartender said, "you're as lost as any of us. And that's saying something." He lifted his own glass to the dusty light. He suggested a toast, and everyone, even the weeping man in the booth, slowly raised their own glasses in response.

THE MELODY OF THE THING

Hot wind sent newspaper scraps scrambling across the intersection. Triple digits for three days now; diesel reek, garbage spilling from trashcans, the thunder of traffic. But waiting for the bus, on my way to Teresa's to work on the set, I was buoyed, even with the heat. Afloat, man. As if I'd asked God to crack open my ribcage and pour light inside. I looked at everyone around me with a grand sense of absolution, an almost haughty sense of permissiveness. Stefan's email had come thirty minutes before: *Matt, we love the demo, we love all the songs, we definitely want to talk to you about releasing it. Long story short, let's do a record. I'll call you tomorrow.*

Sweat-slicked under the relentless sun, my left hand did its constant work, forming the chords of song after song. A lifelong habit. Other people milled around; a cluster of kids from the Catholic school down the street, a few old men with their walkers sitting at the bus stop bench, chatting in some private, hushed tone. Endless traffic. I thought about texting Teresa the news, but wanted to tell her in person.

A couple walked past, a man and a woman. Haggard and sunburned and thrumming. Dirt-rimmed faces pocked in speed-scabs. The man's jaw worked overtime. I wondered if there was an industry that meth hadn't touched— hadn't decimated—but the bar scene and the music scene weren't those. Playing music for as long as I had, as unsuccessfully as I had, I straddled both worlds and had seen it lay ruin to them each. With these two walking by, you did not need to be an expert. The woman was a lanky bottle-blond, mascara ringing her eyes, wearing jeans that had been white once. The dude, small and surprisingly compact, wore a bleach-stained tank top pocked with cigarette burns. The sole of one shoe slapped the pavement like some proclamation. They both carried plastic garbage bags, and the woman wore a nylon backpack shaped like a panda head. Just people, right? We've reached the point in history where the veneer grows thin, I thought—and was there ever a more grandiose thought? A more self-centered one? My hands formed the chords of my songs, I thought of the slow collapse of society, I thought of album artwork, of the press we'd get. Stefan's label was a respected indie one; his bands had gone on to other, larger labels, had won Grammys, toured in cars larger than Camrys, earned guarantees more significant than drink tickets. I felt that the world was a flower opening up to me.

"I'm just saying I'm sick of it," rasped the woman. She plopped her garbage bag down and I heard the clatter of cans inside.

The man's jaw worked and worked. "You're sick of it," he said, incredulous, nodding. "*You're* sick of it." His hair was shorn short and jagged, like a rush job done in the dark, a haircut given while bombs fell outside. His teeth were mustard yellow, leaning, seemingly placed at random. "*You're* the one that's sick of it."

The trio of Catholic teenagers watched this with sly, veiled glances. One boy frowned at the ground, trying not to laugh.

The man grabbed the woman's T-shirt—I saw veins leap in his arm—and pulled her closer to him. "That's what this is? *You're* sick of it? Who owes who money, Denise? Who the fuck owes who forty bucks from the fucking last time, is what I'm saying. That's a question."

One of the old men turned rheumy eyes his way, rattled that he should watch his language, and was roundly ignored. The guy had that bristling, jagged energy of someone right in the middle of a run. Just spun, like any number of musicians or bartenders I'd known in my life. My legs vibrated; I felt diminished in some integral way. I was nonthreatening, a beta, a bearded asshole in a fedora and an ironic, tie-dyed T-shirt.

"All you fucking do is rip me off," the man spat, and his backhand was loud enough to be heard over traffic. The woman's head snapped back, her hand covering her face. Cans spilled out of her bag.

The kids walked away fast, not a word spoken between them.

"Hey!" I said, surprising myself. The man turned. He strutted up to me, dropping his own black garbage bag with a rattle. He didn't even reach my chin. His pupils were pinhole small, his body this close was rife with a sour electric smell. Like standing next to a lightning storm.

Traffic was everywhere. Pedestrians. The old men were right there leaning on their walkers. I thought, *Surely someone will do something.*

"You're talking to me?" he said in a reedy rasp. He could've been thirty, fifty. "What do you have to say to me?"

I pushed my glasses up on the bridge of my nose. "You just slapped that woman." I sounded petulant, pleading my case before a judge.

"So the fuck what?" he said, tilting his head. Eyes rolled in his sockets, eyes that could incinerate planets. He blinked and gave his head a little snap, jaw endlessly rolling.

"So," I said helplessly, "we don't slap people."

"Damn right," said one of the men at the bench.

Cars just kept on going by.

"We what? We what?"

"We don't slap people," I said.

"Oh, we don't?"

"It's fine if you disagree," I said, my voice trembling, feeling that bad electric snap come off him, loathing how small my fear was making me, "but you shouldn't—"

I never even saw it, that first jab to the eye.

There's nothing there for the rest of it. Like I was just unplugged. A vague memory, later, of seeing a scattering of my teeth on stained cement. Great gouts of blood on my T-shirt, a smashed and sun-faded Big Gulp cup next to my face. Cars—moving cars, cars driving by and not stopping—throwing knives of chrome beneath the sun.

That, and just planetary explosions of pain.

• • •

I was in the hospital for three weeks. I kept thinking the fight—if you could call it that—was something that I should be able to rewind and do over. That it had happened so fast and been so far out of my wheelhouse of lived experience, surely I should get another chance at it. Surely nothing so momentous should happen like that, in a span of seconds. The first few days in the hospital were a collection of blurred snapshots: I remember Teresa sitting in the chair next to my bed, her fiddle held in her lap in a way that I'd never seen, like she didn't know what to do with it but she didn't want to set it down. And also my brother, Tobias, ripped and muscle-laden like some upside-down triangle, the logo on his T-shirt stretched indecipherably across his chest. His face like a storm cloud, like a closed fist, but then he touched me on the shoulder and he softened. I don't know, I was on a hell of a lot of painkillers.

The guy had knocked out four teeth. Cracked the ocular bone around my right eye. Fractured a cheekbone. Nine stitches in an ear. He'd pulled me into the street and laid my arms against a curb and jumped on them. All these people, this busy street in the middle of summer. Radius bones in both forearms broken. He jumped on my hands, shattered them like crockery. That was perhaps the most terrifying snapshot of all: laying in a hospital bed and seeing my hands enveloped in huge swatches of gauze, not even my splint-caged fingertips visible, my arms immobile in their casts. The EMTs had, miraculously, found my glasses.

The man had taken a bite out of my fedora, spat it on the ground.

The gas station next to the bus stop had a security camera. The police were able to identify the man as Chad Laughlin, a UFC fighter who, five years before, had tested positive for anabolic steroids and been disbarred. A detective interviewed me while I lay in a dope-haze. Laughlin had a record, he said—possession, assault—and was now wanted.

"I don't know if I want to press charges," I said. Right then, Chad Laughlin could have walked in and sat on my chest and I wouldn't have cared. They were giving me the good shit in there. The world was soft-edged, feathered in light.

"Well, it's not really up you, Mr. Haimes," the detective said. "That's the DA's call, and given this guy's history and propensity for violence, and the fact that there's video of the whole thing, it'd be negligent not to pursue the case."

Like my brother had suggested during an earlier visit, the journey from steroids to meth was perhaps not the most difficult leap imaginable. Laughlin had ended his pro career 6-7, a not even terribly notable run. The detective said he'd get back to me if he had any questions.

Three weeks later I listened to Tobias flirt unabashedly with the nurse as I was wheeled out of the hospital.

"You look like you work out," my brother said.

"Hardy har har," said the nurse. "You're a funny one."

"I'm serious, you've got that lean, cut look. Lot of reps, low weights—"

"Jesus, dude," I said. "Chill."

Tobias pretended to be shocked. "I'm just saying. I'm just pointing out the obvious. This is a guy that takes care of himself."

I was pushed through the lobby out into the sun, and with a *hang loose* shake of his hand, my brother winked and went to go get the car.

"Sorry about that," I said.

"It's cool," said the nurse. He was a nice guy. They all seemed nice. I would miss them, my caretakers, my suture-removers, my catheter-inserters. The pain was still a distant thing right then. Someone else's problem, an event taking place down the hall.

• • •

Tobias settled me in to my apartment. Propped me up on the couch and loaded up the fridge with microwave dinners, yogurts, a flat of protein shakes he was hustling as a side gig. It still hurt my face to chew.

All my plants were dead. Tobias and Teresa had switched off gathering the mail while I was in the hospital. The apartment, never big to begin with, felt small and closed in. With a grunt, I stood up and hobbled over to the window. It was an old, temperamental thing, painted shut and then yanked open throughout the decades. Trying to open a window with splinted hands and a pair of casts was like trying to perform, I don't know, a tracheotomy with a shoe and a dead bird. Just this sad, dumb clusterfuck of a thing. I was standing there sweating, already near tears, my face pressed against the window, when Tobias walked in holding a toilet brush. My giant little brother, cleaning my bathroom, tilting against the whirlwind of entropy.

"What're you doing, man?"

I shut my eyes. "Just trying to open this window. It's roasting in here."

"Teresa got you a fan. It's in the bedroom. Hold on."

He walked into the tiny square of my bedroom and came out with a standing fan. He plugged it in, pointed it at me. The cool air pushed my hair back on my brow and I felt a little better.

"You want me to put some music on?"

I stood there, staring out at the street. The parked cars. The trees. "Music?" Tobias said. "Something on the stereo? That fiddle-de-dee Irish stuff you like? Some sad emo band to reflect your inner world?"

"I don't want any music."

When I turned to look at him, Tobias's face, those vast brick-like planes, was darkened with concern. "Dude, for real?"

"I don't want any fucking music," I said, and turned back to the window, where I watched galaxies of dust, tormented by the fan, go swirling through a band of sunlight.

• • •

Heard about the accident, read the email from Stefan. *That's some rough stuff. We're here for you, my man. We're still a go on the album, as long as we're all on board for a tour soon. Gotta sell some records! Best of luck, and a speedy recovery.*

I stared at my laptop. It'd taken me minutes to painstakingly type out my address, check my emails. I kept misplacing my phone between couch cushions, forgetting to charge it. And it felt like a weight, honestly, the phone, the way it tethered me. It was nighttime, and I watched a moth land on my laptop screen, this trembling silhouette.

If I could have, I'd have cupped it in my hand, stood up and released it back into the night. But the window was still closed and they were club-like things, these hands, the bones knitting together with an itch and a snarl. I had surgery scheduled for the following week; steel pins to be put in the metacarpals, architecture to keep the delicate jigsaw of the bones in place. Some fingers would be coming out of their splints as well. If it'd only been a finger or two, I'd have been fine by now. But Chad Laughlin had turned my hands into chunks of glass candy. It was a new world.

I stared at the keyboard leaning up against the bookshelf, a little Yamaha I'd written a bunch of songs on over the years. The guitar stood on its stand next to that, this beautiful cherrywood Gibson acoustic Tobias had given me when I'd dropped out of Berklee—always with the consolation prizes, Tobias. He'd already landed clerking work in a firm by then, and this, as much as anything, had signified our respective trajectories: mine bumbling, meandering, full of missteps. At best, I had occasion to mine a decent tune out of it here and there. Tobias just seized the world and lifted it up. Just dipped his head down and ran through walls. Teresa and I got royalty checks twice a year for our two earlier albums released on friends' labels. It'd be enough for dinner, a nice bottle of wine. We sold some CDs at shows, kept talking about putting them out on vinyl. Tobias had been paying my bills, keeping the lights on while I was in the hospital. That was another way our trajectories differed—he had things to give.

The fan pushed hot air around the room. I didn't like Stefan's casualness in that email. I pictured Teresa and I touring in a rented van, me playing the album with these casts on. Teresa dutifully trying to fill the gaps with her fiddle while I . . . what? Smacked the Yamaha like a performance artist? Played the guitar like a drum?

I shut the laptop, trapped the moth there. Picked up an orange pill bottle from the coffee table, rattled it next to my ear.

• • •

Days uncoiled slow and lazy and hot. Days stacked upon each other, or unspooled like a winding string. I spent a lot of time crying and sweating, or lost in some feathered haze. I grew heavier. My beard grew wild. I taped forks to my casts to eat and when the tape came off and a fork dropped to the floor, I left it there and tilted microwave dinner trays to my mouth, poured congealed turkey giblets and Szechuan chicken into my face like some ruinous king. I coasted on Oxy. I started double-dipping my meds. My casts sometimes itched so bad I jammed coat hangers down into the darkness until I fantasized about blood dripping down my wrists.

Sometimes there might have been knocks on the door, sounds that pulled me from this kind of half-sleep I often found myself in. I'd open the door and the hall would be empty. Other times I just couldn't be bothered. The faintest ghost of pain sent me to my little orange bottles, plunged me again and again into the great soft tide they offered.

• • •

My brother came to take me to my surgery and found me splayed out on the couch. The fan, every time it finished its rotation to the left, went *creeeeeaaaaaaaak*.

"What the hell," Tobias said quietly. I'd forgotten he had a key. He stood in the doorway, surveying the room. "Have you showered? Did an animal die in here?"

With my eyes half-lidded, I made a pained, gloriously slow fart noise with my mouth.

Tobias walked over to me and grabbed a fistful of my shirt, pulled me up like someone lifting a sack of laundry. He smelled like hair gel and Tic Tacs.

"You have surgery today, dude. Have you showered?"

My legs kicked out like a baby deer's. He was insanely strong.

I tried to sound haughty and put out. "Recently, yes."

"How recently?"

I tried to shrug, but it was hard with him holding me up. And I was sleepy.

"How recently, Matt?"

"A day? Yesterday."

"Yeah, right." He set me back down on the couch. "You got refried beans all over your pants there, genius. At least I hope to living Christ that's what it is."

I tried to shrug again, did a little better this time. "It's gravy," I said.

"It's gravy," he repeated. "You look like total shit. It's gravy." He stood there before me, his hands on his hips, and the anger—like he had a clue, like he had a right—cut through the fog in me.

I leaned forward and swung at him, clipped him in the groin. A good, heavy shot with a lot of cast in it. It would hurt my hand later, terribly so, but I felt nothing right then but a rip of savage vindication.

Tobias let out a yelp and sank down next to me with his hands cradling his junk, his lips pulled back in a snarl. I could see the veins bunched in his temples.

"If you don't want help," he gasped, "I won't help you."

"Good," I said. "I don't want help." I leaned back, splayed my casts on each side of the couch like a guy enjoying his day. I watched lines of ants trundle across the coffee table, a picture of industriousness and teamwork.

Tobias bent forward, dry-heaved.

"You've always done this," he said. "You've always just let the world happen to you. You always just take what it hands out."

"Spare me."

"You're letting this thing get the best of you," he said. "You know that, right? Healing is one thing, but this is something else."

I shut my eyes. "You're about to earn another dick punch."

The fan creaked back and forth, pushed our misery around the room.

• • •

I avoided my email like it was radioactive. I put my dead phone in the refrigerator. I wanted no anchor to the outside world. I watched entire seasons of childhood sitcoms in one go, stopping only to check my orange bottles or hobble to the bathroom for grueling, rabbit-small shits. I occasionally picked at the endless stacks of microwave dinners in the freezer. My beard grew ever wilder. My gut bloomed while the rest of me winnowed down, a strange transformation. Days and nights were interchangeable save for the shards of sunlight beneath the pulled shade.

I listened to our demo, those twelve songs, songs that had at times set couples to dancing, set people to lifting their glasses to lamplight in celebration. That some people—scant few, but some—had claimed to be moved by. These things Teresa and I had culled from nothing. I listened, remembered the way my fingers roved the fretwork of my guitar before I'd met Chad Laughlin. Before he'd happened to me.

At some point I took well past the recommended dose of pain meds—I'd been doing that for some time now, but this time it was a lot—and then cut the gauze off my fingers with scissors, removed my splints. Tried to flex the stiffness from them. Tried to make a chord. A, C, E minor. My fingers were like unruly children: They heard my wishes but didn't care.

No, that wasn't it.

They cared but were incapable.

• • •

Teresa came over. It was cloudy, and seemed as if God had stuffed all of the summer's heat into my apartment.

I opened the door to find her in a short sleeve button-up with little unicorns on it, a pair of cut off shorts. Sweat had pasted whorls of hair to her temples. She didn't have her fiddle this time, but she was holding a pint of strawberries and a tub of whip cream. The smells of the hallway crept in—cumin, mold, carpet cleaner. I felt like an animal caught in the spotlight of her gaze.

She gave me a quick once-over. The robe, the stained sweatpants, the armada of flies buzzing the room.

"Did my brother send you here?" I said.

"Hi, Matt," said Teresa. "Jesus, really nice to see you too."

"Hi," I said. I felt a moment's worth of shame and opened the door. Her eyes pinballed around the room, taking it all in.

"I brought a snack," she said, holding up the strawberries. "Do you want them now? Should I put them in the fridge?"

"I'm not really hungry," I said, scratching my beard. "Fridge is good." I exhaled slowly. "Thanks. Thank you."

She padded into the kitchen. I heard the fridge open and then, quite a while later, heard it close again.

When she stepped into the living room again, she put her hands on her hips and stared at me. Those long, tapered fingers that could do a walk like it was something akin to breathing, that could nail the trills or crossings in a song like she was sleepwalking through it. That tattoo on her shoulder of a butterfly, a stick and poke done by her girlfriend when she was twenty, her one year abroad in Ireland. We'd never dated—I was more afraid of her than I'd ever say—but the songs we wrote fit somewhere close enough to that for me.

"So your face is looking better," she offered.

"Is it?"

"Yeah. It's not so swollen. Does it still hurt?"

"Yeah," I said. "It all hurts still."

"Your teeth look good."

"Plates."

This grand distance between us. *You've always just let the world happen to you.*

"Do you want to go for a walk? Get some air?"

"I need to go to the pharmacy, actually," I said.

"Your pills."

"Yeah."

I could see it on her face.

I sat down on the arm of the couch. "So it's kind of a double-teaming, I guess, you and Tobias. An intervention. Maybe you want to lecture me on the addictive nature of pain medications?"

"No."

"The vast moral high ground of the uninjured is what it feels like. This moment, I mean."

"No one's lecturing anyone, Matt."

Teresa had always been better than Tobias at deflecting my arrows, my hurtful little volleys. We'd played music together a long time. She was a better musician than I was, and we both knew it. It afforded her a certain grace.

Maybe, I thought, I just wasn't a very nice person.

Teresa scratched her elbow, shrugged. "I'll walk with you to the pharmacy if you want."

Tobias, he'd always been versed in absolutes: worked insane hours as a clerk, lifted weights, lived religiously by the calendar on his phone, every hour formatted and planned. He believed exclusively in the removal of bad things, and the inclusion of good ones. He'd always been like this, even when we were kids. Precise. His world was carved in black and white. Teresa's was full of music, the lilt of a note, the understanding that you could play something quickly or slowly, inflict upon it either menace or love. Teresa understood nuance. And right then, I couldn't stand either of them. I couldn't stand myself.

"I'll walk with you," I said, like it was some gift.

• • •

Outside, the casts on my arms hung like leaded weights. When they finally opened these wretched things up, the rot on the inside would be enough to rend the world in half. I wore shorts, felt my scalp tighten under the boiling coin of the sun. I cursed my bone-white legs, desperately missed my fedora.

We walked, dodging sun-baked dog turds and stopping to marvel at the dahlias and marigolds on people's lawns that hammered color into our eyes. My face, my arms, my hands, they all ached and pulsed with my heartbeat. Any pain was too much pain, I had come to believe. Sweat darkened my collar, tumbled down the terrible valley of my ass. The pharmacy was still blocks away. The world yawed wide open. Occasional bursts of hot wind scoured the neighborhood, sent the flowers trembling.

Chad Laughlin was the plane overhead. He was the passing car. The joyful drone of a barking dog, a lawnmower.

"I can't go," I said. I bent over, my hands on my knees. "I'm done."

"It's just a little further," Teresa said, kindly.

"It's not cool, Teresa. Don't make me."

"Okay. I'm sorry."

"Jesus."

"Matt." Her voice changed, softened. "Have you checked your email recently?"

"I'm not on the computer much these days," I lied.

I looked up at her face the same moment a hank of hair blew across her eyes. She squinted and tucked it behind her ear. "Stefan," she said, "isn't doing the record anymore. He emailed us."

I stood back up, nodded, stared off at some middle distance.

"It's not like we can tour," she said. "Not right now."

"I get it."

"Maybe when you're better."

"I get it, Teresa."

Her hands on her hips again, her chin trembling. Was she about to cry? I understood. I felt the same way, even. My hands were broken plates. Gun-shy animals. The songs were good, but they were lost now.

"I still think we should put it out," she said. "Like, just online. It's a good album. It's fucking great."

I let out a little laugh. "That's what you came here to say? That we should put the record on the internet? Really, Teresa?"

"You just vanished, Matt. I mean, it's been months. I've tried texting you, calling you. I knock on your door and it's like you could be dead in there. What was I supposed to do?"

"Nothing. You're fine."

"Look," she said. "I'm playing with Tender Scrimshaw now."

An old woman in a golf visor passed by. Her little dog sniffed my ankle in passage. The woman's eyes were cast downward, presuming, I was sure, that we were in some lover's quarrel.

I said, "Tender Scrimshaw? Those people are butchers, Teresa. They cover 'Hot For Teacher,' are you kidding me? They're a bar band!"

"Bills are bills," she said quietly. Her eyes were hard, crystalline. "Not everyone has a rich brother, you know?"

I raised my arms up like bird wings. Like some extinct species, relegated to running on land. A flightless, pill-popping bird, heartbroken and shitty and afraid. "He broke my fucking arms!" I crowed. "I tried to stop a guy from hurting someone and he broke my arms!"

"It's true," she said. I dropped my arms and Teresa touched my cast and then let her hand fall back to her side. "And what happened after that?"

"Then I focused on healing," I said, and Teresa laughed. "Come on," she said.

"Fuck off," I said. "Have fun playing Smashmouth to a bunch of frat boys, Teresa."

"Matt—"

"I've got to go," I said, and stormed off as quickly as I could, which wasn't terribly fast. I waited to hear if she'd call out for me, but she didn't. I walked toward the pharmacy until the panic finally widened inside me—Chad Laughlin with his red brick-like face, his yellow eyes, how he could come out of that door, or that one, or that one there—and then I turned around and went home.

• • •

Oh, the bitter morass! The lovely alchemy of self-flagellation and self-pity. It was glorious but brief: need overrode all. I'd grown used to double and triple-dipping my pills, and I'd finally exhausted the supply. I called a rideshare to take me to the pharmacy. The driver looked like he was in middle school. He parted his hair in the middle and called me "chief," and we listened to Jefferson Starship on the radio and I wondered if maybe I was going mad, just a little bit. I could feel a sheen of oily sweat at my hairline.

"Looks like you're in a bad way there, chief," the driver said, glancing at me in the rearview mirror.

I grunted, watched as the route on his dash-mounted phone slowly diminished.

"You got someone to wipe your ass for you, a setup like that? Both your arms broke?"

I caught his eyes in the mirror. They were guileless, unafraid; this was the youth of today, or perhaps just the impetuousness of this particular mustachioed young man. "What did you say to me?"

We pulled up to the curb and the driver slung an arm over the seat, looked back at me. "I knew this kid in high school, right? Foreign exchange student. Italian, I think. Kind of an asshole, really. He tried to jump over a tennis net after a match once, got his foot caught. Broke both his arms. He had casts like yours, big ones like that. His host mom had to wipe his ass for him for the rest of his stay. For months! You, chief, smell like hell. Like, monumentally unwashed. You smell like a long-lost baby diaper tucked behind a couch and forgotten." He scratched his nose. "I understand me telling you this probably means a one-star rating kind of situation, which I'm okay with."

"How old are you?"

Jefferson Starship ended and, no kidding, Tender Scrimshaw's revved up, idiotic version of "Sally MacLennane" began playing over the speakers. Atonal, exuberant, the fiddle sounding as if it were hurling joyous blood everywhere. I thought of Teresa doing that and felt like I'd been stabbed in the heart.

"Old enough," the driver said, "to know that you're not even trying to get from Point A to Point B. You seem pretty stuck to me."

I opened my mouth to say something more—what?—but the driver shook his head, ran a finger across the fuzz of his mustache as if he were zipping his lips shut. Then he told me to quit stinking his ride up and bid me good day.

• • •

I filled my prescription and hobbled home. I resisted the urge to spin the cap on the orange bottle right there beyond the pneumatic doors of the pharmacy, there in the parking lot strewn with bedraggled housewives and men feverish in their can-counting. Instead I walked home, through the aches, through the stilled day. I thought about piano trills, chord progressions on the guitar, things I'd hardly considered in months. I thought about the scathing email I would write to the rideshare customer service people. All the while Chad Laughlin lived on my shoulder, galloped his way through the meat between my ears.

What'd the child-driver meant that I wasn't trying to get from Point A to Point B? There seemed to be a grand surplus of people who hadn't been broken in half by a meth-seized UFC fighter, people who were suddenly happy to tell me how to live my life.

By the time I made it back to my apartment, I was once again puffed up with righteousness and grandiosity.

I bounced a few Oxys in my palm, thought of that ocean they offered, that deep fog. It would be so easy to sink back into the folds of the couch, lay upon its beautiful stinking skin. Tender Scrimshaw, Stefan, Teresa, my brother—who gave a shit? I could drift out to sea, lulled to thoughtlessness, enveloped in a sitcom's canned laughter. I'd earned it. Pain—or even the ghost of pain—could be decimated.

I cursed, dropped a single pill into my mouth, spun the cap back on as if the plastic were hot.

Hobbling to the bathroom—which had become a horror show in its own right—I peeled off my clothes, stiff as animal pelts by then. Rubberbanding bread bags to my useless arms, I stepped under steaming hot water, my body splayed out like a half-assed crucifixion.

Ready for one single thing to perhaps be different.

• • •

Unsurprisingly, I stepped out unbaptized. Nude and furred and waterlogged, I turned off the spigot and heard a knocking on the front door.

"Matt, it's me," Tobias called out. "Open up."

I stepped out of the bathroom with a towel around my waist. "I just got out of the shower."

"That's good, at least."

"Bite me."

"Seriously though, open up. I've got a key, remember?"

I opened the front door. Tobias was wearing his work clothes—dress shirt, maroon tie, Oxfords, an earpiece. "I tried calling you. Get dressed." He walked in, started picking up clothes and tossing them at me.

"Where are we going? I don't know if I want to go anywhere." I picked up the clothes and padded into my bedroom, one hand around my towel. "I'm kind of done with doing stuff for the rest of the day, honestly."

"I found him," Tobias said.

"Who?"

Tobias looked disappointed. "Who the hell do you think, dude?"

• • •

We walked into an alley behind a strip mall. My brother had zip-tied Chad Laughlin to the leg of a dumpster next to the back door of a Noodlepalooza. Laughlin sat cross-legged in the alley's filth. He was smoking a cigarette and raised his head when we rounded the corner. He looked emaciated, carved-out. That live-wire electricity in him was gone. I knew this look, too. This was a guy on the ragged end of a dope run, a man who'd been up for days. It galvanized me; Laughlin had run slipshod through my every waking moment since the assault, and he was reduced to a stick-man now, sagging and small.

"I saw him looking through the garbage out front on my lunch break and grabbed him. Tied him up back here."

"What? With zipties?"

"Yeah!"

"Why do you have zipties on you, Tobias?"

Tobias looked disappointed again. "In case I came across this asshole right here!"

"You've been carrying around zipties since I was in the hospital?"

"Yeah," he said. "You're my brother."

"Jesus."

"Aren't you stoked? We found him. I'm gonna let you beat his ass for exactly one minute and then I'm calling the cops." He said to Chad Laughlin, "We call that justice, friendo."

"I can't believe you work in a law firm," I said. "They'll disbar you for this."

"I don't have a law degree, Matt, and no one's disbarring anybody."

"I'm not beating him up."

My brother stepped so close to me I could see the pores in his chin. "Look what he did to you," he hissed.

"It's gross. I can't beat up a guy tied to a dumpster."

"Then I'll untie him."

"No," I said. "Look at him. He's a scarecrow. He's sick, man."

"Exactly," said Tobias.

"I've never hit anyone in my life."

"Today is a good day to start."

"You guys know I can hear you, right?" said Laughlin. Even his voice seemed diminished, smaller. He picked a scrap of tobacco from his tongue with his cigarette still in his mouth.

My brother said, "He almost killed you, Matt." He turned to Laughlin again. "You almost killed him."

"Wasn't me," he said.

"Bullshit."

"Must've been some other guy."

"You jumped on his arms."

And then it was like a slow-motion wreck, the way Laughlin's face crumpled, the way recognition unspooled in ugly waves across his eyes, his mouth. "I don't really remember it," he said, his voice trembling. "I'm sorry, I don't really remember that. Nothing along those lines." And then he kept cry-talking about how sorry he was, his head dipping down toward his lap. I saw a long, infected scratch snarling across the top of his head.

"You're a shitty liar," Tobias said.

The back door of Noodlepalooza opened up, and a teenage girl wearing a hat that made it look like she had really long hair made of noodles peered out of the door and just stared at us for a second. "What's all this about?"

"Nothing," my brother said. "Don't worry about it."

"Is that guy tied to our dumpster?"

"It's a citizen's arrest type of deal," said Tobias.

Laughlin sniffled, raised his red face and pointed at my brother. "This gym candy motherfucker handcuffed me," he gasped.

"Hey," Tobias said, taking a step forward. "I don't juice. You're the steroid user, not me."

Laughlin ran his free hand across his nose and laughed. "I know a stacker when I see one. You juice."

My brother looked at me and smiled. "If you don't kick his ass, I'm going to."

"Well, whatever, I'm calling the cops," the Noodlepalooza girl said.

"Do that," I said. I hobbled over to the dirty brick wall beside Laughlin and slowly slid down until I was sitting next to him. It would not be easy to get back up. The alley was hot and shadow-dusted, smelled of garbage juice and whatever gastronomical travesties Noodlepalooza was committing.

I sat at this crossroads, this understanding dawning in me. "Why'd you hit that lady?" I said quietly.

The look Laughlin gave me was sly, suspicious, and guilty all at once. "Who?"

"Blonde woman, carrying bags with you. You hit her."

He spent some time looking down at his lap again. His cigarette was a tiny nub by then, like an extra tooth. "Yeah," he said, quietly. "Denise, you mean."

"So why?"

"Because he's a piece of shit," said my brother.

I looked up. "Can you go wait for the cops out front so they don't shoot us when they come back here? That'd be great, thank you."

Laughlin and I watched him walk around the corner. This whole thing was an unexpected act from my brother—an act jagged and strange and very unlike him, but crafted from his love for me, however misshapen and wrong the idea itself was. Laughlin pitched his cigarette away. "I don't think he really juices. Dudes just get super pissed when you say that stuff."

"You wrecked my life," I said.

He looked me over; the begrimed casts, my splinted fingers poking out. The dented aspect to the right side of my face. "I did all that?"

I nodded.

"I must've been high," he said.

"Yeah."

For a moment it looked his face would crumple again but then he sniffed and ran the back of his hand over his nose. "I got a problem," he said, sounding almost prideful.

"What's that?" I said, though of course I knew.

"You ever do dope?" Laughlin asked me.

"Kind of," I said. "I'm kind of doing it now."

"Is it a problem for you?"

"Maybe," I said. "I feel like I'm right on the cusp of it being a problem, actually."

"Got any on you," he asked, and laughed a brittle, fake laugh. We both knew he wasn't really kidding. He wiped his pant leg like he was trying to get a stain out.

We sat there. I'd thought so much of what I would do if I ever saw him again, and there we were and it was nothing like any scenario I'd ever imagined. I wondered if this was one of those moments I would always want to do over. We listened to sirens that eventually grew louder. I thought of my sizable pill collection at home, and the songs these healing fingers might eventually make, and the way that I would need to craft other chords if I wanted to move forward. Simpler ones. It would be a kind of starting over. I would need to sing completely different songs. I would need to play the piano like a club. I'd need to use the guitar like a bludgeon. The finesse had been shattered out of me. I'd need to find a new way.

If I still wanted to play, that is. If it still mattered to me.

And so I started singing then, just this song I made up, trying something new, and I could see the chords in my mind, could hear the way they'd play behind me. The melody was like a brick through a window, this time, instead of a winding river.

Laughlin scratched his thin beard and looked annoyed. He was not a fan. The police were coming, after all, and in the grand scheme of things his life was soon to become much more difficult than mine. But I'd earned this song, I figured, and so I kept at it, just these words coming out of me, this melody butting up against the brick walls. The words just kind of roiled out, and I have to say, for a brand-new song I was just making up on the spot, it wasn't too bad.

BRAD BENSKE AND THE HAND OF LIGHT

Splay-legged in my recliner, I've just returned from putting another note under Marcus's door *(In the next life your penis shall be multipronged, insectile, hot and bristling with pustules, gloriously prone to infection)* when someone knocks on my door and I choke back a cry, startled. It's midafternoon and my social life, never strident to begin with, has atrophied in recent months. Who could possibly be knocking? Reluctantly, I rise from my recliner and pull on my robe and, realizing at that moment that it might actually *be* Marcus, a Marcus angry about the insectile penis-note, and all the other notes, I open the door with a mad flourish, trying to be as intimidating as possible.

The day seems obscenely sunny, garishly so. I wince and blink. The man in the doorway is a stranger, and he takes a step back when he sees me. He's wearing some kind of uniform—a blue shirt with a nametag and a pair of blue shorts. A little clipboard.

"Brad? Brad Benske?"

"Yes," I say. It comes out tremulously; for a moment even I feel unsure. Is this who I am? And then, more confidently, "Yes."

The man marks something off on his clipboard and flicks his thumb against one of his nostrils and says, "Brad, hey, what's up. I'm with the water bureau."

"The what?"

He says, "Water bureau. Your water?"

"Oh."

"You're late with your payment."

"Am I?"

"Really late," he says, and consults his clipboard. "Couple months late. As in, if you can't pay it by the end of day today, we have to shut it off."

"The water?"

He seems to see me for the first time then—the robe, the dishevelment, the haphazard leaning mess of the inside of the house that he can spy through the open doorway. I have a zit on my cheek that has over recent days gotten woefully infected and is now nearly the size of a ping-pong ball. Fifty-one years old and getting zits, if you can believe it. *I need to drink more water,* I think, and then have a moment of shock as I realize the water guy is right here in front of me. It's like some kind of weak serendipity, some petulant magic.

"Are you okay?"

"Oh, I'm fine," I say.

The nametag above his pocket says *Cameron*, and he looks like a Cameron. A beefy young man with big calves and a certain dumb purity, someone who did keg stands in college and can differentiate between different types of vape oil. A man who wears a hemp bracelet and sleeps on a futon, I decide, a man who sniff-tests his socks. Cameron peers into the dank chamber of my little house and his nose wrinkles. I step out onto the porch and shut the door behind me.

"Oh man, my grandma got shingles," Cameron says, pointing a blunt finger at my face. "She was only sixty-two. It messed her *up*."

"This is just a zit."

"Oh. Sorry."

The world beyond my yard writhes with life; a little boy wheels by on his bike, leaves on the trees tremble and sway, and I can hear the bass-heavy thump of music strobing through the window of a passing car. The air is rich with the smell of cut grass. And everything trills a memory. Emma has been gone for nine months now. Nine months! I spend a moment hoping Marcus's penis becomes riddled with pustules in *this* life, and draft an internal note saying such.

Cameron clears his throat.

"My checkbook's inside," I say. "How much is it?"

He gives me a number. It seems a reasonable enough amount if I haven't paid in months—Emma handled the bills, and it's yet another instance where I have lagged, where I am lost without her—but he sounds unhappy about it.

"It's okay," I say. "You're just doing your job."

"I mean, I'm in a band," Cameron says. "I do community theater. You know? There's more to me than just *this.*" He sweeps a hand along his outfit, his clipboard.

"Of course there is," I say. I walk inside and eventually find my checkbook beside an old sandwich on the floor that's furred in ants. I write the check and step outside and kind of shake the ants off and hand it to Cameron, and his blue eyes as he watches this are rife with something like pity. "I hope you feel better soon," he says quietly, and it's clear he's not talking about my goiter.

• • •

Melinda says, "So you're still leaving him notes." She lights a menthol and blows the smoke up to the ceiling.

"No," I say.

She laughs outright and flips me off. "Oh my God, you're such a liar. Such a *bad* liar, too."

"I left one today," I confess. *May maggots tumble from thy dong,* it read, and then it had a little doodle of that, a little picture.

Melinda winces. "Honey, why his penis, though? Why talk about his penis?" She adjusts her headband.

"I don't always."

"Well, when you tell me about it, the notes are always penis-related."

"I'm trying to keep it funny. Light. Less worrisome than actual threats."

"Maggots from his dong, though? That sounds like an actual threat to me."

"It's medical," I say.

It had seemed a simple message, one suffused with appropriate dread and then buoyed a little by the silly drawing. I wonder for a moment if I have in fact turned some corner, gone some further distance than I intended. One I won't be able to come back from. Maybe I have crossed some line.

"You know it's illegal, right?" says Melinda. "It's gotta be harassment or something. Menacing. You better hope you don't get caught."

"I won't get caught. Marcus is too enmeshed in his bullshit."

"If he installs one of those cameras above his door. You're done."

"Look," I say, "can you just give me a reading? Please?"

Melinda, when she's working, goes by Madame Ouellette. She has a palm reading and tarot practice out on the jagged stretch of 82nd Avenue, in a weird mobile home kind of thing that rests in an otherwise empty parking lot. She's decked the place out in tapestries and unicorn sculptures and salt candles and incense; the atmosphere goes a fair way toward canceling out the brazen drug deals out front, the endless traffic, the shirtless guy screaming about aliens in his teeth at the Wendy's across the street. Melinda and I slept together once in college, badly, and have ever since been continually thankful of the friendship that has sprung from it. Our shared history buoys us. Emma, at best, had tolerated Melinda during our marriage. Felt threatened by her. Which always surprised me, as she seemed otherwise so sure of everything. "Why can't you just scratch your balls and yell about football with some guy from work? Drink beer and talk about cars?" she'd say, a rare instance where I saw the underpinnings of her insecurity. Melinda gives me readings for free now, and I ask her where Emma is, where they've sent her. If she's happy, if she's safe where she is. This, and bothering Marcus are as close to penance and relief as I get. Madam Ouellette offers me her visions and I imagine that they're true. Half the time it seems like Melinda's just trying to come up with the most outlandish shit she can, and I'm grateful for it. It almost assuredly beats the true narrative.

She makes me a cup of tea as we chat some more. I drink the tea and tell Melinda the story about our wedding day and how Emma had spilled a cup of coffee down the front of her dress, the same dress her mother had worn to her wedding, and had had to wear a last minute back-up dress that showed way more cleavage then she intended. It is a well-worn story; Melinda has heard it a million times. Hell, she was at our wedding, watched the entire event take place. But it's part of the process of the reading, Melinda says. And when I'm done with the tea, she has me upend the cup on a plastic slip mat and we talk for a moment about my hopes with this, what it is I want to get from this. I say something, some bland proclamation. *I want to feel close to her,* I think. *I want to believe that what you're saying is really her life.* We've done this perhaps a dozen times since Emma left me to join the Hand of Light. This is one of the only things I do anymore.

Melinda really gets into character, adjusting her jeweled headband, her hands taking on these exaggerated movements as she tries to withdraw the "intentionality" from the leaves. Tea has started to bead out from beneath the rim of the cup. Eventually she lifts it and frowns at the chiaroscuro of dark leaves on the plastic mat.

She talks, fully Madam Ouellette now. Her voice is clipped, more precise, colder.

She tells me that Emma is in a carwash in Biloxi, Mississippi.

"She's working in a carwash? In Mississippi?"

"No, no. She's *in* a carwash. In a car. Someone's yelling about atonement. Maybe it's the radio. There's a baby in the backseat, but it's not hers. The sudsy cleaning things slap against the window. It's a kind of transformation for her."

"You're so full of shit," I say, grinning. I can't help myself. I'm almost happy.

"She got a haircut. She's wearing sunglasses in the carwash. It's dark."

"Oh, yeah? Did they shave her head? Is she wearing a potato sack, Melinda? Are there snacks?" Part of me relishes these fantasies she makes up. I simultaneously wish they were true and only feel safe when I'm mocking them. I've had a private investigator on the payroll since she's been gone, but he's come up with nothing. He talks to me like I'm an aggrieved husband, speaks respectfully, and part of me hates the guy for it.

Of the two people in the world who know what an utter fuckup I am, one has absconded with the Hand of Light, and the other one's looking at me right now, waving her palm over a bunch of wet tea leaves, offering at least some minute solace.

• • •

The guy from the water bureau is sitting on my front stoop when I come home. He's playing a game on his phone and wearing jeans and a T-shirt. A baseball hat. He's one of those people who even if they shave in the morning they still have stubble by the end of the workday.

He smiles when he sees me and puts his phone away. "Do you remember me?" he says.

"I do," I say. "I don't think my check bounced, did it?"

"I was wondering if you wanted to go see a band play, actually."

I look at him. "You do this with all your customers?"

"No."

I think about the inside of my house. I touch my goiter lightly, hardly aware I'm doing so. "What band is it?"

He says something I don't understand, rich with vowels.

"It's a Swedish black metal band," he says. "But they're not racist."

"Is that a thing? Racist black metal?"

He shrugs. "Unfortunately, yes."

I am feeling expansive: I've showered today. I've paid a bill. I petitioned the unknown via Madam Ouellette and thusly got to hear how Emma's doing, even if Melinda's just making it up. (I know she's making it up.) It's been a good day. I haven't had many good days. My recliner is like a ship marooned amid the wreckage of my life.

The show is at a bar across town. Cameron pays. I feel underdressed and old: Denim and leather abound, and nearly everyone is wearing a black shirt with a band logo that is pointy and indecipherable, barbed wire brought to heaving life. I buy drinks from a solemn bartender with *Cut Here* written on his throat and by the time the band starts, I'm intoxicated and the music is so loud I can feel my ribs vibrate. I haven't drunk in a long time. Cameron is headbanging beside me, and someone is pushing against me, and my cocktail, somewhat expensive, is sloshing down my shirt. The music is a sea to get lost in. It's like a world being born. The singer's face is painted in white greasepaint and he points at us and yowls and we scream back in response. I yell until something in my throat threatens to crack, and still I can't hear myself. It's lovely, really. It's a lovely way to get lost.

After the band stops, Cameron and I drink some more, and he buys a shirt with the band's barbed indecipherable logo on it. There's a picture of a wolf's severed head beneath the logo, and he makes a grand gesture of gifting it to me. I put it on right there over my other shirt.

By now the crowd has thinned, everyone pressing themselves into booths or going out onto the patio to smoke cigarettes and yell at each other. I lift my cocktail—something called a "Norwegian Fuck Cloud" that annoyed the already annoyed bartender when I asked for it—and take a sip and bellow over the jukebox, "My wife left me! For a cult! Nine months ago!"

Cameron frowns and nods. He's put his baseball hat on backward at some point. "That's intense!" he yells.

"I sold our house and moved into a smaller house. I've been living off the profits. Quit my job at the firm I've been at for twelve years. I just manage my investments online and sit around and weep. I've got ants! Ants everywhere!"

"Damn, dude!"

"My best friend pretends to be a psychic and gives me updates on her! Emma— that's my wife—she's always doing mundane stuff! Washing dishes, jogging! Today she was in a carwash!"

"What's the cult?"

"What?"

"I said what's the cult?"

"The Hand of Light!"

"Haven't heard of it!"

I look at him. "Can I tell you a secret?"

Cameron nods, and I go to take a sip of my Norwegian Fuck Cloud and accidentally stab my goiter with the tip of the little black umbrella in my glass. I shriek with the bright white pain of it.

● ● ●

Marcus lives in a duplex on the other side of town. Cameron drives his Corolla with a deep and obvious concentration, his tongue like some minute creature testing the air. We are listening to Sublime—I had to ask Cameron the name— and he is driving very slowly and carefully.

I tell Cameron about Marcus, Emma's brother, and how he was the first to introduce her to the Hand of Light. How she was worried about him and accompanied him to a meeting only as a way of protecting him. Of sussing it out. How she came back from this first meeting still scoffing, but in retrospect I should have seen it—that glimmer of interest, hidden and tucked away. I *know* her, I should have seen it. That fecund possibility of *something more* in her eyes.

Marcus became enmeshed within the Hand of Light and I tried talking to her about it, making sure she was okay. She'd insisted she was. There was an age gap between Emma and I, and we lived with comfortable expanses of silence between us. She had her friends and her brother. I had Melinda and the firm. It was perhaps unconventional, but it worked for us.

But when I spoke to her of her brother, she began winnowing her way onto other subjects. Became evasive. Began coming home late. I started to suspect she was having an affair. I'm not proud of it. Emma is fourteen years younger than I am, and beautiful. My own insecurities took root and bloomed.

At my lowest point, I hired the private investigator, who tailed her to a church in a strip mall—one only slightly more preserved than Melinda's trailer. A dozen pews, stained carpet. A tanning salon next door. He met me for coffee a few days later, where he showed me grim digital photos of Emma at prayer among a scattering of others, her arms raised in a rapture I'd never seen at our most intimate moments. And here was one of her in supplication at the foot of a plastic religious figure, shrouded and forlorn, that looked like little more than a lawn ornament. And here was one of Emma and three other women cutting their palms with a blade and letting the blood (oh, jet black in the photos) drip into a silver bowl. I was mortified.

I waited three days before I asked her about her bandaged hand. She said she'd cut it on a glass that had fallen in the sink. The lie came so fluid, sounded so convincing, I almost wanted to consult the photos again; surely it was someone else, some other blonde woman who was losing weight and had the crazed light of an unswayable piety in her eyes.

I called her a liar. I called her a great number of other things. I wept and quailed and raged, terrified that she was being swept up in some current. She wept too, and said that I didn't understand. That there was a solace she couldn't find elsewhere. This hurt me, her husband, and led me to say more things to her that haunt me now. I left, slammed the front door hard enough that a print fell from the wall, the glass front shattering. I slept in a hotel.

The next day there was a note on our bed. *Gone off, finding what I need. I'll be back if that's what's right.* Her initials. Her initials!

Taillights flash in front of us and Cameron brakes hard. My hands fly onto the dash. "The part I don't get," he says, "is why you leave notes about his dong and stuff."

"What?"

"It seems weird, man. She leaves you and you harass her brother? He's your brother-in-law, right? You threaten his penis because your wife joined some cult?"

"I'm not *threatening* his penis," I say. "I'm threatening *him*. But *obtusely*. So he doesn't *know*."

"That doesn't make any sense."

"He's the one who got her into it. This stupid fucking cult. Do you know what the Hand of Light *is*? What they believe in?"

"No."

I spit, "They do *blood rituals*, Cameron. *Okay*? So spare me your sanctimony."

"Okay. Jeez."

"Thank you. Turn left here."

Marcus's duplex is dark. I root through Cameron's glove box and hand him a ballpoint pen and a scrap of paper.

"Dude, I don't know. I don't think so."

"Come on," I say. "It'll really throw him if it's in different handwriting."

"Nothing about his penis."

"Fine," I say, and dictate another note.

"That seems pretty harsh," he says, but he writes it.

"It's an inside joke," I lie. "It doesn't mean what you think it means." I take the note and creep across the street and slide it under Marcus's front door.

When Cameron drops me off at my house, I wave goodbye. My nodule, speared from the cocktail umbrella and still weeping blood, pulses with my heartbeat. I can't tell if Cameron waves back.

• • •

I tell Melinda about Cameron and the Swedish non-racist black metal band, and she's smiling at me like I've turned over a new leaf. Here I am, out in the world! Showering, making friends, drinking fancy drinks with ridiculous names. I'm like a real person again, and not a stumbling automaton that walks from room to room in his bathrobe, sporadically farting and crying and brushing ants off my cereal as I lament the abject dismantlement of my marriage. Things are happening!

"That's awesome," Melinda says, dusting the display rack of tarot cards with one of those feather duster things. Her cigarette wags in her mouth as she speaks. "Look at you, man." There's a fellow dressed as the Statue of Liberty working on the other side of 82nd, promoting some tax place, and he's really spinning his sign and doing tricks with it. We catch flashes of his hairy legs under his tunic as he whirls around. We watch him for a minute. He's good. It feels nice to watch someone be good at something.

Then I tell Melinda about the note I had Cameron write, the one I put under

Marcus's door *(FYI: The neighbors can hear you when you cry, you sad little fuck)* and the brightness in her eyes goes out like I threw a bucket of water on a fire.

"Oh, Brad."

"I have no remorse," I say, watching the man wave and twirl his sign, and I can't look at her. My voice warbles so badly that it's obvious to both of us that I'm lying, lying, lying.

• • •

Another lawyer in my firm was almost up to bat once during a softball game when he had these chest pains. Years ago, this was. He'd been feeling unwell for a few days, but this day was particularly bad, and the pain in his chest reached an apex right before he was supposed to go up to the plate. He told his friend, the catcher, he needed to go to the hospital. This is a true story.

"Yeah, right," the friend said, and then the guy, the lawyer at my firm, actually dropped to his knees, the pain was so bad. So the catcher realized he wasn't kidding, and he drove him to the ER, where they sat for a little bit in the waiting room before the man's chest was x-rayed. And when the x-ray came back it showed that pretty much his whole body was absolutely riddled with tumors. Just all up and down his chest and groin. The cancer had started in his testicles and spread.

Long story short, he went on chemo for a long time, and it brutalized him, and he lost a testicle, but he beat it. He still works at the firm, actually.

So that evening I'm just looking in the mirror at this bulbous thing on my face, how the skin's grown shiny and taut around it. I'm thinking about Emma and wondering how you define an actual beginning of something. How you trace the exact moment that it starts.

Or, in my case, the exact moment that you started *losing* something.

• • •

My phone rings later that night. I'm in my recliner, willing myself to either masturbate or call the private detective for a progress report. Each seems tiresome and insurmountable. It's an unlisted number.

"Hello?" I say.

"It's Cameron," says Cameron.

"Hey. How'd you get my number?"

"You gave me your card."

"My business card?"

"Yeah. At the show. You wrote your cell number on the back."

"Oh."

"You don't remember?"

"Not really," I say.

"Yeah, you had a lot of fancy drinks for sure. Listen, Brad, I want to let you know that I just don't feel good about what we did. Leaving that note like that. I feel really bad about it."

"It's fine."

"No, it's not. It's not nice."

"He deserves it," I say.

"I think we should tell him."

I sit upright. The recliner squeals in protest. "What are you talking about?"

"I think we should tell him that it was us. I think you should talk to him. I can come pick you up."

"No. Not a chance. No."

"I think it would be a good—"

I'm officially on sabbatical from the firm—the senior partners have been very gracious in that regard—and it's been nine months since I've drafted an arbitration agreement or a c & d letter or stood before a judge. But twenty-five years of practice is right there, and I let Cameron have it. I am positively stentorian in my volume and dizzying in my vocabulary. I'm listing the myriad ways in which pursuing this line of action is profoundly ill-advised, and I make it clear that I'm prepared to bury him under a mountain of pure unbridled motherfucking will if necessary.

He waits me out. I'm so furious that I'm actually panting when he clears his throat and says, "Brad, it's just that—what if she isn't coming back?"

I hang up.

I call the private detective and hurl invectives and ridicule his parents and threaten any number of lawsuits, and then I triple his daily pay and beg more from him.

• • •

Emma was hired as a record clerk. That's how we met. I was moored in a kind of limbo at the time, stuck as a junior partner, repeatedly watching younger hires land clients that I felt should've been mine. The firm was a place that rewarded ambition and I was feverish with ambition, and so this sense of being moored in one place while others rose to prominence, it angered me. I saw no way to improve things. The very people who I needed to petition were the ones who were rewarding these other lawyers. I lived in a large, mostly empty home that I hardly ever spent time in. I was rude to wait staff and customer service representatives and openly contemptuous of the clerks and paralegals who I worked with. I did not see at the time that my unmet ambition had turned into anger and resentment, which in return festered into more unmet ambition. I was poisoned like that. I was sick with it and didn't know. I had become atrophied and small.

I met Emma when someone had misfiled some court documents that I needed for a case. It wasn't her fault, it wasn't my fault, but at that time I was a man who luxuriated in my anger, who dipped my heart in the smooth, ugly salve of it. That day, I started dressing her down for her incompetence, right there at her desk, among her coworkers, and she looked confused and hurt for only a moment and then her face set into a certain hardness and she shook her head once and said, "Nope. No. Stop."

And I did stop. Who wouldn't have stopped? She was thirty-one at the time, and beautiful, and afraid of me, and entirely unwilling to accept the way I was treating her.

"Excuse me?" I said.

She said, "I will be happy to help you find these summaries, Mr. Benske. I'm sorry that they've been misplaced. But it's not my fault, and I'm just not going to be spoken to that way. I'm just not."

And I stood there before her and was galvanized. There's no other word for it. I saw that she was right, and I saw how much my anger had leached into me, had sickened me, slowly, like the guy in Mergers & Acquisitions with his chest pains. I apologized profusely and told her she was right, and that it wouldn't happen again. And it began some change inside me. And it was only two years later, when I saw her and a friend having a drink in a bar, that I spoke to her outside of work. Two years! And I thanked her again because of what she'd said to me before, and of course she remembered it, and I told her how right she'd been and we talked some more and the friend graciously went home, and Emma and I shared a very chaste kiss at the end of the night and she took a cab home and I took a cab home and I marveled the entire way about how self-assured she seemed, how rooted in herself, and anchored, and I asked her out to dinner the next day, and two years after *that* we were married, and I keep coming back to how things begin, those interminable, indefinable beginnings, because how does the woman who says *I'm not going to be spoken to that way* become the woman who leaves a note that says *Gone off, finding what I need. I'll be back if that's what's right?* How does that happen?

• • •

Melinda's eyeballing my goiter over her crystal ball.

"You're not even paying attention," I say.

"Hon, it's getting really bad. Does it hurt?"

"It's a zit."

"I don't think that's a zit. You need to go to the doctor."

"Just tell me how she's doing."

She sighs and adjusts her headband and caresses the small glass globe in front of her with just the tips of her fingers. She's trying hard to get into character, even as the guy in the Wendy's parking lot thunders his numerous dissatisfactions with invasive spy satellites and the National Security Agency.

"Okay," she says. "Emma's swimming in a swimming pool, Brad, and the water is really blue. But there's all this light reflecting off the water, too. Spears of light. She's wearing a black one-piece bathing suit and her hair is turning just a little green from the chlorine. She's been in the water a lot lately." She clears her throat. "And, oh, there's a man with a mustache on a deck chair. He's reading a book." Her eyes are squeezed shut.

I trace the growth on my face while she talks. If I hold my breath, I can feel it begin to pulse in time with my heartbeat. It does hurt. It's hurt for a long time.

The private investigator emailed me this morning.

"When she rises from the swimming pool, she does it in one smooth, languid motion. She—"

I'm suddenly furious at Melinda, at her ridiculous stories. At handing me these pedestrian fantasies that everything's fine, that Emma is whole and safe. And now she's introducing this *man?* "Where's the baby?" I say, my voice sharp.

Melinda opens her eyes. "What?"

"I said where's the baby, Melinda? Last time there was a baby, and a carwash, and all that shit. Now she's what, a mermaid? Swimming in a swimming pool?"

"Brad."

"She's fucking him, right? That's what you're implying? She's fucking this dude with the mustache? She's moved on to other things by now? I've lost her. That's what you're saying, right?"

Melinda stands up and I can already see the glittering of tears in her eyes and it's like some depthless hole has opened up beneath me and I'm falling, while also knowing that this hole is so deep and I'll be falling for a long time.

"Get out," she says. "You think I'm doing this for *me?*"

"I'm sorry."

She chops a hand through the air. "Get out of here."

Outside, the world is as thriving and mad as ever. Dirt and blacktop and exhaust, a thousand uncaring, beautiful colors flung across the day.

• • •

I drive aimlessly and then head home because there's nowhere else to go. I park in the driveway and see that Cameron is standing on my porch again. He's in a dark suit and his hair is combed back.

"Go away," I say wearily as I trod up my steps.

He holds out an envelope. "Here's your money."

"What?"

"Your water bill money." He smiles a little sadly. "I'm not really with the water bureau."

He is clear-eyed, clean-shaven. He even stands differently.

I get it. "Community theater, right? You're an actor."

Cameron nods.

"You're with the Hand of Light," I say.

He nods again, puts his hands in his pockets. "She's in Memphis, Bradley."

"I know," I say.

He offers me the dignity of being surprised. "You do?"

"I hired a private detective. Months ago. He finally found them, it just took a while."

He nods and looks down, scuffs the porch with the toe of his shoe. "She doesn't want to see you, but she wanted me to relay a message. A few messages."

I'm whole, I tell myself. I'll be whole after this man walks off my porch. I'll be whole after he says what he says. I'll still be as whole and ruined and piecemeal, as willing to be in love with her when he leaves.

"She wants you to stop leaving Marcus notes."

"Fine."

"Marcus didn't stay with the group very long. He wants nothing to do with us. If you'd actually talked to him, you'd know that."

"I'm sorry."

"It's not me you should be apologizing to," Cameron says, and it's so sanctimonious, and I feel that familiar feather-stir of anger. That anger that I wish, maybe more than anything else, that I could just spit out like a seed. That I could just be free of.

I tell him I'll apologize to Marcus.

"She wants you to be kind to Melinda. She says your world is pretty small and you should hold tight to it."

"I will," I say, thinking of the work that will require, ashamed of myself.

"And she's asking you to wait."

I stare at him; it's like he's telling me the band name again. Like he's speaking some other language.

He says, "She's only asking. She understands you're not obligated."

"Obligated?" I say. "She used that term? It doesn't sound like her."

Cameron, a messenger relaying a message, is afforded the luxury of just shrugging.

And I wish this was the part where my goiter broke open in a wash of blood and all the illness poured out of me and I was whole and good and unblemished. Or where I put Cameron in a severe, uncompromising headlock and walked him to Tennessee and used him as a human shield so I could see my wife and recount to her the grand litany of things I had undoubtedly discovered about myself on the journey. Or where something else happened so that I did not feel so adrift and scared and uncertain. But none of that happened: I was still the same person. Cameron and I shook hands and he walked around the corner and I was alone. I went inside my house and took a broom from my closet and went out and swept my porch steps and my sidewalk free of leaves. Maybe eventually I would work on the inside of the place. But when I was out there a neighbor boy rode by on his bicycle and he was carrying a little toy gun in one fist and I pretended like he'd shot me, like he'd wounded me, perhaps mortally, my hand to my chest, and he rode away, his head swiveling so he could stay with me even as he pedaled and laughed, and oh just the sound of it, that laughter, I have to tell you it was really, really something.

ACKNOWLEDGMENTS

A tip of a giant hat to the editors that grabbed these stories up. Also, a huge thanks to the writers groups I've belonged to over the years, SSC and, most recently, TUSC: James Mapes, Mo Daviau, Brandi Dawn Cornelius, Tracy Manaster, Leslie What, Marc Ruvolo, and Nathan Cornelius. On those rare occasions I get asked about writing advice, I often have few kernels to throw out there. But one of them is to consider joining a writing group. Writing can be a solitary, lonely endeavor, and the fellowship of other authors counts for a lot. Huge thanks as well to Tricia Reeks and Meerkat Press. We've done four books together now, and I'm profoundly grateful for the opportunities these books have given me. She's tireless, dedicated, and works fiercely for her authors. Thank you, lastly, for Robin Corbo, who continually chooses to navigate the world with me, and does so with grace, humor, and bravery. I have a lot of terrific people in my corner, and I thank you all. These stories would not have been possible without you.

ABOUT THE AUTHOR

Keith Rosson is the award-winning author of the novels *The Mercy of the Tide*, *Smoke City* and *Road Seven*. His short fiction has appeared in *Cream City Review*, *PANK*, *Outlook Springs*, *Black Static*, *Phantom Drift*, *December*, and more. He lives in Portland, Oregon. More info can be found at keithrosson.com.

Did you enjoy this book?

If so, word-of-mouth recommendations and online reviews are critical to the success of any book, so we hope you'll tell your friends about it and consider leaving a review at your favorite bookseller's or library's website.

Visit us at www.meerkatpress.com for our full catalog.

Meerkat Press
Atlanta